Flora's Suitcase

Flora's Suitcase

a novel

Dalia Rabinovich

HarperPerennial

A Division of HarperCollins*Publishers*

A hardcover edition of this book was published by HarperCollins Publishers in 1998.

First Perennial edition published 1999.

Designed by Elina D. Nudelman

The Library of Congress has catalogued the hardcover edition as follows:

Rabinovich, Dalia.
    Flora's suitcase / Dalia Rabinovich.—1st ed.
      p. cm.
    ISBN 0-06-019137-6
    I. Title
  PS3568.A237F58 1998
    813'.54—dc21   98-16837

ISBN 0-06-093249-X (pbk.)

99 00 01 02 03 ❖/RRD 10 9 8 7 6 5 4 3 2 1

To Scott

Acknowledgments

The publication of *Flora's Suitcase* is one of those "dream-come-true" stories. In the summer of '96, Barbara Rabinovich, my mother, spotted a flyer for the "Best Seller Contest" in Borders, and on blind faith insisted that I enter. In May of '97, Olivia Goldsmith, sponsor of the contest, rang to say that I was a finalist. In July, she called with more good news: I was the winner and *Flora's Suitcase* would be published by HarperCollins.

Writing a book is a journey. The words on the page lead you to the most unexpected places. At times it feels very lonely, but you're never alone. While writing *Flora's Suitcase*, I acquired many new friends and rediscovered old ones. Their support during my endeavor will always be remembered.

My family—and their love of a funny anecdote—inspired me to write *Flora's Suitcase*. My father, Saul Rabinovich, put pen to paper and gave me a wealth of material. Shrimpy sat in the sun for hours and talked into a microphone. David and Marcia Rabinovich, Leon and Molcale Manevich, Moises and Estela Farberoff, and Ester Goldenberg all shared their stories.

This book began at the Writer's Voice under the gentle instruction of Elaine Edelman. It moved on to Brooklyn

College, where Peter Spielberg saw potential and kept me on track. His enthusiasm never wavered. Peter, along with Jonathan Baumbach and my M.F.A. peers, suffered through rough drafts and offered sound advice.

At HarperCollins, a hearty thanks goes to David Rakoff and the staff that plowed through 7,000 manuscripts. Sharon Bowers, my first editor, made what was supposed to be hell loads of fun. Fiona Hallowell stepped in two-thirds of the way along and gently ushered the project to its completion. And of course, many thanks to my fellow author Olivia Goldsmith for her desire and determination to sponsor new writers. Your generous spirit made my dream reality. I promise to pass on the torch.

Laurie Zelnick, Rick Pressler, and Ellen Sackelman proofed and proofed. Eduardo Escallón made sure my history and accents were all up to par and the last line precise. Diana Pinto and Miguel Uribe gathered tidbits on Colombia. Samantha Segal Veyne and Tina Harris answered Paris questions via email. Diana Stoll took care of Italy and explained grammar. Jimmy Vines at the Vines Agency searched me out and became my advocate. My sister, Claudia Modlin, read contracts and kept me out of trouble. Patrice Goldman, Maria LoConte, and the folks at LGD FedExed dresses and lent technical and emotional support. Dave Driemeyer got me running after the crash. Marty Seely talked me through twenty years of fashions. Lisa Cameron made posters, bought Crystal, and took pictures in the cold. Camilla Slertman snapped *the one* in the studio. Amy Bazil Beaumont and Abby Strauss held my hand during TV and reading engagements. David and Lorraine Singer provided solitude in Atlantic City as well as a story or two. Thea Goodman's gentle coaxing, enviable work ethic, and pedicure/manicure incentives inspired me. Catherine Moore kept me focused.

A special thanks to: Ruth Diamond, Bruce Ahlstrand, and Ellen Sackelman, who always knew *Flora's Suitcase* would make it to print. Judith Hirsch, who told me to make an appointment with the computer every day. Phyllis and Albert Pressler and Barbara Rabinovich for being my groupies. My sister, Adriana Rabinovich, and brother-in-law, Marc Balhetchet, for brownies, biscotti, and laughter. Joyce Pearl for lending me her dolls. Mary Larkin, Vicky and Sanford Klapholz for the lucky dollars. Helena Alviar for cooking up *sancocho* on demand. Alejandro Escallón, who helped clean house so I could get back to work quickly. Gail, John, Paul, Robert, and my boys: Andrew, Jeffrey, Daniel, and Mookie.

Finally, all my thanks and love to my husband, Scott. You make everything I desire reality. You brighten my life with your love, wisdom, and presence. More than you know, Mr. Man.

Flora's Suitcase

$\mathcal{F}$lora Grossenberg turned her back on the river, unable to comprehend its betrayal. Her weary eyes drifted to her feet where her husband, Dave, lay prone on the deck, his right cheek and shoulder pressed against the railing. "Make sure you get all the dirt off." Flora pointed to the pile of soiled diapers that stood between them.

Dave didn't look up. He stretched his arm toward the murky puddle below him, one of the few pockets of moisture that had yet to evaporate under the glaring sun, and submerged the diaper. It was only 7 A.M. and the starch Flora had ironed into her husband's shirt was long gone. Perspiration had turned the white cotton into a diaphanous veil, and Flora could see the ribbing of Dave's undershirt and the patches of dark coarse hair that grew along his back and shoulders. The baby squirmed on her hip. Flora shifted Sol onto her chest and wiped away the slippery sweat from between the folds of skin behind his knees.

The steamboat, *La Zaragoza*, had run aground in the middle of the night, tossing its crew and passengers from their hammocks. Fortunately, Flora had emptied her suitcase and made a bed for the baby inside, lining it with one of the bolts of cloth from the trunk of wares Dave had brought to sell. When the ship hit the sandbar, the suitcase sailed across the cabin, into a wall, and slammed shut. Dave and Flora groped around in the dark, tripping over the other passengers, who sat stunned on the floor. When they finally found the suitcase, they were horrified by its silence. Dave opened it tentatively, as he was certain the child inside was dead. Sol lay very still upon the silk. Flora bent down, and his warm breath brushed her cheek. Needing to be assured that Sol's sleep was not induced by injury, she pinched his chubby arm. He awoke irate and howled until dawn.

Daylight revealed that the boat had caught up with the drought that was following the course of the Río Magdalena. Formerly home to over a thousand species of birds, the river was a graveyard. Steamboats littered the riverbed. Relics of another era whose fate it was to spend their final days traveling the obscure river, half the length of the Mississippi, they lay perched on their sides, mourning their glorious past. Their lofty staterooms, where presidents and emperors had slept under sheets of silk, were now crisscrossed with hammocks. From the majestic ballrooms, where cancan girls once pranced across stages, came the bellow of cattle that were being transported down the river.

On the bank, a caiman yawned lazily before it slipped off its perch into the riverbed. The reptile slithered past, slicing through the viscous mud that had encased the boat and held it captive for the last four days. Fish flopped in puddles, slowly poaching as the sun boiled away the water surrounding them. The hundred-year-old parrots that once guided conquistadors toward golden treasures had gathered the vibrant colors of the jungle on their feathers and flocked to undiscovered rivers. Vultures, mute from the fumes of the boats, soared silently above. Their shadows, the size of steamers, rippled and bent over the hardened mud that was beginning to crack.

"Why didn't another boat telegraph the port and let them know?" Flora asked Father Belisario, a priest on board who had befriended the couple. Educated in England, Father Belisario practiced his English with Flora and Dave. He served as their translator and imparted Colombian tradition and protocol. "The drought is only a nasty rumor," he replied.

In a land of roads that vanished into jungle without warning, the Río Magdalena was the only way to reach Colombia's interior. The river flowed the entire length of the country, bisecting the tablelands between the Andes mountains. The steamers traveled from north to south and back, feeding off the trees that grew along the Magdalena's shores. They carried cargo, mail, cattle, and occasionally passengers. For a brief time gentry used the steamboats for leisure river tours reminiscent of those along the Nile. Foreigners in pith helmets shot caimans and exotic foul from the upper decks. But the hunters had been frightened away by the soldiers of the endless civil wars who too often mistook the sport for enemy gunfire and shot back.

For Dave and Flora the river was the last leg of a journey that Dave proclaimed was the beginning of their life together. But as Flora watched the beads of sweat trickle down her husband's temples, she could only think that this was not a beginning but rather an end. Was the sun draining the water from their bodies to replenish the river? A faint burn crept up Flora's torso as Sol's knees rubbed her dress against her moist skin. She shifted the baby back onto her hip and was comforted by his fat thighs that gripped the sharp angles of her bones. In the month-long journey from Cincinnati, Flora had lost the thick pad of flesh that cushioned her body. Her cheeks now sunk between the bones of her jaw, elongating her face and widening her eyes.

Had Flora known that a mango sealed her fate, she would have lunged toward her husband and pushed him overboard. But her brother-in-law's letter didn't mention the fruit that would change the course of Grossenberg family history. It was an exuberant account of Harold's travels to a land that had invented nothing but mountains and rivers. A step back in time, he claimed, rich only in potential. The mango was not mentioned, but it was there, sealed inside the fibers of the paper, and dismissed as a watermark. For as Harold scribbled the letter, he had taken a bite of the fruit, and its yellow juice dribbled onto the page. When Dave opened the envelope, the honey scent, trapped inside for months, wafted out and momentarily turned the Paris winter air into spring.

Dave rinsed the last diaper and stood up. He gathered the pile and began to drape them over the railing. "Rinse them again," Flora said.

"What?"

"You didn't get all the soap out."

Dave knew better than to argue. Afraid to spark another argument about how he had broken his word, he stripped the diapers off the rail. Dave sighed and got back down on his knees.

Before they married, Dave had promised Flora that they would live forever in her hometown of Cincinnati. He would make many other promises and break them, but that was the one for which he would always be held accountable. It was to be the dormant root of every argument, rarely hurled as an accusation but always present, implicit. What Dave did not know was that Flora, at her mother's suggestion, had asked him to make a promise that she was sure he could not keep. "A broken promise goes a long way," Shana advised her daughter.

"What did you ask of Papa?" Flora inquired.

"I don't remember." Shana smiled mischievously. "But what's important is that he does."

That afternoon, the silence of the siesta was interrupted by the rustle of feet cutting across the underbrush. A group of women and children made their way toward the river. The women walked swiftly despite the weight of the baskets balanced on their heads. They stopped at an odd clump of trees that somehow had escaped the axes and stood frozen behind them, waiting for the caimans to fall into their catatonic midday sleep. Then, the barefoot women and children tiptoed down the bank gripping the slippery mud with their toes. The women kneeled and set their baskets down at the river's edge. "Papaya, *piña*, mango." Their nasal voices vibrated across the empty waterway, waking the passengers and crew from their naps. From the lower decks of the steamboats they shouted out their requests to the women. The children skipped across the sandbars to deliver the fruit.

"They must come from far away." Father Belisario wrapped his rosary around his fingers. "I believe past those trees lies a valley." He was right. After the line of trees, where the earth dipped, a small village, inhabited solely by women and children, clung to the side of the mountain range. As soon as the hair on a boy's face coarsened and his voice cracked, the jungle reclaimed him. Their land was rich in fruit-bearing trees—guava, banana, and soursop. The ground was carpeted with melon vines. Instinct told them to harvest the bounty, as it made them climb the precipice toward the river. They tossed the coins gathered from the passengers into a nearby lake. It was the lake of their Indian ancestors, searched for endlessly by conquistadors, explorers, and archaeologists, on account of the rumor that a city of gold stood intact under the water's surface.

Flora stood apart from the group gathered at the railing. She watched the women on the shore slicing fruit. One set a coconut on a tree stump, and using a curved knife the length of a man's arm, she split it in a single blow. Below their boat stood a boy ankle deep in the mud. In his thin arms he held a papaya. Too heavy to throw, he climbed up the rope ladder and handed it to the cook. Just as he jumped down, the mud rippled below his feet. Flora saw the tail of the caiman before the snout sprang up from the mire. She screamed but it was too late. The crocodile had already clamped down on the boy's calf. The women on the shore looked up from their carving as the boy wrestled with the reptile. A few men went for their rifles, but before they could take aim, one of the women from the shore was out on the river. Fearless, as only a mother could be with regard to her own child, she held the knife above her and lowered it onto the creature's neck, severing its head. She retrieved her child from the caiman's startled jaws and carried him back to the shore.

The sleep of the crocodiles was over. The mud was alive with their movement. The children on the riverbed collected the coins around their feet and scampered up the bank, back to their mothers. While the women waited for the children, they tossed fruit scraps, prickly pineapple tops, coconut shells, and bitter melon rinds into the river to distract those crocodiles that drew too close. All the children safe, they set the baskets back on their heads and disappeared into the jungle.

Flora stood frozen at the railing. She clutched Sol so tightly that he cried out in pain. Dave, worried that she might faint, led her to a chair. "How can they let the children in the river?" Flora asked Father Belisario.

"Poverty, Señora," he replied, handing her a cup of water. His face reflected his Spanish ancestry. His complexion was fair. Brown eyes were framed by dark brows that dipped down onto the bridge of his angular nose. His great-grandfather had come to Colombia when it was still a colony and his family name was one of the oldest in the nation. One day, his nephew would be president. The second son to his parents and denied an inheritance under the law of primogeniture, he'd been forced to choose between the military and God as a profession. Father Belisario had taken a vow of poverty, but his last name allowed him to lead a comfortable life. His church was in Bogotá, the capital, and his congregation was made up of the men and women with whom he had spent his entire life. He baptized their children, listened to their sins, blessed their unions, and offered them salvation. He went to their parties and was often a weekend guest at their country homes.

"But they must know it's dangerous," Flora persisted.

"Poverty curbs their fear, dictates their actions," Father Belisario explained.

Silence returned to the river. The caimans, uninterested in the fruit, congregated on the bank. They yawned lazily while the vultures stood a few feet away and picked at the scraps. In the four days they had been stuck on the river, not once had a caiman attacked a vulture, no matter how close the bird happened to be. They seemed unfazed by the vultures that hovered by a kill in an effort to speed up the transfer of ownership. The reptiles even allowed the more brazen birds to share a kill.

The oppressive heat of the day continued. Flora could not stay awake. Her eyes grew heavy watching Dave playing with Sol. The dull thud of the wooden blocks against the deck and Sol's predictable squeals slowly waned as Flora drifted off to sleep. When she awoke, the heat was the same, but the light on the river had changed. The crew was busy lighting kerosene lamps. The cook stood a few feet away from her, bent over the papaya. He split the womb-shaped melon in half. The green waxy skin yielded easily to his knife. The meat of the melon was the same deep orange of a sunset and the concave center held hundreds of glossy black seeds.

The papaya appeared on their plates at dinner. "At lunch and dinner it is typical to have a piece of fruit or a glass of juice as a first course," Father Belisario explained to them. Dave followed Father Belisario's example and sliced the meat away from the skin and then cut the wedge into sections. Flora wanted to taste the papaya, but its peculiar odor stopped her.

"Smells like woman." The captain winked from across the table. He lifted his fork to his nose and inhaled deeply before putting a piece of papaya into his mouth.

Flora felt the blood rush to her face. He was a short, mestizo man with enormous hands that were out of proportion to his compact frame. Flora was the only woman on board, and from the beginning of their journey, he had been quite attentive to her state of mind and comfort. As a special favor to her, he had brought his Victrola onto the main deck. "For your pleasure, Señora," he had said in broken English, bowing his upper torso slightly. He insisted that the couple dine at his table at every meal and was genuinely concerned after he noticed that Flora barely touched the food on her plate. One day at breakfast he leaned over and whispered to her, "Señora, perhaps you might like to go down with the cook and pick out the calf we should slaughter for dinner."

After the steamboat hit the sandbar, the captain had little to keep him occupied. He spent a good portion of the day winding the Victrola, playing the one record that he owned over and over again. Flora felt she would go mad with the incessant tune. Even at night, the melody persisted as the captain, unable to sleep without the surge of the river beneath him, roamed the decks, humming the tune, which was fixed in his head. The only time the annoying organ-grinding tune ceased was during the siesta, when the captain stood under the blaring sun gazing up at the sky in search of the many rain clouds that the telegraph operators, with whom he was in daily contact, insisted were headed in the direction of the river. But by the time the clouds reached the sky over the boat, their dark bellies had evaporated and they were nothing more than wisps of white sailing across the brilliant blue vault.

Flora was surprised to see the women and children emerge from the jungle the next afternoon. She pressed her knuckles into her eyes, thinking perhaps she might rub away the silhouettes walking slowly toward the bank. Flora moved toward the rail, leaving Sol on his blanket. As the children scampered out from behind their mothers' skirts onto the sandbars, she scanned the riverbed for movement. The sun had lifted all the pigment and moisture. The earth was the color of sand, fissured and barren. Flora noticed a group of caimans congregated under a slab of rock that jutted out over the bank. They lay in the shade, inert from the heat. Flora felt an arm on her shoulder. Father Belisario stood next to her, pointing to the ground. The baby had crawled off the blanket and sat dangerously close to the railing. Flora scooped Sol up from the floor.

"Señora, I was thinking. Tomorrow is Sunday and I am going to say mass. Perhaps you might wish to have him baptized," Father Belisario inquired politely.

"Baptized?" Flora asked.

The priest assumed he saw fear on Flora's face and was quick to add, "I do not mean to worry you, Señora. The drought will end soon. It always does. But in the case of a child's soul, we must not take any risks."

"Father, we are not Catholic." Flora walked back to her chair.

"What church do you belong to?" he asked.

"We do not belong to any church. We are Jewish."

"¿*Turcos?*" Father Belisario knew the Jews of Bogotá. He had been inside the bric-a-brac shops that they owned downtown in La Candelaria. They spoke Spanish with thick accents. It was rumored they all came from Turkey, and most people referred to them as "*los turcos.*"

"No, Jewish," Flora repeated. She saw Dave approaching. He held two dusty cans in his hand.

"Look, Flori. Look!" Dave's brown eyes twinkled. He offered Flora two soup tins. Although the labels were faded and somewhat torn, the familiar logo was still clearly recognizable.

"Where did you get them?" Flora asked. She reached out and took the cans. Tomato and chicken rice.

"One of the children," Dave said. He pointed to a girl on the river.

"Where did they get them?" Flora wiped the dust off the top with her thumb.

"Probably from the banana company. They have stores on the plantations," Father Belisario explained.

"They look old. They're probably spoiled."

"Flora, I'm sure they're fine." Dave turned to the priest. "Could you ask the cook to prepare one for dinner?"

Flora did not want to eat the soup. She wanted to hold the cans and feel the connection with her home. "Are you trying to kill me?" she shrieked.

The smile faded from Dave's lips. He had paid a peso, almost the equivalent of a dollar, for each can. He dug his hands into his pocket, stabbing his finger on the tortoise-shell comb he bought to replace the one Flora had dropped and broken at the beginning of their trip. She'd salvaged a small section, but the jagged edges snagged her fine hair. Dave pulled the comb from his pocket and placed it in Flora's lap.

Father Belisario broke the uneasy silence that followed. "Señor, I am worried about your child's soul."

Dave looked at Flora. She responded by shrugging her shoulders.

"Please consider having him baptized. Children are fragile creatures."

"We do not baptize our children, Father." Dave picked up Sol and began to walk toward their cabin. "Come, Flora."

"I'll pray for his salvation," the priest called out after them.

"Pray for all of our salvation," Flora muttered under her breath.

In the cabin, Dave was visibly angry. "Why did you tell him? Why couldn't you have said he was already baptized and left it at that?"

"I do not hide my religion," Flora answered.

"Flora, we are in a land where there are maybe twelve Jewish families, at best. We are outnumbered and alone. We must be discreet." Dave sat down on the hammock. He felt the familiar fear well up inside his throat. The wood panel of the cabin reminded him of the armoire in his mother's house in Gomel. He had spent hours hidden inside, listening as the soldiers ransacked the house. He wondered what harm would come to his son if he did allow the priest to baptize him. After all it was only water and words. But he knew Flora would never agree. She had no concept of his fear. She was first-generation American. Both her parents had immigrated to the States as young children.

◆

The next few days felt as if they were all caught up in the same recurring dream. In the morning, the captain would gather the passengers and crew and tell them the telegraph operators' predictions of rain. But by noon it was apparent that the day would end as dry as it had begun. Every day, Father Belisario asked to hold Sol. Flora would release her child into the arms of the priest. She'd wave good-bye as they strolled off cheek to cheek. When they returned twenty minutes later, Sol's ample ears were hot, swollen with prayers for his heathen soul. After the siesta the women and children would come through the jungle. Their slow gait never implied weariness but rather an unhurried, carefree manner. The fruit they brought was always sweet to perfection. Sometimes they carried earthen jugs filled with fresh water.

None of the people aboard the boats feared going hungry or thirsty. What they did fear was that someone would go mad from the dull repetition of days. If one person succumbed to delirium they would all be forced to surrender to its infectious nature.

On the sixteenth day, a gust of wind unfurled the boat's flag from its pole. It whipped back and forth all morning, ridding itself of the dust it had accumulated. Silt swirled around the boats, and every so often, it shot up into the air like a geyser. By midday the sky was black. From behind the jungle there rose a mist. It seeped through the trees and rolled onto the river, swallowing up the boats. Flora and Dave sat with Father Belisario under the canopy of the lower deck. The baby played on a blanket at their feet. Flora looked down and noticed Sol's newborn hair up on end. They rushed inside. Lightning cracked as the door closed behind them. Then came the hollow sound of rain hitting the wood over their heads. The noise grew louder and louder and then abruptly subsided. They waited a moment to see if it would resume, but nothing happened. Dave and the priest stepped back out onto the deck. It was covered in ice. The riverbed was blanketed with hailstones, some as large as a baby's fist. The sun burned away the clouds and the daylight returned. Bands of steam rose from the river as the sun bore down on the ice. The boat began to rock as the earth beneath them loosened its grip. When Flora awoke the next day, the boat was moving down the river to the interior of the country.

ime would weather the Grossenbergs' collective memory, allowing the family Boswells to take liberties with the fruit that shaped their destiny. Benzi, Dave's cousin and brother-in-law, placed the mango at the end, a witty denouement to his account of why a clan of Russian Jews decided to make their home in Medellín, Colombia. Benzi portrayed himself as the financier and cast Harold as his Columbus, in search of a land where the Grossenbergs might make their fortune. "I put my money on Colombia and the Canal Zone," Benzi liked to say. "Panama was the perfect spot for an import/export company. Boats from around the world at our doorstep. Little did we know that the French were digging out the swamp with a teaspoon." Benzi insisted that it was he who ordered Harold to board a banana boat headed for Colombia's main port, Sabanilla. In the weeks it took the boat to cross the Atlantic Ocean, the contract with the French corps of engineers dissolved. "The men were as flimsy as the paper it was written on," Benzi would scoff. The few remaining workmen who hadn't died of malaria or been devoured by caiman fled. Excavation came to a halt, leaving the country's neck fissured and ready to crack. Forced to wait while the Colombians pondered their canal's dismal future,

Harold dragged his trunk across the plaza and checked into Sabanilla's only hotel.

Once the ships left port, lethargy blanketed the town. The wind ceased, along with the current. The sun ironed out the breakers, and the ocean grew taut like a piece of canvas stretched on a frame. Inertia turned Sabanilla's residents into ghosts. They lingered in shadow behind doorways and window shutters.

In the morning, Harold passed the time circling the empty square until the church bell announced the noon hour. He then stepped across the plaza to the restaurant, hungrier for the clatter of plate against plate that emerged from the kitchen than for the food placed in front of him by invisible hands. After lunch Harold, preferring the sun's rage on his neck to insipid patches of shade, retraced his footprints, still intact in the dusty street from his morning walk.

After the sun dropped into the ocean, the town was engulfed by the same fog that once curtained Sabanilla from pirates and explorers who combed the shores of the Atlantic at night. For centuries it kept the depth of the natural harbor a secret and protected the local Indians from the Jesuits who slipped into villages after dark and demanded one god by sunrise.

One night, unable to sleep, Harold returned to the plaza. Still awake at dawn, he watched the mist as it rolled off the ocean. The fog infused with brine coated his body in a film of salt. His eyes burning, Harold stumbled back toward the hotel. As he crossed the street, brakes screeched.

"The fender of a car is almost up his ass, but Harold can't see it because the fog is so thick and his eyes are stinging from the salt," Benzi would chuckle. "The driver keeps honking the horn, but Harold doesn't know which direction to move."

Harold stumbled forward, scraping his shin on the grate. He groped his way around the car until his fingers stumbled upon glass. He rubbed away the condensation to find two men staring out at him. Both wore turbans.

"Harold just stares at them." Benzi would laugh and slap his thigh. "He thinks he's dreaming."

The engine grunted and the car slowly pulled away. Harold followed the sound of the motor through the fog. When it stopped, he was at the pier. The sun had melted the mist over the ocean. Ships lined the horizon. Life ebbed into Sabanilla as the boats from the United Fruit Company, the Royal Mail Lines, and the Compañía Transatlántica entered the harbor. Taxicabs flocked into town. They circled the plaza, depositing street urchins and beggars on the steps of the church, the door of the hotel, and in front of the restaurant. At the wharf, the drivers waited in their cars, motors idling, for passengers traveling on to Barranquilla, a neighboring coastal city, located at the mouth of the Río Magdalena.

Colorful horse blankets unfurled over the cobblestone square. Women sold soaps, cocoa butter, and bowls carved out of wood and tortoiseshell. Clapboard stalls sprung up from the dirt, each a cornucopia of fruits and vegetables ripening under the morning sun.

The men in turbans stood at the end of the wharf. The silk of their tunics flapped around their legs as the waves drew the ships closer to the port. Harold approached them with caution, fearing they might vanish along with the breeze and the sweet scent of coconut milk bubbling up from a cauldron outside the restaurant.

They did vanish, momentarily, into the hull of one of

the ships, emerging behind several crates that were jammed into the trunk and strapped onto the roof of the car. Harold quickly hailed one of the taxis.

"Harold tries to tell the driver that he should follow the car with the Turks. But he can't speak Spanish," Benzi would continue. "Luckily, as only Harold's good fortune would have it, there is only one road and it goes to one place: Barranquilla."

An hour later, he arrived at Barranquilla's central plaza, where the men in turbans had multiplied into a small crowd. They stood around the two original, inspecting silver candelabras, coffeepots, Persian rugs, and bolts of cloth inside the crates. Minutes later the crates were empty and the turbans dispersed. The two men Harold had seen in Sabanilla walked across the empty square. He thought about the items in his own trunk. A set of silverware, an iron, some dead bolts and doorknobs, useful household objects. "After all," Benzi liked to point out, "peasants don't need Turkish coffee pots. A box of nails, on the other hand . . ."

Encouraged by the sweet jingle of coins coming from their trouser pockets, Harold followed the men along crooked streets and past Spanish colonial palaces. They slipped into an alley and disappeared through a wooden door. The sun was at four in the sky, and Harold swore he heard the beginning of the Sabbath prayer from behind the whitewashed wall.

Harold returned to Sabanilla. The next morning, he strapped his trunk onto the roof of a cab and drove back to Barranquilla. His plan was to sell his merchandise to the men in turbans. Then he'd wire Benzi to send more. Harold expected to have to wait until after the Sabbath to approach them, but when he arrived at the plaza, they were there, doing business at the market.

"Sephardim." Benzi's voice never hid his disdain. "More Arab than Jew. Saturday morning they were at the market, filling their coffers with gold."

Harold dragged his trunk over to the two men. He opened it, and like a magician pulling rabbits from a hat, he drew the crowd's interest. Within five minutes, the foot-locker was empty. Harold smiled at the men in turbans, extended his hand to introduce himself, but their leathered faces were creased with anger.

"I'll get more," Harold started to say, thinking the men were upset because they hadn't had the chance to purchase anything. "My cousin . . ." Harold's slender body rose off the ground. It sailed across the market, swiftly into the street. The empty chest followed him, splintering as it hit the sun-baked earth.

"The bastards ran him out of town. They must have wired their relatives in the capital because when Harold arrived in Bogotá, they were waiting for him."

Harold wandered around Bogotá with money in his pockets but nothing to sell. The Jews downtown marched him out of their shops when he tried to introduce himself or buy some of their merchandise. The local businessmen were also suspicious and generally unfriendly to the young man with slightly slanted eyes, sallow complexion, and a family name that no one had ever heard of.

Harold attributed his chilly reception from the "Rolos," the nickname for the people of Bogotá, to the frigid air of the Andean plain. The entire month he was there, bitter rain battered the city and its residents. The women, cloaked in thick mantillas made of coarse wool, sealed the cold into their hearts, while the men let it seep out through the sides of their ponchos.

"Eventually they would be good customers." Benzi always gave the Bogotanos credit for the success of the factory. "Loyal customers. But that was after we became established in Medellín."

The incessant rain and the wariness of the "Rolos" drove Harold from Bogotá. Cupped between two mountain ranges, he found Medellín, a small city in the department of Antioquia.

"The last letter we received, Harold said he was going to Medellín. After that we didn't hear from him again. After six months I assumed the Indians had eaten him, but for the sake of his sisters, I sent Mule, my brother, to find out what had become of him. I gave Mule some merchandise to finance his trip and he headed off to Colombia."

Mule discovered his younger cousin eating mangos in the Medellín plaza. Tired of traveling, Harold decided to stay tucked in the valley, where the climate was temperate and the people friendly.

"He was sitting on a gold mine," Benzi would say, laughing. "The place was ripe for industry. But Harold didn't know that. People had money, but there was nothing to buy. Mule wired me to send him more merchandise. I sent him anything I could get my hands on: shoes, dresses, matches, even a box full of porcelain Madonnas that I hadn't been able to unload in Cincinnati." Religious statues were to be our bread and butter until we started the factory.

Mule's version of events depended on his audience. In the company of men, the hotel in Sabanilla was a brothel. He'd found Harold not in Medellín, but in Sabanilla eating mangos with the prostitutes. The shoes in the box Benzi sent him were all one size and for the same foot.

For the "ladies," Mule transformed the brothel into a

monastery where the kindest nuns nursed a delirious Harold back to health by feeding him teaspoon after teaspoon of mango nectar. Both chronologies ended the same: in Barranquilla and Bogotá the competition was already there. Mule scoured the land and discovered Medellín. He set Harold up and returned for the rest of the family.

The mango always flavored the narrative. Tossed in haphazardly somewhere in the middle of the story, it belonged at the beginning. The fruit touted to make tone-deaf men sing on key, cure impotence, and forever end constipation was always Harold's pursuit. His quest led him to Asia— Indochina, Burma, Siam—where the blistering sun ripened the mangos too quickly, rendering them a mushy, tasteless, inedible mass. In India the mangos grew so high up in the trees that only birds could enjoy their honey sweet flesh. "The mango belongs to the mynah," women in saris claimed. "It gives them the gift of words." And through the trees, Harold heard the conversations of the parrots. They spoke of a land, skirted by ocean and sea, the shape of a witch's head, where twenty-five different varieties of mangos grew. Harold sat under the trees and studied his maps in search of the clues the parrots offered. All the while, he endured the wrath of the monkeys that bombarded him with sticky pits, stole his satchel, and tugged at his hair. Harold located the boot of Italy and the cougar in the fingers of Norway, Sweden, and Finland. But, he could not find a witch.

His money spent, Harold returned to Paris. It was winter and the cobblestone streets were slick with frozen patches of soot-covered snow. A dull gray sky cast its hue over the city. Chilled to the bone, Harold wandered Rue Montorgueil in search of fruit. A patch of yellow leapt out from among the brown potatoes and pale cabbages. He approached eagerly and pointed to it.

"*Banane?* Monsieur?" the vendor offered.

"Where are they from?" Harold asked. He peeled one open and bit into the creamy flesh.

"*La Colombi,* Monsieur. *La Colombi.*"

Harold returned to his atlas. He located Colombia at the tip of South America. As he gazed into the country of rivers and mountains, the features of the witch came to light. Her hat jutted into the Caribbean sea and her nose and chin pointed into Brazil. A week later, Harold set sail from Marseilles.

After three weeks at sea, Harold landed in Sabanilla. He stepped off the plank and a group of black women with baskets perfectly balanced on their heads surrounded him. It was market day. They circled him twice chanting, "Papaya, *chirimoya, banano, piña.*" Their dirge was perfectly orchestrated in a canon. As they splintered off, their nasal voices rose up through the din of the market. Then Harold heard the word that brought his search to an end— "mango." He followed a barefoot woman across the plaza. Her hips swayed to her song. She stopped and lifted the basket from her head. "¿Papaya, *chirimoya, piña?*" she asked, pointing her long brown finger at each fruit. Harold pointed to an oval fruit with orange and purple skin. "Mango?" He nodded. She pulled a knife from her basket and cut the mango into sections, offering him a piece from the tip of her blade. He took the nectarine-colored slice and popped it into his mouth. The sweet meat obscured the slightly bitter taste of the skin.

3

*A*s a boy, Harold was always bringing home strays. Goats, dogs, cats, chickens constantly turned up in the backyard. He once mistook a cow tied to a post for abandoned and dragged her home. Guita took the heifer back to the farmer and explained that her son had seen it alone in the field and thought the animal lost. "I know your boy," the farmer replied. "Last week I caught him trying to free my chickens. Tell that Saint Francis of yours to keep away from here."

Harold's interest in animals dwindled as he grew older. His attention turned toward strangers. He dragged people home and displayed them like trophies for his mother. Most were shoved off the porch by Guita and her broom. She could smell a horse thief, a pickpocket, or just a plain troublemaker Communist. Her nose was a finely tuned instrument. She often sniffed out betrayal, fear, and death among her family and neighbors. But no matter how often he was scolded, Harold continued to bring his outcasts to dinner. With her husband, Sol, dead from consumption and her eldest son, Leon, frail from the same, Guita needed someone to watch out for Harold. Dave was only eight. Therefore, she entrusted her nephew Benzi, who lived with the family, to keep an eye on her son.

Benzi kept his promise to Guita and rarely left Harold out of his sight except one afternoon, when business required him to speak with the CHEKA, the secret police, who were in need of some horses. Harold was instructed to wait outside, as a bar was no place for a fourteen-year-old. A group of Russian soldiers noticed him shivering in the cold and invited him inside. They offered Harold his first taste of vodka.

Benzi spotted his cousin in the canteen but knew the risk of interfering with the soldiers' fun. He quickly concluded his business and sat discreetly behind the group, listening to them convince Harold that he should join their army unit. After two shots, Harold agreed. They emerged from the bar and were about to lead their newest recruit to the captain's office, when Harold made a simple plea. "I must tell my mother where I am going. She'll worry." Normally, the soldiers would have scoffed at this request, but the possibility of other boys in the home enticed them. A few more recruits.

Benzi raced ahead to warn his aunt, only to be chased back outside with a broom.

"You! Get out!" Guita cried shoving the bristles into Benzi's face. "You think I can't smell what you're up to? What is the matter with you? You want cross-eyed babies with eleven fingers?" For months Guita had been trying to decipher the smell that had invaded her home. At first she thought it was love. But then Guita remembered the fragile fragrance love left behind, like rose petals scattered between sheets, faint, demanding close attention. This scent was different, musky as the deer in the forest and yet ripe like an aged cheese. Guita had pressed her nose into her older boys' heads and clothes in search of an answer. After all, Leon was seventeen and Harold fourteen. But all

Guita could smell was Leon's mediciny weakness, and the sweetness of Harold's naiveté. The odor intensified in the presence of her eldest daughter, Reesa. But no matter how many looks mother gave daughter, the younger's eyes refused to divulge any secrets. It wasn't until Guita saw Benzi and Reesa together that she knew the first cousins were lovers.

"Harold—" Benzi managed to blurt out, shielding his face with his hands. "He's with the soldiers."

The broom that hovered over Benzi's head spun in the air and landed, bristles down, at Guita's side. "My boys will not fight their wars," she muttered. A gust of wind whipped down the lane, leaving autumn leaves shuttering in its wake. "You better hide," Guita hissed at Benzi as he followed his aunt into the house. She opened the armoire and shoved him inside. "Quiet. Who knows what else that boy told them." Guita went to the kitchen, scattered flour onto her hands and sunk them into a bowl of bread dough. As she pulled the sticky paste out onto the wooden table, Harold burst through the door.

"Mother, I've come to say good-bye. I'm joining the army." His face was ruddy from the alcohol and his speech somewhat slurred. The soldiers followed Harold inside, strolled past Guita, into the other room. From the dark armoire Benzi could hear the floorboards creak under the weight of their boots as they searched the house. They returned to the kitchen. One of the soldiers demanded the key of the wardrobe.

Guita began to search the drawers for the key, tossing around her neatly folded linens. "I have another son, if you want him," she said, slamming open the cupboard.

The soldier turned away from the armoire.

"He's seventeen. He eats me out of house and home. A

good-for-nothing. Probably took the key to the armoire, just to spite me. I guess you'll have to break the lock." Guita returned to her dough. She worked it into a smooth ball. "If you come back tonight, he'll be here. You can take them both."

"But Leon . . ." Harold interrupted. Guita punched her fist into the dough to silence him.

"I have eight children. Three sons and five daughters. The youngest boy is still a baby, or else I'd let you have him, too. The girls are worthless. Hopefully someone will marry them. But who knows? They are as ugly as their father, may he rest in peace."

"Where is the boy now?" the soldier asked.

"Off being lazy. Probably with the whores. Who knows with that one. But, he always comes back for supper." Guita concentrated on the dough, stretching and pulling, listening for the soft clicking of the yeast as it burst. "We eat at six. Come before seven or you'll miss him."

"Okay, we'll be back." The soldiers lifted Harold out of the chair by the elbows. "Let's go."

"Leave him here for now," Guita suggested. "If the older one comes home and the entire family isn't here, he'll grow suspicious. I'll have them both packed up to go."

The soldiers eyed Guita. She could smell their distrust. It hung in the air, sharp, like old cabbage. How could she convince them that she was sincere? "Okay, take him. But I guarantee you, the other one is going to be on to us. I've already tried to have him arrested. I tell you, he's a louse."

The soldiers consulted. "We'll be back." One soldier brushed by Guita. Guita avoided his gaze and continued to work her dough until after they left. When their scent dissipated, she pulled her shaking hands out of the dough. She took the armoire key from her pocket and opened the lock. Benzi spilled out of the closet, his limbs bent and twisted.

"You've made quite a mess for us, Harold," Benzi said, slapping the boy's head with his glove. "You'll get us all killed with your stupidity." Harold slunk down into the chair, too drunk to fend off his older cousin.

Guita shooed him away. "Benzi, he is just a boy. Innocent. That is his gift. Now we must think of what to do."

When the soldiers returned they found Guita alone. She swirled the tea in her glass with a spoon, ignoring their threats. She did not know where Benzi had taken them; she had declined the knowledge. "I will see you in my tea leaves. It's safer that way."

Bound to Gomel by her daughter Ganesa, Guita flatly refused to go with them. Ganesa studied in Kiev. Mule offered to stay behind and wait for her return to Gomel. Then the three of them could make the journey together. "Mule, forget about Ganesa. She's a stubborn girl who believes the revolution will bring changes for us. You know she will never leave Russia," Guita told him. "And I will not leave Ganesa here alone."

Before her family departed, Guita insisted that they sit down. "An old Russian custom," she lied. In truth, she wanted one last look. The sweet memory of her children sitting side by side would stay with her the rest of her life. "Your son will be weak but your daughter will be strong," Guita whispered in Reesa's ear when they kissed goodbye. She clutched Dave to her bosom. "These are your parents now, Dovid," she said, entrusting her youngest son to his four older sisters. "Mind them as you would me." Guita then took hold of her nephew's hand. "Benzi. Never forget that Harold's innocence is a gift. Trust it. It will make you a rich man."

$\mathcal{F}$

lora and Dave said good-bye to Father Belisario at Puerto Berrío, a frontier town off the Magdalena named after a prominent warlord of the nineteenth century. What was supposed to have been a nine-day trip down the Río Magdalena had taken almost a month. "Just a few more days, Señora, and you will be in your new home," the priest called out to Flora as the boat pushed away from the wharf. The couple stood on the dock waving to Father Belisario until the steamer disappeared into the smoke of its own engine. It sailed south, toward Honda. From there the priest would travel by railroad to Bogotá. Conquistadores dubbed the capital and plain surrounding it El Dorado because the tableland in the upper Andes teemed with gold. The Chibchas, the Indians of the region, hammered the ore to make headdresses, jewelry, and bowls. When celebrating the gods, they ground gold into dust and blew it through reeds onto wet skin. They even ladened their dead with trinkets to take on to the next life.

"He was a kind man," Flora declared, unaware that Father Belisario had secretly baptized her child. The opportunity had presented itself, like a sign from God, in the form of a washtub left unattended. On his way back from communion, the priest spotted his chance to save the child and sprinkled some holy water onto the suds. Flora returned with Sol swaddled in a towel. She noticed Father Belisario lurking behind the engine pillar. But Sol's impatience at the sight of his bath distracted her. She tested the temperature and then gently placed the baby in the tub. Father Belisario watched as Flora moistened Sol's shoulders, back, and belly using a cup made from the outer shell of a coconut. Water cascaded down his newborn skin, leaping over rolls of baby fat. Flora dipped the cup and doused the baby's head. As the water streamed down Sol's forehead, the priest whispered the baptismal prayer. Father Belisario would always consider it divine intervention that Flora herself had consecrated the blessing. When she wiped away the soap above Sol's eyes, her fingers swiped a cross upon his brow.

With the aid of a porter, Flora and Dave gathered their luggage and walked to the station, where twenty emaciated Ayrshire cows were being pushed up the plank of a freight car. The porter led the couple to the front of the train, climbed on board, and then extended his hand to help Flora inside. The compartment was empty except for an old man sitting on a makeshift bench. His pants were rolled up to his knees and over his shirt he wore a cotton poncho. On his lap he held a wire cage that contained a prize-fighting cock. Flora and Dave smiled politely and sat down opposite him. The man, in turn, bent his body slightly forward and tipped his hat.

Although the cargo had already been unloaded, the wooden slats of the car were impregnated with the scent of fresh roasted coffee. The rich aroma masked the stench of cattle being transported into the valley and erased the green scent of bananas brought to the river basin from the lowlands. Flora inhaled deeply and the shabby interior of the train seemed to dissipate. She leaned her cheek against the window and prepared herself for another delay like the one in Puerto Colombia.

Unfamiliar with the alternate moods of indolence and activity of the Costeño, the people of the coast, Flora and Dave had sat inside the sweltering train for six hours, waiting for the engineer. The railroad, a recent addition to Sabanilla along with its new pier and name, was supposed to cut the travel time to Barranquilla in half. But the engineer, like his fellow brethren, lived by the philosophy that if something was not accomplished on the day said, there was an infinite number of days remaining in the good Lord's calendar in which to finish the task. Mornings were for sleeping, an appointment called for noon could happen anytime between twelve and three, and the night was meant for drinking and dancing. Meanwhile, bananas waiting to be transported from the steamships to the port freckled in the sun, and mail from abroad faded, the ink on the pages sometimes vanishing as time withered the relevance of their messages. The Costeños' carefree nature arose from circumstance. He never feared hunger. His ocean was filled with conch and sweet shrimp; his neighbor's yard was overgrown with papaws and guavas. Money fell into his idle hands by the death of a rich uncle or a large jackpot at the cock fight. His life was uncomplicated in every way, except for love. For the Costeño with a wife surely had a girlfriend. It was not a question of fickleness, but rather a question of a large heart. The Costeño made love to his wife in the morning with the same sincerity and passion that he made love to his mistress during the siesta. His affection for one did not negate his desire or devotion for the other.

But at Puerto Berrío, the train pulled out of the station five minutes after the couple boarded. It left the Río Magdalena behind and headed west, clambering up the central cordillera of the Andes. Two miles up the mountain, the shadow of the Tolima, the tallest peak of the range, fell over the car. Large raindrops began to strike the window. They shattered upon impact and turned to snow.

Dave noticed Flora shivering in her cotton dress. He removed his suit coat and placed it on her shoulders. "The baby," Flora whispered. Sol had fallen asleep in the crook of her arm. "Get a blanket."

The old man got up and took off his poncho. "Señora," he said, offering it to her.

"No, thank you." Flora shook her head, but his arm remained outstretched, and she felt obliged to take it. She wrapped the baby in the nubby cotton cloth and held him close to her body to keep him warm.

At seven thousand feet above sea level, their ears began to seal from the pressure. The steady hollow tap of the rain against the tin roof waned, as did the rattle of the train and the howl of the wind. The old man's head hung limp over his chest. His mouth was slightly open and his breath gurgled each time he inhaled. Flora watched Dave also succumb to the thin mountain air. While his left eye fought to stay awake and maintain vigil, the right one closed, unable to resist the sweet indulgence of sleep. The weight of his head kept propelling his body forward. He'd jerk awake for a split second only to fall limp the next, until his neck finally collapsed into his shoulders. Flora rested her head against the cold glass. By the time the train reached the top of the mountain and began its descent into the valley of Antioquia, once the richest auriferous deposit in the world, she too was asleep.

The western flank of the cordillera was studded with vein mines and small towns with biblical names—Jericó, Nazareth, Armenia. Late in the sixteenth century, twelve Jewish families had sought refuge in the foothills. They lived in harmony with the Indians of the area, observing the Friday Sabbath and the festival of lights until Spanish explorers discovered the valley was filled with gold. The settlers vanished, leaving behind a trace of conjecture and rumor that the people of the land, the Antioqueñians, were descendants of the missing Jews because of their skill as merchants and moneylenders.

Flora awoke to Sol writhing in her arms. His face was red and streaked with tears, but his cries sounded distant and muffled to Flora's congested ears. Sol's fingers tugged the cartilage of his ear. Flora nudged Dave awake. "The baby," she said.

The old man opened his eyes and his lips eased into a grin. "*Los oídos,*" he said, pointing to his own ear. He rummaged through his *carriel,* an accordion-shaped satchel made of leather, and retrieved a flask. He took a swig, pressed his hand to his ear, and then offered the bottle to Flora.

"No thank you," she said, shaking her head.

"Don't take it," Dave cautioned. Before they sailed from New York, Dave had received a letter from Benzi giving him instructions on how to get to Medellín. At the end, Benzi had written, "Beware of anyone offering you food or drink. The country is teaming with bandits. They drug foreigners and steal their money, their suitcases, even the clothes off their backs."

"Of course I'm not going to take it," Flora hissed. "Who knows what germs are on that bottle." But the man kept waving the flask under her nose and pointing to Sol's ears.

"No, thank you," Flora repeated. She pushed his hand away. The man took another swig, this time exaggerating the swallow and yanked his earlobe. It was then that Flora understood. She reached into her bag and pulled out Sol's bottle.

"¡Sí! ¡Sí!" the man laughed. His eyes twinkled and Flora was embarrassed for having been so rude. She slipped the nipple of the bottle into Sol's open mouth, but he turned his head and screamed even louder.

As the train made its way down the mountain to the steady howl of the child, the thick forest ebbed and was replaced by tidy parcels of low-lying plants. Each tract was delineated by plantain trees whose broad spiny leaves shaded the dark green shrubs and their crimson fruit from the sun. Every few miles, a large house loomed. Most were the same, rectangular white adobe structures with terra-cotta shingle roofs. The shutters were either red or green and always closed to keep out the heat and the soot. From the train window, Flora could see people working in the fields. They moved in pairs along the rows of bushes. While one grabbed the base of the plant and shook it, the other collected the fallen berries into a satchel made from hemp. Women sat at tables sifting through the crop. They looked up at the passing train and continued their work, able to define a ripe bean over a green one solely by touch.

Flora held Sol up to the window and tried to distract him by pointing out objects on the vast green slopes. "Look, Sol! Look at the pig. See the horsy? See the cows? What does a cow say? Moo." But it was to no avail. He continued to sob. Inconsolable, he pressed his face into the glass, streaking it with his tears.

Flora paced the length of the car, holding Sol, who continued to wail. The train came to a stop. Flora noticed a group of people standing on the platform. Three women boarded. They paused for a moment, under the arch of the rear entrance, to collect their breath. The skin on their faces was flaccid and crisscrossed with lines. Wisps of coarse yellowed hair poked out from under their frayed kerchiefs. They moved down the aisle as one, shoulders and hips touching. When they reached Dave, the one in the middle placed a thin, talonlike hand on his shoulder. "Dovid?" The strength of her voice shocked Flora, for it did not match the withered body.

Dave looked up confused, almost frightened. Then his eyes registered something familiar in their faces. He burst out of his seat. "Reesa!" he cried. The three women swooped around Dave, concealing him with their arms and bodies. "Fanny! Hava!" Dave pulled out of the embrace and kissed them each on the cheek.

Flora watched the reunion, waiting for Dave to introduce her to his sisters. She had expected them to be younger, even though she knew that Dave, like herself, had been born to parents who thought their child-rearing days had long passed. Millie, her oldest sister, was twenty when Flora was born; Joe, her only brother, eighteen. Each one of Dave's sisters looked old enough to have been his mother. Their faces reminded Flora of schoolmarms whose tight-lipped smiles implied a stern reprimand was imminent.

At the other end of the car, Flora recognized Harold by his shock of brown hair and his wild blue eyes. They had met in Paris while Dave and Flora were on their honeymoon. Strolling by the Opera, Dave had spotted Harold sitting on the steps, surrounded by orange peels. "Harold! What are you doing here?" Dave had cried.

"Eating oranges," Harold answered, as if there were

nothing strange about the coincidence of their meeting in Paris.

"Flora!" Harold ran toward her. In his hand he held a bunch of miniature bananas. "Flora!" he exclaimed, squeezing the sobbing baby between them. "Isn't this place amazing?" he asked. "You have to taste this. It's sweeter than a regular banana." He began to peel one.

"Welcome to Colombia, Flora." A man dressed in a double-breasted tweed suit stood before her holding a bouquet of flowers.

"Flora, this is Mule," Harold explained over Sol's incessant crying. "He's our cousin. Benzi's brother." Harold pointed with the banana to a man who was patting Dave on the back.

"Well you made it!" Benzi walked over to Flora. He kissed her on both cheeks. He was the opposite of his brother. While Mule was tall and slender, Benzi was short and his skin was thick, which made him appear stout. His nose had the same beaked arc like Dave's and his sisters'. "We've been waiting weeks!" His English, although perfectly understandable, emerged rough from his throat. "We were beginning to think something happened to you. This place is full of hustlers. You have to be careful."

"Flora! These are my sisters," Dave interrupted. "Reesa, Fanny, and Hava, this is my wife, Flora. And this is my son, Sol," Dave said, beaming.

"*Sof kol sof, shvegerin.*" Reesa extended her hand.

"I don't speak Yiddish." Flora smiled shyly, just brushing the icy hand with her own as it quickly retreated. The conversation in the car waned. Sol reduced his sobs to a soft whine, and the cock beat its wings against the cage.

Flora noticed a little girl staring at her. She was partially hidden by Mule's body. "Who is this?" she asked, trying to break the awkward silence that had descended.

"This is my Bluma," Mule said, stroking the girl's head. Bluma took hold of Mule's neatly manicured hand and came forward.

"What a lovely daughter you have." Flora bent down to greet the child.

"No, no." Mule laughed. "This precious girl belongs to Reesa and Benzi. I'm not married."

"Okay, we better get going." Benzi began to direct everyone off the train. Two boys were unloading their trunks. Someone took the baby from Flora's arms, and she was left standing with Bluma on the makeshift platform. As she looked around the depot, Flora realized she was standing in the middle of a pasture. There was nothing there except for a few cows nibbling the sweet grass growing along the track. There was neither station, nor office, just a few wooden planks that shifted under their feet. "Oh my Lord," Flora mouthed softly. "This isn't even a whistle-stop." From the moment they set foot in Barranquilla, she had felt a pit in her stomach. Now, a wave of nausea rose in her throat. She drew a few deep breaths to keep from fainting.

"Do we have everything?" Benzi asked.

Flora looked around her. "My suitcase!" she cried.

The train was already moving away from the station. Benzi ran alongside, calling out to the engineer. But he did not hear. The clamor of wheels and steam had long ago settled in his ears, eclipsing every voice, including his own.

"What's the matter?" Mule came up behind them.

"Aunt Flora's suitcase got left on the train," Bluma explained.

Benzi walked back toward them. "Well that's the last we'll see of that. I hope you didn't have anything too valuable inside."

"My clothes . . . my shoes," Flora stammered.

"Maybe we can catch up with the train in Medellín," Mule suggested.

"You'll be lucky if you get back just the empty suitcase. But it's worth a try." Benzi walked ahead of them toward two cars.

"This isn't Medellín?" Flora asked.

"Oh no." Benzi laughed. "This is El Limón. We're about thirty kilometers away from Medellín."

"What happened?" Dave asked when he saw Flora's face.

"My suitcase . . ."

"Don't worry," Mule said as he helped Flora into the backseat of one of the cars. "We'll find it."

"The baby? Who has the baby?" Flora tried to control the tremor in her voice.

"My mother has him in the other car," Bluma answered as she climbed in next to Flora.

Benzi started up the engine of his Franklin sedan. The passenger door opened and a portly man eased himself into the seat, shifting the weight of the car. He turned around and held out his hand to Flora. "Hello, I'm Zamie." The corners of his lips filled with saliva as he spoke.

"Aunt Fanny's husband," Bluma clarified. "Your dress is beautiful," she added. The girl ran her index finger over the ocean pearl buttons sewn on the sleeve of Flora's dress.

"Thank you," Flora answered. She looked out the window. Mule pulled the other car alongside them. Dave rolled down the passenger window. The three sisters sat in the backseat. Reesa held Sol on her lap. He continued to cry as fingers adjusted his clothes and stroked his downy pate.

Mule leaned over Dave to speak to Benzi. "Let's drop

them off at the house and then we'll go to the train station."

Benzi nodded and pulled out ahead onto the dirt road. Flora looked back at the other car and saw Sol's small arms reaching out toward her.

The two cars snaked down the mountain road. The descent seemed eternal to Flora. Every curve led to another. The winding of the road made her dizzy as did the proximity of the jagged precipice. Her head began to spin and her stomach felt queasy. Flora closed her eyes and the nausea subsided. When she opened them a few minutes later, the terrain was completely altered. A forest of eucalyptus had sprung up from the side of the mountain. Their trunks were white from the lichen that fed off the bark. Crosses dotted the side of the road bearing the names of individuals who had been lured to the edge of the mountain by the phosphorescent fungus and had thrown themselves into the brilliant abyss.

Flora leaned forward on the seat, trying to spot her new home, but the city below was obscured by the fragrant, silvery green leaves of the trees. The smell reminded Flora of the vapor rub her mother used whenever anyone in the family had a cold. Flora stifled the sob caught in her throat but was unable to hold back her tears. They spilled down her cheeks faster than she could wipe them away. She felt Bluma's eyes upon her. Bluma slipped her hand into Flora's. "Don't cry, Aunt Flora," Bluma whispered to her. Ashamed, Flora closed her eyes and allowed herself to be soothed by the child's soft hand stroking her own until they reached the house.

he house stood in the middle of the block, its terra-cotta shingle roof and red trim looking sorely out of place among the Greek Revival government buildings that stood on either side. Originally it was a farmhouse, surrounded only by pastures. One morning a maid had opened the shutters and noticed the city inching across the fields. By nightfall, the house stood on a main avenue and the land behind it was sprouting masonry.

The women in the valley were as fertile as the soil under their feet, bearing sometimes fifteen or more children. Therefore, it had not been hard for Benzi to find a house large enough to accommodate the three families as well as Mule and Harold. He had signed the lease despite Reesa's protests that the house was too big. "We don't need eight bedrooms!" She kept complaining about the expense and waste of space even after Benzi reminded her that her brother Dovid was on the way with his family, and more of the family was bound to come once the business got going.

Reesa felt vindicated on the first night. Uncomfortable by the space between them, the entire family ended up sleeping in the living room. Accustomed to the close quarters they had shared in Russia, where everyone slept in the same room—families divided only by sheets strung across a wire in the evening and taken down in the morning—the clan passed a few restless nights of wandering the halls, and congregating in the kitchen for a glass of tea and a biscuit.

Eventually they eased into the house, spreading out among the adjacent rooms. Unfamiliar with walls and their ability to relay secrets, tongues that had been checked a lifetime lashed out with venomous candor. Dormant rivalries rose to the surface and years of resentment bled through the walls. Accusations flowed back and forth through the adobe until the air in the house became so hostile that all the plants in the garden died.

During the day, the three boys and Bluma played in the empty rooms. At night their toys—a wooden spoon, a pot, a dingy cloth doll, two leather satchels, and a growing collection of miniature paper boats—were stored in an empty trunk, and the children returned to their parents' rooms to sleep.

One day, as Reesa was sweeping the upstairs hallway, she overheard Bluma and Conrado, Fanny's eldest son, in a heated discussion.

"Your father eats too much." Bluma's voice mimicked her mother's. "He's eating us out of house and home."

"Well your father always pushes everyone around," Conrado retorted.

"If it weren't for my father, your father couldn't make a living."

"Bluma, come here," Reesa called from the door. Bluma rose and followed her mother out into the hallway. Reesa grabbed her arm. "Why are you saying such horrible things?"

"But you said that Uncle Zamie . . ." Bluma felt the

burn of a pinch on her tricep. She looked up into her mother's stern brown eyes.

"You have big ears, little girl. But worse, you have a big mouth," Reesa hissed. "We're better. But they are family and we need to stick together in this new land."

They found themselves divided. Nothing was forgotten or forgiven. They resuscitated their parents' and grandparents' old feuds and clung to them as children do to blankets. The men's quarrels were strictly about business. They screamed at one another, shouted obscenities. But the domestic disputes that erupted among the women were far more murky. They sent chills up the men's spines because a fight over soiled linens or dusty cupboards was never just about soiled linens or dusty cupboards. They were catalysts designed to blow open a bag filled with serpents that slithered around the house and curled up in dark corners waiting to strike. And no matter how hard the men tried to remain neutral, they always found themselves staring into the eyes of a hissing cobra.

Throughout the years it was to become progressively worse. The children would awake in San Cristóbal, the family farm, to find lines drawn in chalk, dividing the patio. Overnight, long after they had been sent to sleep, someone, during a game of cards or the last cup of tea, would have said something to offend or recalled an old grudge and triggered another family feud. The children ate their breakfast aware of the silence that had descended upon the house. They waited to be called aside by their parents and told whom they could play with and whom they should avoid. As the day grew hot it became clear by the clusters of adults around the pool who was speaking and who wasn't. Once, during a big family blowout, where even the tightest alliances had split and everyone was angry at one another, someone took a bucket of white-wash and extended the lines drawn on the patio down the grassy knoll that led to the pool.

In the house and on the patio the children respected their parents' battles and remained within the boundaries. But in the pool, the cool water erased the admonitions from their minds, and slowly they drifted together and began to play. No matter how many times their parents pulled them out with the pretext of a lip check and whispered a reminder not to play with so-and-so, as soon as they dove back in, they quickly forgot and resumed their splashing and dunking. After numerous reprimands they learned to devise covert water games so that on the surface it appeared they weren't fraternizing. They spent most of their time on the bottom of the pool swimming back and forth, coming up only for a gasp of air and then sinking back down again.

*T*hat afternoon Flora fell asleep during lunch. Mule was asking her if she'd gone to a particular café while they were in Paris, and Flora, in the process of answering, stopped midsentence and closed her eyes. He waited for her to continue, thinking she was trying to remember a name or a street. But she just sat there, eyelids pressed together and her right brow slightly furrowed. Embarrassed by Flora's extended silence, he tried to draw her back into the conversation with another question but soon realized that she had dozed off.

"Poor girl. She must be exhausted," Mule whispered.

Twelve hours later, Flora awoke to find herself still sitting at the table. "On Saint Germain," she said, rubbing the back of her neck with her hand. She turned to face Mule and realized no one was there. Outside it was pitch black and the air was so cool that Flora wondered if the suffocating heat of the afternoon had been a dream. A low light emanated from under the kitchen door. She got up and walked toward it. "Yes, it was on Saint Germain," she repeated, wandering into the kitchen. She stopped under the door frame, startled by a shadow cast against the wall. The image, a twisted body with three heads, sent a shiver down her spine. It moved slightly, causing Flora to cry out. Reesa stepped forward. She held a candle in her hand. Sol was laid out on the kitchen table. He was whimpering, still holding his ear. Fanny and Hava stood beside him.

"What's the matter, baby?" Flora gathered Sol in her arms and doused his wet cheeks with kisses. Then she noticed an enema bag on the table. "What are you doing?"

"The baby is sick," Hava explained. Fanny hiccuped.

"Sick?" Flora touched Sol's forehead.

"He has a temperature. This will bring down the fever." Reesa picked up the bag.

"He has an earache! See? He's holding onto his ear. I don't think an enema will make him feel better." Flora's voice hollowed out on the last sentence as the wrinkled faces before her flattened and buckled. Cold hands were on her body, lifting the baby from her arms and guiding her up the stairs toward one of the bedrooms. She felt them loosening her clothes and pulling off her stockings. Unable to fight them, she leaned back on the bed and went back to sleep.

Flora woke up three days later, wiggling her toes. Outside the window, daylight was fading quickly, streaking the sky in purples and pinks. She arched her back several times, gently lengthening the bones in her spine. She rolled over to ease the stiffness out of her left side and came face-to-face with Dave. She lay there for a moment, tracing the curve of his hairline with her finger, trying to remember his name. She shook his arm to wake him. "Who are you?" she asked.

"Dave," he answered. He flopped onto his back with a loud snort.

"Dave?" Flora peered closely at his silhouetted face. She sounded out his name. It felt unfamiliar as it rolled off her tongue. "Dave."

Another name welled up in her throat. "Sol. Sol." Her heart began to race as she looked around the room in search of her son. She pushed back the covers and fell out onto the cold tile floor, trying to make her legs, rubbery from sleep, obey her. She stumbled down the stairs, clutching the banister for support.

Sol sat in the middle of the kitchen surrounded by pots and pans. He announced his mother's arrival by clanking a wooden spoon against a metal pot. The Sisters looked up from the peas they were shelling. Flora hobbled toward the table. Her vision was blurred and her head felt inordinately heavy on her shoulders. "I feel so strange," she said, pulling out a chair.

"Too much sleep," Reesa remarked, making no effort to conceal the accusation in her tone. She had forgotten. They all had. Those first few days in their new land had been drained from their memory by a viscid sleep that descended upon the entire family after they boarded the train at Puerto Berrío.

As the train had spiraled up the mountain, leaving the valley and the river below, the air in the car had grown thin and everyone began to yawn uncontrollably. They pursed their lips, tried to swallow, but still, their jaws pulled apart, demanding more oxygen. When they arrived in Medellín, Harold boarded the train and found the entire family fast asleep, curled around one another like a bunch of cats. He managed to wake them, just long enough to get the group into the two cabs he had hired. But as the cars pulled out of the station, they nodded off again. At the inn, Harold could not rouse them. He yelled into their ears, pinched the flesh on their arms, but they refused to open their eyes. With the aid of the innkeeper and the two cabdrivers, Harold carried everyone inside except for Zamie, whose massive frame was wedged into the backseat. Six men tried to pry him out, but he was too heavy.

Harold left Zamie in the cab and the driver, eager to bandy with the chambermaid assigned to clean the rooms that faced the street, agreed to wait. He flirted shamelessly with her for a few hours, accepting the hot chocolate, *buñuelos*, and sweet candied figs that she filched from the kitchen. But as supper drew near, the cabby blew her a good-bye kiss and went home to his wife with Zamie in the backseat.

He returned the next morning (after dropping off a few fares) to find a frantic Harold pacing back and forth in front of the hotel. But Zamie, like the rest of the new arrivals, was still fast asleep. After much discussion, Harold, unwilling to spend the money to hire the cab for the day, agreed that the driver should go about his business and return Zamie when he woke up. Afraid that a passenger might try to rob the sleeping giant, Harold emptied his brother-in-law's pockets. He then gave the cab driver a peso and promised him another on the condition that he bring Zamie back as soon as he woke up.

For an entire week, Zamie rode around Medellín in the back of the cab. He awoke with an extensive vocabulary of street names: Junin, Sucre, Palace, and knew the way to the market, the central bank, and the post office. He could navigate the city better than any local. He knew every crooked backstreet and what main avenues they transversed. Many years later, when Benzi and Dave bought the plot of land in La Pilarica, sight unseen, to use as the Jewish cemetery, only Zamie knew where it was. When it came time to bury the first member of the community, Zamie rode in the hearse so the driver would know how to get there.

Divided among four rooms, the rest of the family lay asleep at the inn. While Harold was busy trying to extract Zamie from the cab, the innkeeper, unsure about the conjugal and familial relationships, had placed Benzi, Grecia, and Mule in one room, the three sisters in another, and the four children in Harold's room. Rather than move everyone again, Harold decided to let them stay as they were.

The men slept soundly. The hum of the city came through the open window and, like a lullaby, dragged their souls deeper into the abyss of slumber. But the Sisters' sleep was discombobulated. They screamed, threw punches, and kicked up the covers. They ground their pelvises against mounds of sheet and blanket, saturating them with their sour discharge. Reesa called out to her two sisters, urging them to get up. They did not respond. She rose from her bed and fell on top of them. Shamelessly, Hava and Fanny arched their hips toward Reesa's face and grabbed at her torso with their legs. Moaning, they twisted themselves into a human braid.

The first to wake were the children. One morning, Harold returned from the market to find them sitting up in bed. He greeted them first in Yiddish, then in Russian, but they stared at him with their black marble eyes and said nothing. When he offered them some fruit, they ripped the bananas and oranges from his hands. Harold worried that his niece and three nephews had become mutes. They followed him everywhere he went. At night, he could feel their breath upon his face as they watched him sleep. He became wary of their silent stare, wishing desperately to shake their parents awake. "It's the sleep of the valley, my friend. When you arrived you slept for ten days," the owner of the inn reminded him. But Harold did not remember. The memory of his first days in Colombia were linked solely to the sweet coastal mangos and the lean muscular arms of a mulatto prostitute in Sabanilla.

Grecia was the first adult to awake. The chambermaid accidentally bumped his bed as she was sweeping, causing him to stir. He seemed to be afflicted with the same speechlessness as the children. He sat on the bed, brooding while the children played with the rings on his fingers and rearranged the fine strands of hair on his head. They brought him food and fed it to him with the tenderness of mothers. Harold thought it ironic that his brother-in-law, renowned for his political diatribes, had been rendered silent. But there was no one there to enjoy this irony. Everyone who knew Grecia was either asleep, voiceless, or far, far away.

Harold was relieved when the rest of the family rose from their beds and their voices, although groggy from lack of use, responded to his own. A few days later, Reesa found herself searching for the Russian word for *house*, and Benzi could not remember how to say *hello*. Within a month the only thing they could remember about Russia was that they came from a place called Gomel, but no one could remember exactly where it was. All their memories of Gomel had been wiped away, only the name remained, tenuous and fragile on their tongues.

Gone as well was the memory of the harrowing journey from Russia to Colombia. No one recalled the treacherous night under the bridge, where they waited for hours, their feet numb and heavy from the cold. They forgot the fear on one another's faces as the Chinese border sentries searched their pockets and their own surprise when each contained a small pouch filled with coins. Sleep had erased the uneasy silence that followed in the hotel room in

Manchuria until Benzi ripped apart their overcoats to show them the gold watches, gemmed rings, and filigree bracelets he had sewn into the linings. "Our money is worthless here," Benzi had explained. "This, on the other hand," he said, admiring a ruby ring, "is worth something." The scarlet stone faded from their memory along with their laughter. Years later, when Bluma turned fifteen and Mule gave her a ring, almost identical to the one Benzi had pulled from the lining in her sleeve, no one noticed the resemblance between the two, or even recalled the incident, except for Grecia. He held Bluma's hand up to the light to admire the ruby and then wiped a tear from his eye.

The children regained their voices, but the language they spoke was not Russian nor Yiddish, but rather the one of the land. They whispered it among themselves until one morning Bluma betrayed their secret by asking a vendor at the market the price of guava paste. When Reesa admonished Bluma for not having shared her knowledge, her wrath emerged from her lips in Spanish. Reesa paused, midsentence, and turned to her two sisters. Fanny and Hava stood with their eyes closed, listening to the calls of the market women. What had been gibberish a minute before, now made perfect sense. Back at the inn, Reesa told Benzi what had happened. "I know," Benzi replied. He and Mule had made the same discovery a week before.

Grecia, however, never regained his ability to speak. The words would form clearly in his head, but as they rolled off his tongue and collided with the air, they disintegrated into blather. He was permanently afflicted with nostalgia for Russia. On melancholy days, Grecia, dressed in a high-collar embroidered shirt, sat by the Victrola, sifting through stacks of old Russian records. He drank vodka and danced the Kazachok for the children, stomping and pirouetting until he was bathed in sweat. Inebriated, he forgot his speechlessness and tried to sing along. His stunted lips, which never uttered another intelligible word other than Hava, his wife's name, would always betray him.

After the family bought the farm in San Cristóbal, Grecia could be spotted in the town dressed up in his Russian military uniform riding his white freckled mare with the sawed-off tail. Over the years, as he aged and his belly swelled, the uniform began to pull at the seams and had to be let out several times. The material became shiny, then threadbare. One day Hava left it soaking in a bucket and it disintegrated. Nothing remained except the gold crested buttons. Afraid of Grecia's reaction to the news, Hava took a photograph to the seamstress. A week later, another uniform hung in Grecia's closet. Even though Hava had washed it several times, beat it against the stone scrub board to make it look worn, Grecia eyed it with suspicion. He put it on, and for the first time in many years, it fit the way it had when he was a young officer in the czar's army. He appeared at breakfast all smiles, and when Hava handed him his tea, he shot her an all-knowing wink.

The sun and the dense oxygenated air that wiped Gomel from their minds also changed their appearance. The children, always gaunt and undernourished, developed thick rolls of fat on their thighs, arms, and stomachs. The men lost the greenish tinge of their skin, and the dullness in their eyes was replaced by a mischievous twinkle. But it was the Sisters who suffered the most drastic transformation. Their youth had evaporated. The year-and-a-half journey from Russia to Colombia had taken its toll. The hot sun drained all the color from their hair. It shriveled their skin, along with their wombs. They shrank several inches in size. The bones in their spines bunched up near their shoulders, permanently stooping them, and their ankles lost every ounce of flesh. They complained about aches and pains that started at the base of their skulls and ended in their kidneys, but that didn't stop them from hauling buckets of water from the cistern or walking a mile from the market carrying sacks of potatoes and onions. They squinted so much that their eyes became slanted. It wasn't that their vision had diminished. On the contrary, their eyesight had become so keen that they could spot a thin film of dust under a candy dish over twenty feet away and noticed smudges and stains invisible to the naked eye.

*F*lora's suitcase made several trips in and out of the valley before Benzi was able to locate it. When she popped the latch, the smell of coffee wafted out into the room. The aroma from the beans on the train had seeped into her clothes, locking into the fibers. For years, the suitcase would exude the smell of coffee, the odor adhering to anything packed inside. It wasn't until the material lining, worn with age, was replaced, that the scent would fade.

Flora had purchased the leather-bound case at a shop in Paris. At the tail end of their honeymoon, as the couple prepared to return to Cincinnati, Flora realized that she needed another valise in which to pack the items they'd accumulated during their stay in France. Dave had rented a small apartment to cut the expense of the trip, and although the flat came furnished, Flora had bought a few embroidered tablecloths to cover the shabby wood table in the kitchen and some linens to supplement the one set provided. Dave had surprised her with the French silverware she'd admired in a shop on the Champs-Elysées. He'd splurged and also purchased a cherry wood box for storing the entire forty-piece set.

The shop in the Marais carried two sizes of luggage.

Flora initially bought a smaller piece, confident that it would hold everything. But after Dorothy and her aunt presented the newlyweds with a Limoges cake stand, Flora exchanged it for a larger one.

Dave and Flora had met Dorothy on the ocean liner to France. Dorothy, a few years older than Flora, also hailed from Cincinnati. Traveling with her elderly aunt, the young woman was desperate for company her own age. She spent so much time with the honeymooners that people on board assumed that Dorothy and Flora had known one another in Cincinnati and had always been the best of friends.

Flora, like the rest of the passengers, was smitten by Dorothy's blue eyes that sparkled when she smiled and her jet black hair that never ruffled, not even in the strongest wind. Her infectious laughter warmed the frigid, rainy sea days. She shared the most delicious secrets. "Don't tell me anything!" Dorothy would exclaim. "I can't be trusted!" Yet no one took heed. Her sympathetic manner drew people to confide their transgressions. She listened and gave sound advice. Then, the moment they stepped away, she'd relay their story, adding flair and innuendo.

Although Flora enjoyed Dorothy's company, she felt cumbersome in her presence. From the moment the two women met, every article in Flora's trousseau fit awkwardly. If the foursome played bridge, she threw out the wrong card, costing her partner the game. During their strolls around the promenade deck, Flora always tripped on a loose slat or slipped in a puddle. After a few days at sea, a bruised Flora longed for some distance between them. She wanted the ship to pick up speed so they might go their separate ways.

When the ocean liner finally docked in Marseilles, Dave

insisted on escorting Dorothy and her aunt on to Paris. He purchased their tickets and helped them arrange for their luggage to be transported to the station. During the entire train ride, Dave chatted about the fabulous sites he wanted to show the three women. "But, Dave," Dorothy laughed, squeezing Flora's hand. "You're on your honeymoon. Perhaps you should spend some time alone with your bride. After all, Paris is the most romantic city."

"We have our entire life to spend together," Dave answered, uncurling the smile on Flora's lips.

During their two-month stay in Paris, Dave and Flora had seen Dorothy almost every day. In the morning, they met for coffee and then toured the city together. Dorothy's enthusiasm was infectious. With her as their guide, a painting in the Louvre moved through history and took its place on the wall behind it. The stained glass in the Sainte-Chapelle glittered when Dorothy pointed out a certain panel. Every bell tower deserved to be scaled and each gargoyle demanded a close study. At dusk when they parted, Flora, Dave, and the aunt fell into their beds, exhausted. Dorothy, on the other hand, changed her clothes and set off to explore Paris at night.

Flora wrapped a tablecloth around the plate and another two around the silverware box to dull its sharp corners. She placed both inside the leather-bound case, wedging a sheet between them. Having tightly secured them, she placed the remaining bedding and towels on top. When Dave returned to the flat, he found Flora sitting on the suitcase, trying to close it with the weight of her body.

"Here, let me help you," Dave said. He pushed down the top of the suitcase with his hands. The latches caught and Flora hopped off.

"Did you find out about the train to Marseilles?" she

asked as Dave washed up for dinner at the porcelain sink located in the corner of the room. Thinking the water had drowned out her words, she asked again.

"Do you like Paris?" Dave took the towel off the handrail and wiped his hands.

"What do you mean?" In the short time that they had been married, she'd learned that a simple question from Dave was not idle chatter. Generally a quiet man, he spoke only when necessary. Yet, for all his economy, he was not direct. He was slippery, just like the ice on the rink where their courtship began.

Flora and a group of girlfriends were skating when her brother Joe and a few of his coworkers from the bicycle factory stepped onto the ice. Among them were Cyrus and Branya, and Branya's youngest brother, Dave, who had recently moved to Cincinnati after living in Japan for a number of years.

Flora skated over to say hello. "Dave needs a partner, Flora. Want to skate with him?" Joe had asked. Unable to say no to her brother, she joined their group. During the first loop, Flora stumbled. She grabbed Dave's arm to save herself from falling. A gentleman, he continued skating, even though he could feel his wrist turning blue. A week later they were teamed again in a game of charades. They lost because of Dave's limited knowledge of American culture. During a game of badminton in the spring, Dave hit the birdie into a clump of poison ivy after the third serve, ending the game.

Between encounters, each thought little of the other, and after, they secretly vowed not to allow the pairing to continue. When Branya and Cyrus moved to New York, both felt confident that their acquaintance would end. But coincidence took charge of their destinies. The doorbell rang one afternoon, and there stood Dave, with a suitcase, asking if the lady of the house was available. Both blushed below the gills. Dave tried to make a quick getaway, but Shana, passing through the foyer, ushered him in to inspect his merchandise. Joe came home a few minutes later and found his friend's brother in his living room. He sealed their future with an invitation to a good home-cooked meal.

"It's no use," Dave whispered to Flora the moment they were left alone. "I will have to marry you or else my future wife will be quite annoyed at your constant presence." He looked into Flora's eyes and believed he saw a twinkle. It was really a tear. It was too hard to fight fate alone. They said their "I do's" one month later.

Their first night of matrimony was spent aboard a train to New York, in a car with several other passengers. Their second, on a ship set sail for France, caught in choppy waters. Their skin turned green like the sea and their breath sour. They slept on deck chairs until the cool Atlantic wind forced them back inside their cabin. The next morning, Dave discovered vomit in both his shoes.

By the fourth day, the swell in their stomachs had settled. Unsure as to how to broach the subject, Dave waited until after lunch to suggest a nap. Even though she never slept during the day, Flora agreed. She was eager to end the awkwardness between them. But it was already embedded in their lives, impossible to extinguish, feeding on every gesture, word, kiss.

Flora stomped over to Dave the sink. "Why do you ask?"

"Well, I was thinking of setting up an office here. With Paris as my base I'd be able to buy goods from all over Europe and send them to Benzi in the States." Dave tried to step around his wife, but unlike a tango he'd once seen where the dancers wound gracefully in and out of the space between them, she'd boxed him into a corner.

"No."

"No what?" Dave inspected his fingernails in order to avoid his wife's fierce eyes.

"No, I don't like Paris. I want to go home like we planned."

"I've already put money down on a lease, Flora."

"Get your money back." Flora hoisted the suitcase from the bed and dragged it over to the side of the room.

"I can't get my money back."

"Yes you can. You haven't moved in yet . . ." The week flashed through Flora's mind. They had been busy getting ready to leave. She'd been buying a few presents, packing up. Dave, she assumed, had been out finishing up business, collecting merchandise to take back. But he'd been leaving early in the morning and not returning until after five. Lunch, usually spent together, had been impossible. "That's where you've been going all week, haven't you?"

Dave nodded.

"Why bother asking me if you already made the decision?"

"I thought you liked Paris."

"Whether I like Paris or not is irrelevant. It's the sequence of events," Flora mumbled. "It's the sequence of events."

The next morning when Dave awoke, the suitcase stood upright by the door. Flora sat by the window, gazing at the crooked rooftops with their terra-cotta shingles and blackened smokestacks. The suitcase remained at the door for two weeks until it was shoved under the bed of the apartment they rented near the Opera.

Flora was determined to remain angry, but Paris absorbed her anger, replacing it with romance and enchantment. During the day she roamed the streets, always ending up at Rue Montorgueil, to buy spicy sausage and a fresh baguette for the evening meal. They were greeted by name at Café de la Paix, where Flora taught the headwaiter the art of the double-decker sandwich. Flora couldn't even seem to find anger when Harold showed up at their doorstep, asking to stay a night and leaving two months later. The three settled into the tiny flat, making room for the occasional visitors Harold brought home. Expatriates, a Romanoff princess who worked as a chambermaid in a local hotel, even a Communist rally leader spent a few nights curled up on their floor until Flora sent him marching after she found Dave reading one of his pamphlets.

Harold disappeared before Christmas. He left one morning and never returned. Dave's nonchalance augmented Flora's anxiety. No matter how many stories he told limning Harold's free spirit, Flora still worried and pondered the lack of a note, or a good-bye. A few months later, the letter arrived.

Harold's letter brought Flora relief but left Dave anxious. The market that year had been bleak, and the streets of Paris smelled of impending war. Benzi and Mule wrote letters urging him to quit the Paris office and head south. When Flora announced she was pregnant, Dave pried the suitcase out from under the bed, scuffing the leather on a slat.

"Pack. We sail tomorrow," he declared.

"Why?" she asked.

"I do not want my son to be a Frenchman," Dave replied.

Convinced they were going back to the States, Flora didn't bother to argue the sex of their first child. Ocean liner tickets, left on the bureau, confirmed another destination. Bile rose to her throat, coating her heart with its bitterness.

"I'm going back to the States," Flora told Dave that night. "You've broken your word. I don't care where you go, but I'm going home." The determination of Flora's voice caught them both off guard. They'd mistakenly assumed that Paris had smoothed the fissures in their marriage. But once again, they were stumbling.

8

The days in Medellín were indistinguishable, each a repetition of the previous one. The Sisters were up at dawn, punching out dough that had been set in a cold oven to rise the night before. From her bed, Flora could hear the soft hiss as the swollen mounds sank to the bottom of their bowls. Then came the knocking of the butcher-block table against the kitchen wall as they rolled out the dough into long strands and braided them into thick, uneven plaits. While the Sisters waited for the bread to rise one last time, they drew water from the squeaky pump in the courtyard. They filled two dented cauldrons and set them on the stove to boil. All the water needed throughout the day was drawn from those two pots, even that used to wash the dishes. "Invisible parasites! Eat away at the intestines. Consume people from the inside out," the Sisters cried any time Flora forgot and accidentally opened the tap.

As soon as the men sat down to breakfast, they disappeared behind sheets of newspaper, inattentive to the plates and cups being pushed in front of them. Benzi sat at the head of the table with Mule to his right and Harold at his left. Grecia and Zamie usually sat somewhere around the middle, scattered in among the four children. Until

Dave and Flora's arrival, the seat at the other end of the table had belonged to Reesa. But on their first day there, Reesa had offered it to her brother. "Dovid, you take it," she said, keenly aware her offer tinkered with an unspoken family hierarchy. "I never sit, so you might as well." None of the Sisters sat at meals. Instead, they hovered around the dining room slicing bread, replenishing the juice pitcher, and picking stray seeds off melon wedges. Each tended to her own husband and fought over the privilege of taking care of Mule. The moment he looked up from his newspaper, the three women fell around him, fighting over who should fill his teacup or give him another helping of food.

Dave's arrival gave the Sisters someone else to dote upon. They always served him first, assuring that he got the plumpest egg or the best piece of fruit. They fetched his tea, bickering among themselves about whether he preferred cream and sugar, or just took it plain, completely disregarding the wedge of lemon Flora always placed on his saucer. Harold, on the other hand, they regarded with suspicion, calling him "Meshugneh" under their breath. They were frustrated by his eccentric food habits. No matter how much the Sisters pleaded with him, he wouldn't eat any meat or eggs. He ate only fruit and raw vegetables and drank an entire pitcher of juice at every meal.

Flora always sat by the corner of the table, her chair jutted out at an angle so she could hold the baby while she ate. If she attempted to get up and help serve or clear the dishes, a firm hand always pressed her back into her seat. Sometimes Mule or Bluma would translate something for her, shifting the conversation momentarily to English. But then their tongues drifted back into Yiddish. Flora tried to pay attention, tried to decipher their words, but her memories took hold, sending her back to a café in Paris where she'd tasted her first *salade niçoise*, to the park near her home in Cincinnati where she had climbed an elm tree with Joe, to a song her mother always hummed while she starched and ironed Flora's father's shirts.

Not until the men's and children's voices trailed outside the doorway, and the engines of the cars faded, did the Sisters sit down to eat breakfast. In the momentary stillness that fell upon the house, they picked at the leftover fruit, ate the heels of the bread, and drank their tea, which had become bitter and tannic from oversoaked leaves.

After breakfast the Sisters sat in the kitchen, peeling potatoes, trimming carrots, and braising beets for lunch. "Can't I help?" Flora asked every morning.

"No. No." The hands gently pushed her out of the kitchen.

Flora spent her days in the courtyard with Sol. He was her only connection with the world, but he too spoke a different language, filled with grunts and squeals that Flora could not comprehend. She longed for the day when he would learn her words. One morning as they strolled around the courtyard, she began to sound out words for him. "Pebble. Peh-bel," Flora enunciated as he pointed to the round stones surrounding a withered flower bed.

"Ech, ech." He stretched his body toward the fountain in the center of the courtyard.

"Foun-tan. Fountain," Flora repeated.

Sol turned to face her. He cooed and then squeezed her cheeks between his palms.

"Ponem," Sol squealed. He pulled her face toward his.

"Ouch," Flora said, trying to loosen his grip. "Face." She pointed to his face. "Face."

"Ponem," Sol countered.

"Face, cheeks." Flora touched his small nose. "Nose."

"Ponem!" he insisted.

"Okay, ponem," Flora said wrapping her arms around his unsteady body.

He looked at her, satisfied. Yet to make sure she agreed, he repeated the word once more. "Ponem." He squirmed free from her embrace. From inside the house came the clatter of silverware and plates.

Flora wandered into the kitchen and set the baby down on the floor. She took a bowl from the cupboard and went to the stove. As she lifted the lid off the pot, the steam from the soup blew up into her face. The blast of hot air reminded her of the manholes in the streets of Cincinnati. During the winter, they billowed clouds of thick white air. Once, crossing the street with her father, Flora had tried to stop the vapors' escape by stepping on one of the holes. It had burned through the sole of her shoe and scorched her foot.

She ladled out some broth into the bowl. The Sisters returned to the kitchen. Their chatter echoed in Flora's head as they talked among themselves. She put the ladle back in and dug around until she located a piece of carrot. "Carrot," Flora said and blew on it. Sol crawled over to her and plunked himself down on her foot. "Carrot." Flora offered it to Sol.

Sol took it from his mother's hand, pressed the slice to his tongue, and let it drop from between his lips. Flora retrieved it from between the folds of his shirt. She handed it back to him. "Carrot."

Sol admired it for a second, then raised it above his head and tossed it on the ground. He grinned. "Solly." Flora sighed. She swooped him off the floor, reached for the bowl on the counter with her empty hand, and sat down at the rickety kitchen table. She dipped a teaspoon into the broth and blew it, creating a ripple across the liquid. As she lowered the spoon toward his lips he twisted his head away from her. "*Fein,*" he said.

The Sisters' voices ceased. They looked at the baby and then at Flora, who held the spoon to Sol's scrunched-up face. "*Fein,*" Sol repeated.

Reesa took an egg from the basket and held it out to Sol. "*Fein kochen, mamashana?*" she cooed at him.

"*Kochen!*" Sol cried.

"What is he saying?" Flora asked, bewildered by Reesa's enthusiasm. "What?"

"He wants a scrambled egg," Fanny translated.

"How do you know?" Flora asked.

"*Fein kochen* means scrambled egg, in Yiddish."

"*Fein!*" Sol demanded.

"That's right, *mamashana*. What a *ponem,*" Reesa said, pinching Sol's chin.

"*Ponem!*" Sol squealed.

Reesa lit the burner and placed a dollop of butter into a frying pan. The sweet aroma filled the entire kitchen.

During lunch, the scent of egg lingered on Flora's clothes. What Sol hadn't eaten, he had smeared onto her dress. She sat there, staring into her soup bowl. It was eighty degrees outside and they were eating soup. Flora picked out a slice of cucumber from the salad and placed it on her tongue, hoping to absorb some of the fruit's inherent coolness. The men stooped over their soup bowls. Beads of sweat slid down their temples. Flora took two slices of cucumber and placed them on the back of her neck. No one noticed. She had become invisible.

fter lunch the shutters on the houses closed and the entire city fell into a deep sleep. The sun's midday glare created an eerie white haze so intense that it silenced the smell of the flowers and temporarily drained them of their vibrant colors.

Unaccustomed to sleeping during the day, Flora wandered the neighborhood, pushing Sol in his perambulator. The squeak of the wheels of the carriage, interspersed with the click of Flora's heels, echoed through the empty streets. Every day she ventured a little farther from the house, another block east or west, despite the family's warnings of sleepwalking bandits. "Rob houses, clean them out, even pull the nails out of the walls," Benzi claimed. "They steal children," Hava had hissed in her ear. And although Flora hadn't believed them, something made her anxious during her walks. Perhaps it was the weight of the air, or the vultures perched on the rooftops that stared down on her with gargoyle eyes.

Flora, herself, had been dubious about her inexplicable desire to escape the cool shade of the house and venture out into the ninety-degree sun until the day she spotted the house on Carrera Simón Bolívar. The white rectangular structure was quite plain except for the mustard stucco trim surrounding the door and the row of agave planted along the front wall of the house. It was the hand-printed sign in the window that caught Flora's eye—SE ARRIENDA.

She knew that meant "For Rent" just like she knew how to say *thank you* and *please* in Spanish without having been told. It frustrated her that while she had completely understood the woman who came to the door looking for work one day while the Sisters were out, she had yet to figure out the conversation at the dinner table. Yiddish slipped through her head like flour through a sifter. If it weren't for Bluma, she'd be unable to understand her own son, who spoke only Yiddish and stared at her quizzically when she addressed him in English.

Flora paced up and down the sidewalk, trying to discover the layout of the house. But the barred windows revealed little except for the fraction of a second when Flora thought she saw an old woman staring at her. She memorized the street name and number and walked back home.

Unable to lift the carriage up the stairs of the house, Flora picked up the sleeping baby and went inside. Sol stirred for a moment as if he might cry. Flora gently swayed him in her arms until he fell asleep again, his lips sealed in a pout. A thin strand of hair lay pasted across his forehead. He looks old, Flora thought.

Upstairs, the men and the Sisters were in the deepest cycle of sleep, where dreams become lodged, trapped inside crevices of the brain and lost forever. Zamie brushed past a man identical to himself. "Do I know you?" he asked. "Yes," the man replied. The man spoke again, but this time he was an infant. "You chose to breathe, Zamie." His voice fell to an angry whisper, and Zamie understood that he had broken a covenant with the blue, shriveled baby. Harold dreamt he was being embraced by Guita, his mother. But as he went to kiss the soft cheek, her face faded into Reesa's. Harold struggled to salvage the image, but Guita was gone. The loss settled in his throat and tears collected under his eyelids. Dave inspected a swatch of wool cloth. Flora took it from him and handed it to Sol, who pulled on a loose thread. The entire piece unraveled before Dave's eyes.

As Flora sat in the living room, waiting for the veil of sleep to dissipate, her own eyes grew heavy. The baby sunk into the curve of her arm as she leaned back into the sofa. Her chin rested in the hollow of her throat, tugging her jaw apart. She began to dream about a man who whistled so loud that she was afraid he would wake Sol. But his song was so beautiful that she could not ask him to stop. So she listened, holding her child's ears. His song went on and on. He never paused to inhale and Flora became concerned. "You'll choke," she cried. She put her mouth to his lips. As his breath ran through her body, she flinched, waking Sol.

The baby's cries resonated throughout the house, spinning the fabric of the Sisters' dreams. They became the roar of vendors at the market who accused Hava of stealing lemons, the sound Fanny heard as the butcher's ax severed a chicken's head, the screech of the violin that Benzi played for Reesa. Then it returned to what it was—the lament of a startled child that drove the Sisters from their beds with sleep still clinging to their eyes. They found Flora in the foyer bouncing Sol on her hip to quiet him.

"He's sick," Hava insisted.

"No. Just frightened," Flora answered.

"He's boiling," Fanny said, pressing her lips to Sol's bright pink forehead. She tried to take the baby but Flora moved away from her.

"He's fine. I'm sorry he woke you. I'm sorry we've been here this long," Flora added.

"What do you mean?" Reesa asked.

"You know, the old proverb. Guests and fish, after a few days they both smell. We've been here so long we must stink to high heaven." Flora laughed. Her mirth was countered by the Sisters' stern faces.

"Where else would you be?" Reesa's eyes bore down on her.

"Well, in our own home," Flora said slowly. The tension in the room drew Sol's interest. He looked to his aunts and then up at his mother. His sobs reduced to a mere whimper. From outside came the snip snip of a gardener trimming a hedge. Before Reesa could say anything, Flora understood. She brushed past them and went upstairs.

Dave was in their bedroom brushing his teeth over the basin on the bureau. Flora walked in and stood by the window. She looked out onto the street to steady the voice inside her head. Women stood in the doorways adjusting their hats. Maids lingered behind their mistresses, holding empty wicker baskets. "That's funny, I saw that woman at the market this morning. I recognize her by her hat. Always wears a cloche with a black ribbon. She had two porters at the market plus the maid following her around. Poor girl, I thought she was going to collapse from the weight in her basket. And now her mistress is going back again."

Dave poured some water from the pitcher into a glass. He took a swig and spit it back into the basin. "They have big families. Sometimes fifteen, sixteen children," Dave replied. "Hard to carry enough food for three meals in one trip." He looked at her reflection in the mirror. Flora's gaze made him uneasy. "Solly! Solly!" he cooed, waving to the child from the mirror. Sol stretched away from Flora's hip and reached for his father. Dave patted his lips with a towel and walked over to Flora.

"On my walk, I saw a house. A small house. It had a 'for rent' sign in the window." She kept talking, hoping that he wouldn't notice the tremor in her voice.

"What's the matter with this house?" Dave asked. He took the baby from her arms and walked back to the bureau. He took another sip of water and swished it around his mouth. Sol squealed with delight as Dave held the water on one side of his cheek and then switched it to the other.

"Nothing. But we shouldn't take advantage of your brother-in-law's kindness. We should start looking."

Dave spat. "For what?" Sol tried to grab the glass from Dave's hand. "Wait, baby. Wait." He dumped the water into the basin, wiped the rim of the glass with the towel and then refilled it with fresh water. "Here." Dave held the glass to Sol's lips and helped him drink.

Flora knew Dave was being cagey. His way of avoiding a fight was to pretend he didn't understand. He had yet to realize that it worked only to his disadvantage because by the time the discussion rolled around, she was totally enraged. "You don't expect me to live with your entire family, do you?" Flora asked.

"Where else would you live?"

"In my own home, with my own family . . ." Flora stammered. She sat down on the bed.

"This is your home, Flora. We pay our share."

"How could you not ask me? I can't believe you didn't ask me," Flora repeated.

"I thought you understood."

"Understand? How can I understand what I don't know?"

"We need to keep together here. We're alone in this country."

"And that means we have to all live under one roof?"

Flora asked. "We can't be united if we don't all live on top of one another?"

"Flora." Dave sighed. "This is my family. In Russia, family is very important. It comes before everything. Together, we make decisions that are going to be the best for everyone."

"I'm your family!" Flora cried. "Why wasn't I asked about it?"

"You're my wife." Dave walked out of the room, taking Sol with him.

Flora felt her stomach compress into the size of a walnut. She went to remove the glass off the bureau before it stained the wood, but knocked it over instead. I'm the bottom rung of this totem pole, she thought as the water dripped down the side of the bureau. There was a light tap on the door. Flora waited for the knocker to identify themselves. The second rap was as faint as the first.

"Aunt Flora?" Flora opened the door. Bluma held Sol in her arms. "Mother wants to know if you need anything from the market."

Flora tried to say no but was unable to speak, so she just shook her head. Bluma's eyes fixed on Flora's hands. They fluttered against her thighs. Flora clasped them together to stop the spasms, but they continued their awkward dance.

That evening during dessert, the conversation at the dinner table ceased with the rattle of Flora's spoon against the inside of the sugar bowl. The family watched as she drew the teaspoon toward her. Her hand swayed back and forth, spraying the tablecloth with crystals. By the time she reached her cup, there wasn't any sugar left on the spoon.

Dave awoke at dawn, convinced the earth was opening up under them. He leapt out of bed to grab Sol, but as soon as his feet hit the floor, he realized the only thing in the room that was shaking was the bed. Flora's hands lay by her sides pulsating against the mattress. "What is the matter with you?" Dave asked.

"I don't know," Flora whispered. "I don't know."

During breakfast she sat on her hands trying to press out the jitters. Throughout the day, Flora attempted to will the shaking away. But no matter how hard she concentrated, her hands ultimately betrayed her. By lunch Flora had broken three glasses, knocked over a porcelain statue, and accidentally poked Sol in the eye as she was wiping his face. When the men came home for dinner, Hava was applying a hot salve made of mustard powder and witch hazel to Flora's hands. An hour later, the skin on her hands was stained bright yellow and her eyes were swollen from the fumes. Zamie was sent to fetch a doctor.

He brought back an elderly gentleman who smelled of cigars and black licorice. "She'll be dead in a week," the doctor mumbled to Dave after he had examined Flora. He left, stopping on the edge of the porch to wash the taste of death from his mouth with a swig of Aguardiente, an anise-flavored liquor.

While Flora lay upstairs oblivious to her fate, the tenants of the house congregated in the parlor. Petrified of bumping into death as it entered the house and deviating its intended path, they sat behind closed doors, moving as little as possible. Reesa sent Bluma upstairs with a tray. Bluma burst into tears as she poured her aunt some tea.

"Mother says you're dying," she wailed.

"That's ridiculous," Flora replied. She climbed out of bed and strolled into the parlor. "May I please have my son?" Flora took Sol from Reesa's arms.

"Flora, you should be in bed." Dave rose to take his wife's arm.

"I'm not going back to bed. That man is a quack. I'll outlive all of you. Just wait and see." Flora went into the kitchen to prepare Sol's dinner.

The next morning, Flora announced she was going to look for a house. No one said a word. They were afraid to deny the last wishes of a dying woman.

10

*T*wo weeks after they moved into the house on Simón Bolívar, Flora discovered the old woman that she had seen in the window. Her finding explained the rocking chair in the courtyard that creaked back and forth on windless nights, the red corset that appeared on the clothesline the day after Dave had strung it across the patio, and the smell, slightly rancid and definitely old, that hung in the air, defying ammonia and the scrub brush.

It was the smell that led Flora to the room behind the kitchen. Convinced that some animal had decided to draw its last breath in a closet or under a bed, she began a meticulous search for the source of the scent. Armed with a bucket, mop, and a few stiff brushes, Flora scoured every room in the house. She wiped the walls with bleach to brighten them and ran a wet mop across the ceiling to get rid of cobwebs. She pulled drawers from their bureaus, dusted them off, and then set them to air outside, hoping the sun might absorb the musty scent emanating from the wood.

But the odor prevailed. Unable to locate the source, Flora cast the blame on the geraniums planted in the courtyard. Convinced that their bitter, earthy scent was the source of the lingering smell, she decided to pull up the carmine flowers. She grasped the base of the plant, but the roots clenched down into the earth to which they had been attached for hundreds of years and refused to budge. No matter how hard she pulled, they remained embedded in the soil. Infuriated by their stubbornness, Flora took a pair of shears and hacked them down to nothing but stubs. They grew back overnight, four inches taller, and by mid-day were blooming again.

Flora was looking for a shovel when she noticed the door in the patio. She stared at it for a moment, unable to comprehend why she had never seen it before, for the door was not camouflaged by paint or concealed behind boxes. Flora dismissed the oversight as probably a tool shed. Determined to clean every inch of her home, she returned to the broom closet and gathered her cleaning supplies.

The door was under five feet tall. Flora crouched down to avoid knocking her head on the door frame as she entered. Where she expected a mud-caked floor and rusted tools, she discovered a mahogany canopy bed and a woman sleeping under sheets stitched with gold thread. The room was damp, and soft black mold clung to the walls. Over the bed hung a portrait of a man with vacant eyes. He was dressed in a military tail frock coat from the eighteenth century. A sheath of wheat wound along the high open collar of his uniform.

The mop rattled against the edge of the pail and fell to the floor, taking the bucket with it. The woman did not stir and Flora feared she was dead. She tiptoed over to the bed. Age had reduced the woman to nothing but bones, bones held together by leathery skin, dried out, cracked and worn from the sun. Flora looked to the gaping mouth for a sign of life.

"Excuse me?" Flora called out. "Señora?" Flora touched

the woman's bony hand. The skin was coarse like sandpaper.

The woman swatted Flora's hand away, turned on her side, and farted.

Flora ran out of the room. She had no idea what to do. Dave was at work and wouldn't be home until lunch. She grabbed Sol, who was napping in his crib, placed him in the carriage, and ran to the Sisters' house.

Flora found them in the kitchen drinking tea. "Reesa, there's an old woman asleep in my house!" Flora gasped. Flushed from running the ten-block distance between the two homes, she wiped her brow.

The Sisters eyed one another, twitched their eyebrows, and said nothing. They returned to their tea, stirring the amber liquid, their long metal spoons clanking furiously against the glass.

"Do you think you could come back to the house and help me find out why she's there?" Flora persisted.

They sat in silence. Nothing moved except the tea, swirling inside the glasses, sloshing up against the rims. They were still angry that Flora had gotten her way. The moist good-bye kiss each had planted on Flora's cheek had been full of spite and ill wishes. Not only did Flora manage to get her own house, but her victory had also sparked another defection. Leon, their oldest brother, had not been in Colombia a week when his wife, Freida, decided she did not want to live in the house on Guayaquil. At first, Leon had resisted and ignored Freida's vicious attacks on his family. But ultimately she wore him down with her wicked tongue. In the end, no one was truly sorry to see them go. The animosity between Reesa and Freida had drained the house of all its air. The two women ascribed meaning to the most innocuous glance or sigh. Their collective presence made glasses rattle, knocked saltcellars onto their sides, and slammed doors. Nevertheless, the Sisters blamed Flora for placing big American ideas in Freida's small Russian head.

Flora felt the tears welling up in her throat. They began to fall as soon as she stepped back onto the street. Her fingers jittered furiously as she ran the back of her hand across her face to wipe away the tears. She'd only walked a few feet when she heard someone call her name.

"Aunt Flora?" Bluma stood behind her, adjusting the strap on her books. "What's the matter, Aunt Flora?"

Flora managed a faint smile. "Why aren't you in school?" she asked the girl.

"Catechism class. Father finally convinced the nuns at school to let me miss Catechism."

"How did he manage that?" For years Benzi had been pleading with the Sisters of the Holy Ascension to excuse Bluma from religion class. But they insisted that she attend. They were concerned about the girl's soul. So every morning, Bluma sat in the school chapel reciting the Lord's Prayer. While the other girls stood at the altar, taking communion and whispering their secrets to the priest, Bluma knelt on the cold stone floor and pretended to read the New Testament.

"He donated some religious statues to the church." Both the girl and the woman smiled. Bluma put her hand on the carriage, and as they walked toward the house on Simón Bolívar, Flora told her niece about the old woman.

The door in the patio was slightly ajar. Flora and Bluma stood outside, waiting for the old woman to emerge. After a few minutes of listening to her move about the room, Flora regained her courage and knocked on the door. "¿Señora?"

The door yielded, and a woman barely four feet tall

emerged. She squinted up at Flora and said, "What?"

"I beg your pardon," Flora stammered, "but you seem to be living in my house."

"Your house?"

"Yes, we moved in a few weeks ago."

"Well they had no business to do that. This house is a historical landmark."

"Historical landmark? But the rental agent said the house was only a few years old," Flora said.

"That part of the house is new." The old woman pointed to the kitchen. "Constructed after the fire that practically leveled Carrera Simón Bolívar in 1921. But this patio and this room were built in the 1800s. I was born in this room in 1830."

"You were born in 1830?" Flora gasped.

"I'll be a hundred and three at the end of May."

"Where is your family? Were you left behind?" Flora asked.

"I have no family. My mother died shortly after the Liberator was taken by consumption."

"The Liberator?" Bluma stared at the woman's shriveled face. "Do you mean Simón Bolívar?"

"Yes," the woman replied.

"Who is Simón Bolívar?" Flora asked.

"Simón Bolívar is the general who liberated our nation and most of South America from Spain." The old lady's tone grew animated. "The street this house is on is named after him. The plaza downtown bears his name. I am named after him."

Both Flora and Bluma waited for the woman to state her name, but she only smiled. Her gums were the color of dried blood. Her one tooth, the right incisor, was ridged and streaked with black. She laughed, and the air between the three became so rancid that Bluma and Flora were forced to back out of the room. "My name is Bolívariana," she called after them and closed the door.

A fetid cloud hung over the patio making it impossible for Flora or Dave to ask who the old woman was and why she was living in their house. Each time they tried to approach the door, they were overcome by the smell of rot. Dave contacted the real estate company, who claimed to know nothing about Bolívariana. The owners of the house were out of the country. No forwarding address had been provided. The only information they had was the bank account into which Dave had already deposited a check for six months' rent.

In the meantime, Bolívariana became quite brazen. Being at that age where sleep comes effortlessly during the day but is ephemeral at night, she would wait until everyone in the house was asleep and then shuffle into the kitchen. Cupboard doors slammed open against one another as she searched for crackers, store-bought cake, and her favorite, Sol's teething biscuits. She dug her nails into papayas that had been placed on the windowsill to ripen, tearing them apart with her bare hands. Discarded chicken bones were retrieved from the garbage and sucked clean. Any cartilage surrounding the joints was ripped off and the soft tips of the bones were gnawed and drained of their marrow. She ate until dawn, when the mist began to rise off the ground and the sky turned violet. Then Bolívariana returned to her room to find sleep waiting for her.

Flora tried different tricks to stop Bolívariana's ransacking. She loaded a tray with food and ventured out into the stench of the patio. She gave Bolívariana twos and then threes of everything—three slices of bread, three wedges of cake, three pieces of meat, three boiled potatoes. But it was to no avail. Flora tried placing a small bag of groceries alongside the tray. She filled it with fruit, crackers, a loaf of bread, and half a pound cake. The next morning the kitchen was still a mess and all that remained of the other half of the pound cake were the crumbs.

"Remember the raccoon? The one that picked through our garbage every night?" Flora wrote to her mother. "It's moved to South America and is now living in my house . . . I shall miss the first snow, the way it dusts the streets announcing the arrival of winter . . . Time has forgotten us, this place, where every day is the same, hot, humid and eternally green. It's almost December and the flowers are all in bloom . . . When Sol gets mad, his lower lip juts out into a funny pout, and he looks just like Millie when she's concentrating. His eyes are always sad . . . Mule is sailing to New York. He promised to mail this letter as soon as he gets off the boat . . . It will get there faster than if I mail it from here, where everyone and everything moves like molasses." Flora scribbled, thinking about the policeman who had come to the house five days after Dave had filed a report at the police station.

He was not a man, but rather a boy, no more than sixteen, who had yet to shave the soft downy fuzz growing over his lip and under his chin. His clothes were tattered, and he wore no shoes. At first, Flora thought he was a beggar. She had him wait at the door while she searched the kitchen for food. He crammed the two slices of bread and the chunk of farmer cheese into his mouth as if he had not eaten in a long while and then stood there waiting for her to let him in. "Go. Go now," Flora commanded from the step.

"*Soy la policía*, Señora," he said, stepping past her into the house.

"Police? This is the police?" Flora whispered to Dave as

they escorted him into the courtyard. Bolívariana was asleep in her rocker. Her head was cocked over one shoulder and her feet hung five inches off the ground. "Is she dead, Señor?" the policeman asked. His voice trembled. He had never seen a corpse.

"No, just asleep," Dave answered. "We moved into this house and she was here. We don't know who she is or where she belongs."

The policeman reached out and poked Bolívariana in the thigh with his stick. "¡Vieja!" he called. "¡Vieja! Get up."

Bolívariana opened her filmy eyes and sucked in her cheeks. "Don't call me old lady. You should have more respect," she hissed. Her breath was sour.

"Who are you?" he asked.

"My name is Bolívariana."

"Why are you here? You have no right to be living in these people's home."

"Right?" Bolívariana jumped up from the rocker. She stomped her foot like a bull ready to charge. "Come with me." They followed her through the kitchen and into the patio. "Señor, do you see that room?" Bolívariana gestured toward the door with her blue webbed hand. "In 1829, the year before I was born, Simón Bolívar slept in that room. Yes, Simón Bolívar, the liberator of our country." Bolívariana shook her finger for emphasis. "His lungs were weak from the tuberculosis. He was feverish and delirious. My mother, a servant of the house, tended to him. And he in gratitude left her with his seed planted in her belly." A gentle wind pushed across the patio, causing the canopy of bougainvillea and jasmine to stir. "Unlike you, Señor." Bolívariana pointed to Dave. "Who will die in this land and never see your home again, I will die in the room of my birth."

Where will I die? Flora wondered. Her heart grew un-bearably heavy.

The old woman and the young woman stared at each other. No words passed between them.

"Flora?" Flora felt Dave's hand on her elbow. Dave looked at his wife and then at Bolívariana. For the first time he noticed the resemblance between them. The shape of their faces, the width of their lips, and the arch of their eyebrows were almost identical. He wondered if Flora could see past the camouflage of ravaged skin.

The solution, according to Dave, was simple. "We'll move back with my sisters," he said that night as they were getting ready for bed.

"No." Flora was sure if they went back, she'd be stuck in the house on Guayaquil until the day she was as shriv-eled as Bolívariana. She preferred the old woman and her stench to living with the Sisters. The way they moved, as one entity, made Flora's skin crawl. Secretly she had begun calling them the Sisters of Gorgon.

"What do you propose then?" Dave asked his wife.

"We'll wait."

Dave glanced at Flora, hoping to find on her face the compassion that was missing in her voice. It was not there.

Flora punched down her pillow, preparing it for sleep. "We'll wait, Dave. We'll wait."

He understood. Flora was waiting for Bolívariana to die.

But Bolívariana avoided death. Or perhaps it was death that avoided her. Whenever it tried to unthread the soul from her decrepit body, she fought back, screaming "I am not ready. I will go when I am tired of this world, tired of the smell of air and tired of the color of the flowers."

Like with an ugly piece of furniture bolted down to the

floor, Dave and Flora learned to live with Bolívariana. For the most part, she was unobtrusive. During the day she slept in the courtyard, getting up only to drag her rocking chair into the sun. Dave and Flora grew accustomed to the shuffle of feet at night as she roamed the house in search of a spot that might ease the ache in her back and the stiffness in her bones.

One morning, as Flora was locking up the kitchen cabinets, a strategy she had devised to stop Bolívariana's pilfering, the old woman came up behind her and whispered up into her ear, "Sadness will burst forth from your womb." Certain that Bolívariana was still angry about the padlocks on the cupboards and the pantry, Flora dismissed the comment, just as she ignored the queasy feeling in her stomach when she ran into the Sisters at the market later that day.

The three women flocked toward Flora and immediately began to comment on her choice of tomatoes (too firm), her carrots (too big), and her basket (too frail). Flora just nodded her head, wishing only to be out of the sweltering plaza, which smelled like rotting oranges. She quickly said her good-byes, leaving the market before she had finished her errands. On her way home, she ran into an empty lot where two cows were grazing and threw up.

lthough Dave and Flora had been living in their own home almost a year, the Sisters continued brooding. At first, Bolívariana had provided the Sisters with a glimmer of hope. When Flora refused to leave, forcing Dave to live with the old woman, their sister-in-law's strong will enraged them. But it was Bluma's attachment to Flora that pushed them to the edge.

When not at school, the girl spent every waking moment at Flora's house. She came home telling tales of sewing projects, cookie baking, and something called Jell-O. Flora taught Bluma how to curl her hair and let her play with makeup. Reesa tried punishing Bluma to keep her at home, away from Flora, but that only strengthened the bond between them. Flora became Bluma's confidante, her solace from her mother. A letter from Branya offered Reesa an opportunity for revenge.

My dearest Sisters,

I finished my housekeeping early today, so I took my pen and tablet out to the park near my flat and decided to use the free hours to write you a letter. It is spring here and all the trees are pale pink. I love this season, short as it may be. The air is crisp, but the sun is warm on my face. But, soon it will be summer, and summer in New York City can be as cruel as our winter back in Gomel. Everyone sits outside, trying to escape the heat of their apartment. But the air is stagnant and heavy. Last year Cyrus traveled to the ocean. He came back brown and content, promising to take me this year. How quickly time passes. How many years has it been since we kissed good-bye, our hearts so conscious of the likelihood that we might never see each other again? I miss you so much. I am lonely here. Cyrus continues painting and spends most of his time in the studio he set up in the spare bedroom. He stays up all night drawing. In the morning, I find his models curled on my settee. They stumble into my kitchen and I scold them for drinking too much vodka the night before, while I brew them coffee and butter their toast. Cyrus calls them "his cherubs." When he hugs them good-bye or strokes their smooth, hairless faces, I feel a pit in my stomach. Those are the sons which I have denied him. I fear Cyrus will give up on me.

> *Your adoring sister,*
> *Branya*

Reesa read the letter first and then handed it to Hava, who read it aloud to Fanny. It was not necessary to discuss the letter's message. The three women understood Branya's plight. In Russia, it was not uncommon for husbands to return barren wives. The idea that Branya would appear on their doorstep was a constant source of concern. What man would want her with her useless womb? Who would blame Cyrus for sending her back? Perhaps in this new land, she could be passed off as a virgin, her past kept secret. But Branya was no beauty. Even as a child, she never drew the compliments that most babies receive. An older man, a widower with a family, might be the solution. But until then, no one had died in their small Jewish community and the oldest men were their own husbands. The Sisters shuddered at the thought. Branya's letter was a plea for help.

Friday nights the family gathered at the Sisters' house to celebrate the Sabbath. After dinner everyone would wander out into the courtyard to escape the smoke of the two tallow candles burning on the sideboard. The men huddled in a corner of the stone garden to discuss business, while the women sat spread out along the porch divided by piles of socks and shirts that needed mending.

One Friday night, as they sat outside enjoying the first cool breeze to slip over the mountain in weeks, Reesa drew her chair up next to Flora's. It was the time of year the locals called "the dry season," where the wind slackened its pace across the valley and the nightly rains were reduced to an occasional drizzle. The heat of the sun fell like a weight across the town, and a general lethargy settled in among the people.

"Flora." Reesa's hot breath moistened the inside of Flora's ear. "When are you going to announce your little secret?" she asked.

"Secret?" Flora smiled, unaware that Reesa had just sewn the first stitch into the fabric of retaliation.

"Hava noticed it weeks ago. That day we ran into you at the market, you were as green as those tomatoes you had in your basket," Reesa cackled.

"I'm not one hundred percent sure, yet," Flora stammered. She had tried to ignore the dull ache in her bosom.

"Not sure? Look at you." Reesa pointed to Flora's distended stomach.

Flora's eyes filled with tears. She began to sob uncontrollably. The idea of being pregnant in this backward land, away from her mother, terrified her. Yet she knew that Reesa was right. She had already missed two periods.

From the other end of the courtyard, Mule noticed that the women had abandoned their sewing. The chairs were empty and they had formed a circle. He could hear someone crying. Thinking perhaps it was Bluma, he hurried over. "What's the matter?"

The circle opened. Fanny and Hava returned to their seats and Freida went to fetch a glass of water. Bluma stroked Flora's arm. Reesa stood behind them, tapping the back of the chair with her fingers. "Mule, be a dear and get Dave," Reesa said.

"What's wrong?"

"Nothing is wrong. Flora is tired. She wants to go home."

"Don't worry, Flora." Reesa placed her hand on Flora's shoulder. "Your sisters will take good care of you."

12

Dear Mother,

Our roots grow deeper and deeper in this land of peasants and witch doctors. It seems that I am expecting another child. Hava says that it's a girl because I am constantly nauseous. Dave has had a bad case of the flu all month. He can't seem to shake it. He's as queasy as I am.

I'm enclosing a portrait. That handsome boy on my lap is your grandson, Sol.

Love,
Flora

As Flora addressed the envelope, she felt guilty that the letter was so sparse. But as she wrote, she had been distracted by the notion that her parents might never meet the new baby and that they would know her children only through photographs. Her hand lost its momentum and all the events she planned to recount evaporated, leaving nothing to tell. Flora decided to tear it up and start again, but was interrupted by the doorbell.

Hava stood on the step. She held a jar in her hand. Fanny and Reesa waved from the gate. "Do you need anything from the market?" Hava asked. She kept looking past Flora, inside the house.

"No thank you," Flora answered. "I was there this morning."

"This is for Dave." Hava handed Flora the jar. It was hot to the touch. "It will help settle his stomach. You might want to try some, too."

"What's it made of?" Flora asked.

"Sassafras," Hava replied. "Let us know if you need anything." She clipped the chain on her cardigan and joined her sisters. With a shake of her head, Hava let them know that Flora did not need anything.

Flora watched the three women link arms and move slowly up the incline of the street. Another hot day. The rains that tinted the valley green remained elusive. Flora could see the perspiration soaking through the back of their stockings. They pitched their bodies slightly forward, as if to avoid being toppled over by gravity. When the Sisters reached the end of the block, they paused for a moment to collect their breath.

Hava's potions never made it past the sink. The hand salve taught Flora what the family already knew. Even when made with love, Hava's remedies were worse than the illness. Flora set the jar down on the kitchen table. It seemed to be generating its own heat. Flora opened it. The concoction smelled earthy, like cow dung. "Another witches' brew," Flora mumbled under her breath as she poured it down the sink. It fizzed and burned a hole in the porcelain.

The next morning Dave awoke with a small red circle under his right eye. "A bug bite. Or maybe a pimple," Hava declared after she inspected it. It grew, masking his entire cheek and part of his forehead, giving him the appearance of a raccoon.

"He has the mark," Bolívariana commented to Flora. Too hot to sit outside, the old woman had dragged her rocker into the kitchen.

"The mark?"

"A man whose wife is with child always gets the mark. Sometimes it's on the face, and sometimes, if he's lucky, it's only where he can see it."

Flora shook her head in disbelief.

"It's very common," the old woman insisted.

Dave's stomach settled the day Flora's nausea subsided. His appetite returned, and with it a passion for vinegar. He sprinkled it on everything: meat, rice and beans, mashed potatoes, even sliced mango. Dave battled with indigestion and complained about varicose veins. The skin on his abdomen grew taut, and when he walked, he always held the base of his stomach with his hand, as if he were afraid of losing it.

Noting Flora's exasperation, Bolívariana tried to ease her mind. "It will pass. I once knew a man that grew a belly as big as his wife's." Flora stood hunched over the sink. Outside the kitchen window, the thorns of the bougainvillea drooped. The jasmine had lost all of its flowers and its trunk had faded to white. The shrubs that lined the houses on the block were nothing but twigs. Each time Flora turned the porcelain handle, brown water spit out of the tap and then subsided to a dribble.

"How much longer? I don't know how long I can stand this nonsense."

"It's the heat. Makes people crazy," Bolívariana answered.

Weeks passed without a visit from the mailman. The last time he had come to the door, his bag hung limply across his shoulder. In his hand he held two grease-stained letters. He offered them to Flora with a timidity that is the result of recent rejection. One was addressed to a Liliana Gutiérrez, a beauty contestant who lived over twenty blocks away, and the other was for a man who lived in El Prado, the next neighborhood over. Flora shook her head and gave them back. The postman moved onto the next house and warily handed them to the maid who opened the door. Flora had watched him go from house to house, until he vanished around the corner and became the neighborhood beggar, disheveled by insanity, who roamed Guayaquil, clutching two yellowed envelopes that would eventually bear the names of the dead.

As she was straightening up one day, Flora noticed the unfinished letter to her mother buried under a stack of papers in the kitchen. She quickly jotted down a few more lines and placed it in an envelope. On her way to the market, Flora stopped to mail it. The walls of the post office were lined with burlap sacks. Letters that announced the birth of children, declared eternal love, and settled land disputes had become a footrest for the wintry clerk who was suffering from phlebitis and had been advised by a healer to keep his leg raised.

"Do you have any mail for Grossenberg?" Flora asked as she handed him the letter.

"Nothing has come, Señora," the clerk replied. He stamped the envelope and tossed it behind him.

"Perhaps you might check in the back?" she asked politely. Flora thought it odd that the clerk had answered without even bothering to get up.

"Nothing has come, Señora," the clerk repeated.

"But how is it possible that an entire block has not received any mail in over a month?" Flora exclaimed.

"How about an entire city?" the clerk proposed. "What

happens when an entire city stops getting mail?" The clerk made a sweeping gesture toward the wall. "What happens to these letters waiting to travel to distant lands? They will sit here day after day because God has sucked the river down to nothing but mud. What shall happen to me? Am I to be devoured by a sea of paper words or by the words of an angry mob cut off from the world?" His feverish eyes darted back and forth in their sockets.

Flora left the building, shaken by the clerk's words. She stepped out into the dusty street. It was almost lunchtime and the vendors in the plaza were busy covering their carts to protect the produce from the midday sun. Flora cut between two drays. *"Escobas, fregonas, estropajo."* Worn brown hands tugged at the hem of her dress, pulling her toward the colorful mops made from shredded rags, yellow straw brooms, and loofah sponges.

"Jabones para la ropa. Jabones para la casa." Bars of soap made from vegetable fat, stacked one upon the other like bricks, and earthenware bowls filled with brown soap berries beckoned. *"Chumbimbo."*

"Mango con sal. Crispetas con azúcar. Obleas." School children on their way home for lunch stood around the vendors, buying mangos sprinkled with salt and brown paper cones filled with sugared popcorn. They held out their small hands to receive a sandwich made from two oversized hosts filled with creamy milk caramel.

"¿Papaya, Señora? ¿Mango?"

Flora stopped and admired the fruit. The skin of the papaya was the color of a buttercup. Somewhere in this land it had to be raining. She pressed her trembling finger into one end to make sure it was ripe. It was firm, yet it yielded slightly to the touch. The coins jingled in her palm as she handed them to the fruit vendor.

Flora bought a few more items and then returned home. Bolívariana stood on the landing staring up at the sun. "The rain is coming," she said.

Flora looked at the sky. Not a cloud was in sight. She licked the sweat from her upper lip. "How do you know?"

"I can feel it in my bones." Bolívariana shuffled back inside the house.

After the siesta, a single white cloud appeared over the mountain. The children played outside, watching their shadows grow to outlandish proportions and then shrink down to nothing as the cloud expanded across the blue sky. It hung over the valley, slowly turning gray. An hour later, the sky looked like night.

Flora sat in the living room with Sol. She was stacking blocks. Each time they fell over, Sol clapped and demanded that she build another tower. A bolt of lightning flashed. The lamps flickered and then the room went black. Frightened by the sound of the thunder and the sudden darkness, the toddler began to cry. "Hush, baby. It's okay," Flora said. She groped around the coffee table for a candle. Flora struck a match and the orange-blue flame exposed a bullfrog crouched in the corner of the room.

"Out! Scoot!" Flora cried as she stomped around the frog. It hopped lazily around the room, pausing briefly between each leap. "Get!" The frog jumped through the open door. As Flora went to close it, she noticed that the cobblestones in the courtyard had an odd glow to them. She stepped outside into the murmuring air. The stones were moving. She bent down to have a closer look and realized the courtyard was covered with frogs. They seemed to be making their way toward the empty fountain. A frog jumped down from the roof and landed on her head. Flora screamed. She bounced up and down, trying to rid herself of the slimy amphibian, but it was tangled in her hair. She yanked it from her head, along with a clump of hair, and flung it. As she tried to run back into the house, she felt a soft squishing under her feet. She was ankle deep in frogs. Her knees buckled and everything went black.

Flora awoke in her own bed. Bolívariana stood by the window. A frog jumped onto the ledge. It paused long enough for the old woman to snatch it up into her hand. Bolívariana held the frog to her face and ran her tongue over its eye. As Flora began to stir, she slipped it into her pocket.

"Who has Sol?" Flora asked. Her voice was hoarse.

"He's with his father."

"But the baby . . ." Flora tried to get up, but the room started to spin. She fell back onto the bed.

"Don't worry. The baby is fine. Smell."

"What?"

"Smell." Bolívariana ordered. "Take a deep breath."

Flora inhaled. A luscious fragrance, sweet and clean, filled her nostrils.

"The jasmine is blooming," Bolívariana said. "The jasmine is blooming."

13

Three days of steady showers washed away the thick layer of dust that had settled on the city. When the downpour stopped, the houses sparkled as if they had donned a fresh coat of paint. The air was sweet with the smell of gardenia, verbena, and campanula. The rain restored the color to the grass and exposed the invasive nature of the portulaca. It had not only survived the drought but flourished. The mountains that surrounded the valley enveloped the town in a purple halo of flowers.

When the sun finally came out, the children fell into the street. They splashed around the deep puddles gathering tadpoles. They salted the slugs that poured from the rich brown earth and watched them sizzle and bubble on the cement.

One of the first plants to revive was the lycopodium. It shot up, growing almost a foot a day. Women gathered the stalks and lay them out under the sun. Once dry, they stripped away the yellow petioles, ground them, and then sold the fine powder to the pharmacist, who used it as a remedy for intestinal parasites or to make fireworks.

The rain also dissolved the strawberry patch on Dave's face, replacing it with a dull ache in his chest. Loss flooded his body, making him pat the pockets of his trousers and jacket, and ransack the drawers of his bureau. At night, in the darkness of their bedroom, Dave would gaze at the outline of Flora's stomach, swollen with life. He'd hoped Sol's birth would bridge the distance between them. But his son only deepened the chasm. At times, and this caused him great shame, Dave felt envious of the love Flora lavished on the child. Sol secured every one of Flora's smiles. All her laughter and joy belonged to him.

Preparations for the new baby were under way. Dave watched his wife from the bedroom window as she unfurled a bolt of cloth along the flagstones that ran between the kitchen and the courtyard. She got down on all fours and began to trace squares into the cotton, using one of Sol's diapers as a stencil. Despite the size of her stomach, Flora crawled along the strip of fabric with ease. Over her nightgown she wore a poncho cinched with a piece of rope. Bent over her work, she looked like a monk, deep in prayer. The Lilliputian head and the enormous body brought a smile to Dave's face.

When Flora asked Dave to bring her some cloth from the store, he thought she wanted to make a dress. His gut hurt as he watched her rip into the center of the imported gabardine with her shears. "None of my sweaters fit anymore," she said as her head popped through the hole.

"You should let Lucha do that for you." Dave walked out into the courtyard. Lucha was the washwoman. She came every Thursday and always brought her son, Fernando. With Flora going into her last month of pregnancy, the couple decided it might be best if Lucha stayed with them until after the baby was born. At first, Flora had been concerned about having Fernando in the house as well. He was two years older than Sol, and she worried it would be too much work for Lucha to look after them both. But

Fernando was a docile child. He loved Sol's collection of pencils and chalks and could spend hours stretched out on his stomach drawing on butcher paper. He never cried, except when it was time to go home and his mother pried the smooth sticks of color from his fingers.

"Lucha will have enough to do once she gets here," Flora said. Dave extended his hand to help her, but she ignored it. "Are you going to fetch them?" Flora pushed herself up off the ground.

"Yes. Do you need anything?"

Flora shook her head. She followed Dave outside and watched him drive away. Across the street, a maid was sweeping. Flora waved good morning to her. The girl made the sign of the cross and hurried back inside the house.

Seeing her son's interest in drawing, Lucha had dipped into her wages and bought Fernando a pencil and a small writing tablet. Within two hours, the pages were full and his pencil had discovered another canvas—the inner walls of their house in Alpujarras. She'd given Fernando a sturdy beating with his dead father's belt more for his subject matter than for the fact that he had drawn on the tiles in the kitchen and inside the pages of her Bible. The woman in his drawings was unmistakably Flora. Even though Lucha took away what remained of the pencil, portraits of Flora continued to surface. A small one was carved into the front door with a knife. Another appeared on the cistern. For pigment, Fernando used rocks that yielded color when scratched against a hard surface, ground flowers, and leaves. He also discovered that adding water, or his own urine, to earth produced a color very similar to la Señora's poncho. When Flora's likeness began to appear on the whitewashed walls of the houses of their neighborhood, the people of Alpujarras believed that Fernando's hand was guided by God. Her image became the patron saint of the barrio. They called her Nuestra Señora de Alpujarras. Women knelt in front of her, begging forgiveness for their sins, asking her to heal their children, or return their husbands' affections. At night candles burned at her feet and people prayed for her mercy. One day, the owner of the bakery, doña Rosa, returned from the market claiming to have seen Nuestra Señora de Alpujarras in the plaza smelling a melon. A few days later, don Martín, the chemist, swore she appeared at the intersection of Junin and Palace. Even Vic, the street urchin, swore he saw her in a black car. But no one believed him. Everyone knew that saints did not ride in automobiles.

Lucha knew better than to try and explain. The women of Alpujarras would have scratched her eyes out if she had told them that their Señora was an American living on Carrera Simón Bolívar. Therefore, she too knelt down before the lady and prayed for salvation.

The last time Dave had driven Lucha home it was night. As he drove through Alpujarras that day, he noticed the portraits of the woman with a small head and an enormous body painted on the walls of the houses. In some she bore street clothing, but in most she wore a friar's costume. When Dave arrived at Lucha's house, she was waiting for him outside. "Vamos Fernando," she called out to her son. The two scrambled into the backseat of the car.

Lucha kept her head bent in prayer the entire ride. The neighborhood was organizing a pilgrimage to the plaza. They were determined to see their lady in the square.

During Flora's confinement, the Sisters did her food shopping. Every morning on the way to the plaza, they stopped at the house to pick up Lucha. Before they arrived, Flora would go over the list with the maid. "Don't get the big carrots. Get the smaller ones. They're sweeter. Last time you got the big ones. They tasted bitter. Get light eggplants. The heavy ones are all seed."

Lucha would listen to Flora's instructions, all the while nervously chewing the inside of her lower lip. Reesa snatched the list from her hand the moment they left the house. She lacked the courage to tell the Sisters that la Señora wanted the yellow potatoes, not russets. The maid accepted the avocados they handed her even though the tips were as hard as stone, well aware that Flora would be angry. Their ability to pit vendor against vendor to get one more tomato, or half a centavo off a pound of potatoes, shot shivers up Lucha's spine. Las Señoras reminded Lucha of hens, scurrying through the market, checking every price. Then, they would converge on a dray, pointing their bony, dried-out fingers. "How much for a kilo of carrots?"

"Ten centavos, Señoras."

"Eight."

"Nine."

"It's nine over there," they'd lie, flapping their arms at another vendor who also happened to be selling carrots (at two cents more).

They held onions loosely in their palms, ready to drop them back into the crate. "How much?"

"Six centavos."

"Onions were five yesterday."

"*Está bien.* Five, Señoras."

The Sisters wiped down the chairs offered to them by the vendor and sat down. "Five pounds cucumbers. Ten pounds tomatoes. Ten mangos," they barked.

"*¿Tinto*, Señoras?" A young girl offered cups of espresso from a tray.

"Don't drink it, Lucha. They make it with filthy water," one sister would invariably say if Lucha accepted the cup of coffee.

Before the merchant was allowed to pack up an order, every potato, carrot, and string bean had to be inspected. In the meantime, Lucha was sent to hire a porter. Too often the Sisters accused the porters of bruising the produce. "I'd rather sit here in the sun," they'd say when she approached them.

"But it's also for Señora Flora." Lucha knew the porters liked Flora. She tipped well and always gave them a soda before they returned to the market. But Flora's name drew little leverage when it came to working for the Sisters. Lucha had to beg until one of the men took pity on the maid and agreed to help her.

Two hours later, the Sisters strolled into the kitchen. Lucha and the porter tripped after them, clutching baskets of groceries. "You're definitely having a girl," Hava declared.

"How do you know?"

"A girl drains the mother of her beauty," Fanny informed Flora.

Flora waddled over to the table. Her hips and back ached from the weight in her stomach. She took some coins from a jar and gave them to the porter.

"I already tipped him, Flora." Reesa stood in the doorway, staring at Flora's stomach. She had never set foot inside her sister-in-law's kitchen, not even in the three weeks they had been doing Flora's shopping. Instead she always flapped around the door, hurrying Fanny and Hava along, shouting instructions. "Flora, you shouldn't be on your feet," Reesa admonished her.

"I feel better if I stand," Flora lied. In the last few days, she had broken three chairs. The instant she sat down, the wood began to creak and splinter, or she felt the cane center rend under her.

"You go rest." Reesa looked to her sisters. "We'll make lunch for you." Hava and Fanny nodded in agreement.

"Oh, don't worry. I can do it. I've got Lucha to help me." Their eyes were on her stomach.

"Go lie down." Reesa stepped into the kitchen. "We'll tell the shiksa what to do."

She had not slept well in weeks. Too tired to fight them, Flora decided to accept their offer. "Maybe I will try to take a nap."

Flora was still asleep when Dave came home for lunch.

"Dovid." Reesa took him aside. "Our sister is in trouble." She opened her purse and retrieved Branya's letter. "We need to help her," she said after Dave finished reading the letter. Dave understood what his sister proposed. In Russia, it was common for children to be passed between families. Economic hardship had brought Benzi to their home. Dave's father took his nephew in and raised him like a son.

"I'll talk to Flora," Dave said. He kissed his sisters good-bye and asked Lucha to serve lunch.

Flora awoke after Dave finished his soup. She found him at the table, drumming his fingers on the letter as he ate his meat and potatoes. "A letter from Branya," Dave said. "My sister, the one who lives in New York."

"I know who Branya is. She introduced us. Remember? She was at our wedding." Flora sat down.

"Oh, yes. Of course." Dave rubbed his eyes. "It must be lonely for her in New York."

Lucha brought Sol into the dining room. He climbed up onto Flora's lap and began to play with the silverware. "*¿Lucha, el tetero?*"

"*Sí*, Señora." Lucha went into the kitchen and came back with a bottle.

"Doesn't her husband have family there?" Flora tested the milk on her wrist. Sol tried to grab the bottle from his mother's hands. "Wait, honey. It's too hot."

"Yes, but that's not the same as your own." Dave looked at his son. "And she has no children to keep her company." He shoved the letter into his pocket.

"Hot! Pfft." Sol attempted to blow air from his mouth.

"That's right. That's how Mommy cools things down. Blow. Lucha!"

Lucha appeared in the doorway. "Señora?"

"It's too hot." Flora handed Lucha the bottle. "Run it under some cold water," she said to the maid.

"Hot! Hot! Hot! Bears!" Sol clapped. "Bears!"

"That's right. The porridge was too hot so the bears went out for a walk."

"And then that Golda girl—" Dave piped in.

"Goldie," Flora corrected him.

"Goldie came in and stole their food."

"She didn't steal it," Flora corrected him.

"She broke all their chairs, ate everyone's food, messed up all their beds. In Russia she would be arrested." Dave laughed.

"Tete! Tete," Sol demanded.

"Lucha!" Flora called out to the maid in the kitchen. "Not too long! Or else it will be too cold."

"Cold. Too cold," Sol repeated.

Lucha came back with the bottle. Flora tested it again. "Just right," Flora said to Sol as she handed it to him.

"Rye," he repeated and took a sip. "Jus rye." As Sol chewed on the rubber nipple, he reached for the stone on Flora's engagement ring. "Pretty." He smiled up at his mother. The baby settled into the crook of his mother's arm, squeezing her breast as he drank.

Dave got up. On his way out of the room, he stopped to stroke his son's head. Sol looked up at him.

"This one came out good. Huh?" Dave smiled at his wife.

"So will the next one," Flora answered. "Hava keeps saying it's a girl."

"How about we send her to Branya?"

Flora looked up at her husband and was surprised to see he was serious.

"We'll send her to Branya. We'll share our good fortune," Dave declared.

"You want to give away our child?" Flora was incredulous.

"She has no children. We have one, another on the way. We can have more."

"You would give away your own flesh and blood?" Flora cried.

"It is not giving away. It is not like we'd give the baby

to a stranger. We are giving it to family. Giving it to family who are not as fortunate as we are."

Sol's eyes were drowsy and sanguine. He looked up at his father. He would not remember the conversation, only Dave's smile, the way it had faded, abruptly.

"Are you insane?" Flora hissed.

"Why? In Russia families do it all the time."

"I will not give my child away."

"Flora," Dave pressed on. "We are in the position to help her."

"How can you even consider this?" Flora screamed at him.

"They've been married almost ten years, Flora. She has yet to bear him a child. He's been very patient. Cyrus has every right to return Branya."

"Return her? She's not something he bought! For better or worse, Dave. Remember?"

"I'm thinking about what is best for the family."

"Whose family?"

"Our family."

"No, Dave. Not our family. This is not the best for our family," Flora said. "Take him." Flora held Sol up to Dave.

"No. Not Sol," Dave said.

"Why not Sol?" Flora asked, jumping on the idea that Dave had misunderstood and thought she meant to give away Sol. "What's the difference?" Flora eased herself up from the chair.

"He's my son."

Son. Son. The words reverberated in Flora's head. "And if this baby is a boy, a son, will you be so eager to give him away?"

Dave said nothing.

Flora stormed into the bedroom, slamming the door

behind her. She turned the key in the lock and sat down on the bed. She placed her hand on her stomach. "Don't you worry. I won't let them send you off." The baby responded by jabbing her rib cage.

Dave knocked on the door. "Flori. Let me in,"

"No. Go away." Flora closed her eyes. She prayed for a boy. She did not want a daughter, not now, not ever. She suddenly understood Reesa's contempt for Bluma. What did a daughter have to look forward to in this family?

"But Flora," Dave begged.

Flora refused to come out at dinner. Instead she sat on the bed and finished the box of chocolates that Mule had brought her from his last trip to the States, almost a year before. At eleven o'clock, she heard a faint tap on the door but pretended to be asleep.

he sun beamed in through a crack in the wooden shutter. It lit Flora's right cheek, slowly warming the alabaster skin to a soft pink. The dread of having overslept pried her eyes open. Flora sat up. Sol. Who had Sol? Why hadn't she heard him cry this morning? The house was quiet except for a scratching noise coming from the courtyard. Flora opened the shutter. Fernando sat under her window facing the wall.

"Fernando."

The boy looked up. In his hand he held a piece of coal he had taken from the fireplace.

"Fernando," Flora repeated, ignoring the boy's soot-streaked face and hands. "Fernando, go get your mother."

The child rose and wandered into the kitchen. "Fernando!" Flora heard Lucha cry. *"¡Ay Díos mío! ¡Este mucha-chito me va a volver loca!"* Fernando scurried back out into the courtyard with his mother on his heels.

"Lucha," Flora called across the courtyard. "Lucha! Come here."

Lucha approached the window timidly. She eyed the sketch on the wall below Flora. *"Otro. Ay Díos,"* she whispered, certain that la Señora had noticed the portrait drawn against the whitewash. *"Buenos días,* Señora Flora."

"The baby?" Flora inquired.

"He's taking his nap, Señora."

"What time is it?"

"Three, Señora."

"Three? How could I have slept this late?" Flora wondered out loud. She was usually up by six. She had slept almost sixteen hours. "Did you feed the baby?"

"Of course, Señora."

"And don David?" Flora asked, ignoring the maid's insulted eyes.

"He came back to eat lunch, but when he saw you were still asleep he went back out, Señora."

"Probably ate at the Sisters'," Flora muttered to herself. "Fine. Let him eat his meals there." She closed the shutter, and the light withered, leaving the room once again dark and cool. "Let him play that game." Sol would be up soon. His afternoon bottle needed to be heated. Flora was about to unlock the door when she felt a sharp pain cut across her middle. Her hand gripped the porcelain knob. She tried to open the door but another contraction doubled her over. "No. Not yet, baby," she whispered. Flora fell back onto the bed. Fear gripped her. Her heart was pounding, every beat amplified in her head. She tried to get up but another contraction sent her reeling to the floor. "Lucha," Flora moaned. "Lucha." But the maid was on the other side of the house, giving Sol his bottle and could not hear her mistress calling her.

Bolívariana heard Flora's cries for help. She got up from her rocker and wandered over to the bedroom window. "Señora?" She stuck her hand through the wrought iron window bars and pushed the shutter open. Flora was writhing on the floor. Bolívariana went inside the house.

The bedroom door was locked. "Señora! Señora! Open the door."

But Flora could not move. The inside of her thighs felt warm and sticky. She could hear Lucha and Bolívariana wrestling with the knob, pressing their shoulders into the wooden door, hoping to burst the lock with the weight of their bodies. "Don't worry, Señora," Lucha called. "We're going to get help." But Flora did not respond. She was staring at the blood running down her legs.

Lucha raced to the Sisters' house. "La Señora," she panted.

"What happened?" Reesa asked.

"La Señora," Lucha wailed. *"Está grave."*

Ten minutes later the five women stood outside Flora's bedroom banging on the door. "Flora! Flora!" they called, but to no avail. She lay unconscious on the cold tile. The Sisters searched the house for a set of keys but found none. Reesa gave Lucha some money and sent her to fetch Dave in a taxi. When the men arrived, the Sisters were trying to unwedge Fernando from between the wrought iron window bars. They had managed to squeeze his thin body inside the room, but his head was too large to slip through. When they attempted to pull him back into the courtyard he became hysterical. His body swelled up from the tears and they were unable to pry him out. In her quest for keys, Hava had spotted a jar of chicken schmaltz and was busy rubbing it all over the child's body to help free him. Fanny was feeding Fernando candy in an effort to stop his crying. Mule and Harold tried to pull apart the bars with a crowbar. Sol, frightened by the commotion, began to wail. "Mama. Mama. Mama. Mama." His sobs rose above the mayhem.

Flora opened her eyes. A pair of legs fluttered in the window. "Sol," she called out faintly. "Don't cry, baby." Dazed, she opened the door and followed the sound of his voice. It was tucked inside the semicircle of people standing around the window.

They stared at Flora as if she were a ghost. Her skin was the color of her nightgown, translucent. "Señora." Bolívariana took Flora's cold hand and led her back into the bedroom.

"Where's Sol?" Flora asked.

"Don't worry," Reesa said. She took hold of Flora's elbow and helped Bolívariana guide Flora back into the room. "Zamie's bringing the doctor. Lucha, wipe that up." Reesa pointed to the trail of blood running from the bedroom to the courtyard.

The doctor Zamie brought back was a young man. His cheeks had yet to lose the softness of boyhood and were pink as a baby's. "I'll need a sheet and a basin filled with water," he said softly, undoing his cuff links and dropping them on the bureau. He rolled up his sleeves.

"Señora, please." The doctor gently eased Flora back onto the bed.

"Drape it on top of her," the doctor said when Fanny returned with the sheet. She lay it over Flora's body, leaving only her head exposed.

Flora felt the doctor's hands inside of her and gripped the cloth between her fingers. The night she had gone into labor with Sol, nearly two years before, her mother had stayed by her side the entire night, defying the nurse who ordered her out of the room. Shana held Flora's hand through each contraction. When they came to take Flora into the delivery room, her mother had whispered in her ear, "I am with you, my dear child," and it was then that

Flora noticed the purple bruise she had inflicted on the back of her mother's hand.

"Pop." A gush of liquid saturated the bed linens. The doctor dipped his hands into the basin. The water turned pink as the blood ran off his fingers. He motioned for the Sisters to step out into the hallway. "The baby is turned sideways," he said, drying his hands on a towel.

"Sideways?" Hava asked.

"Horizontal. The head is here," the doctor said pointing to the right side of his own stomach. "And the feet are here." The Sisters followed his finger over to the left side of his abdomen.

Benzi sauntered in from the kitchen. "What's the matter?" he asked, taking a sip from the demitasse cup he held in his hand.

"The baby is sideways," Hava answered. "It should be head down. I went to medical school in Russia," she informed the doctor.

The doctor's eyes lit up. "Did you get to deliver a child?" he asked.

"She didn't even get to clean a bedpan," Reesa interjected. "She was there all of two weeks."

"Two months," Hava corrected her. "I was there two months."

"Doctor, can I offer you a cup of coffee?" Reesa interrupted.

"Yes, thank you. If it isn't any trouble."

"Fanny, get the doctor some coffee," Reesa said. "See if Flora has any cake or cookies," she called after her.

"Is the baby in danger?" Benzi asked.

"Well, yes," the doctor replied. "They both are. If I don't get it turned around . . ." The doctor crossed himself. He waited for them to follow suit, but they just stood there, with their hands slack at their sides. "Perhaps you might want to call a priest." The doctor slipped back inside the room, followed by Hava and Reesa.

Flora lay on her side. Her face was partially illuminated by the glow of the lamp. Her expression was peaceful, as if she were just about to fall asleep. Bolívariana stood next to her, softly stroking her hair.

"Señora?" The doctor bent down toward her.

"Yes?" Flora asked. She furrowed her brow, squeezed her eyes shut, and sucked in the air between them.

"I'm going to examine you again." He went around to the foot of the bed and reached under the sheet. The doctor concentrated on his task, his gaze fixed on the ceiling to avoid the look of indignation on Flora's face. As he checked to determine the baby's exact positioning, a miniature hand gripped his index finger. The doctor tugged gently, hoping that he might free the baby from its lateral position. But it refused to budge. He attempted once more, this time with a bit more force. Nothing. He tried to wiggle free from the baby's grasp but it wouldn't surrender his digit. The baby tugged his finger. "Okay," he whispered. "You show me the way. That's it. That's it." The motion stopped. The baby's lips surrounded the tip of his finger and began to suck. "Got you!" The doctor hooked the baby by the gums and gently rotated the head. The baby scratched at his hand, trying to break free of the doctor's firm grip. But he held on, even when gums clamped down on his index finger with such furious strength that they almost severed his skin. He felt the head give way as he gently pulled down. "Good. Okay now you're ready to come out and meet your family," he said. But as soon as he withdrew his hand from Flora's body, the baby curled itself into a ball and flipped over.

Flora screamed just as Fanny entered with the pot of coffee and an assortment of cakes.

The doctor stuck his hand back inside just in time to grab the baby by the ankle. "All right, we'll do this the hard way," he said, tugging the infant. He pulled again and managed to expose a tiny foot to the air. It struggled to climb back inside but the doctor held on tight. "Hold this," the doctor ordered Hava. He grabbed the other foot and tugged.

"Push, Señora. Push!" the doctor commanded.

Flora pushed, but nothing happened. For nearly two hours, the baby clung to its mother's womb, defying the doctor and her aunts, who tried to yank it out. Its shoulders, too wide to pass through the cervix, kept it anchored. The doctor twisted the infant's body, easing the shoulders through. With the cervix closing around its neck, the baby was ready to choose death, but Flora, tired of the ordeal of labor, gave a giant push, thrusting her daughter out into Reesa's open hands.

16

*F*rom the moment she drew her first breath of air, the baby, named Ruth after her maternal great-grand-mother Rebecca, was inconsolable. Outraged by her sex, she screamed night and day at a fervent pitch that seeped through the walls of the house and out into the street. The child's rage intensified at dusk when the sun fell behind the mountains and the jasmine's pale yellow blooms heralded the night with their sweet scent. Ruthie seldom slept. When she did, tears welled up under her blue-veined eyelids and spilled down her cheeks. One morning, Flora looked inside the bassinet and found her daughter floating on a pool of sorrow.

Ruthie unleashed grief buried deep in people's hearts. After Fanny held the baby, her first love, the man who left her at the altar, bubbled up. Once at home, she filled a bucket with ammonia and bleach. Her sisters discovered Fanny inhaling the fumes to burn his memory from her brain. Each time Benzi visited, he shed tears for his son buried in an unmarked grave in Krasnoyarsk. Even Bluma, who usually went to Flora's house straight from school, could not tolerate her cousin's forlorn wailing. She spent the afternoons in her mother's kitchen, nibbling the poisonous leaves of rhubarb, feeding on their bitterness.

Mule and Harold no longer lunched with Dave and Flora on Tuesdays. They claimed it was impossible to carry on a conversation in the presence of a screaming child. Dave tried the same excuse, only to find a packed suitcase waiting for him by the door. "You might as well sleep there too!" Flora cried, eager to vent her rage at someone. Ruthie consumed every ounce of her energy. Flora tried to be patient, but by midday the baby's cries became spiteful, uttered solely to torment her mother. Resolve shattered, Flora's lips fired back. She hurled insults—brat, monster, obnoxious—at her daughter. Flora's words gelled in the baby's memory, never to be forgotten or forgiven.

Ruthie's trilling red tongue drowned the warble of mating crickets, the howl of the wind, and Reesa's desire for revenge. Unlike the rest of the family, who left the house with the infant's despair clinging to their clothes and her rage echoing in their ears, Reesa emerged euphoric. While everyone dabbed their eyes after a visit to Flora's, Reesa wiped the smile from her lips. Flora got what she deserved: a wretched child.

Doctors consulted found nothing wrong. They gave the standard answers—colic and gas. Dave, Flora, and Lucha walked around like zombies, bumping into furniture, walls, and one another from the lack of sleep. The only ones in the house who managed to get some rest were Sol and Fernando, who were blessed with the deep, impenetrable slumber of children, and Bolívariana, who had the selective hearing of an old woman.

Lucha, exhausted by the child's anguish, dozed off at the stove one day while heating a bottle. She awoke to the smell of burning cotton and realized her apron was on fire. The flames spread quickly, and by the time Dave threw a blanket on her, the skin on her thighs was singed so badly that she was unable to walk. She returned to Alpujarras with Fernando, leaving Flora and Dave alone in their misery.

After Lucha's departure, a string of maids followed. Each came boasting a remedy—chamomile to settle the stomach, rum on the gums to ease teething, eucalyptus plasters to loosen congestion—and left claiming that *"la niña"* was possessed by the devil.

Filomena arrived in August. A descendant of the slaves of El Chocó, Filomena had inherited a knowledge of household remedies from her mother and grandmother: burn limoncillo to keep the nighttime mosquitoes at bay, carry a branch of rue to ward off evil, boil the rue and drink the oily tea to loosen an unwanted child from the womb, apply a salve of cruceto to a snakebite and then say a prayer to the Blessed Virgin.

Convinced Filomena wouldn't last more than a day, Flora didn't bother to show her the house. She sat the new maid down in the kitchen and wearily recited the litany of chores. "Breakfast is early. Mr. Grossenberg goes to work at seven." Flora swayed Ruthie, trying to soothe her. "He comes back for lunch at one. We eat dinner at six. I will help you with the cooking for lunch and dinner, but you are in charge of breakfast. Mr. Grossenberg drinks tea. It is in the cupboard—"

"That child is full of sadness," Filomena interrupted.

"She's just a little cranky this morning," Flora lied. "She didn't sleep too well."

"May I hold her?"

Flora handed Ruthie to the maid. Filomena cradled the baby within her burnished black arms. *"Niña. Niña. No llore,"* she sang to wailing child. Filomena bent her head toward the child's mouth and listened carefully to the pitch of her grief. "Don't cry. Filomena will make it better," she hummed.

Sleepless and depleted, Dave and Flora failed to notice the altar that Filomena set up in the children's bedroom closet. It was decorated with a porcelain Christ, three tallow candles, and a bowl made from the shell of a coconut. Inside the bowl lay the ashes from a clump of the newborn's hair and some nail clippings. All through the night, pots clanked and brews boiled on the kitchen stove. But the tea that was supposed to make Ruthie sweat out her sadness only made her cry more fervently. And the jaborandi used to dry her tear ducts only made them more lachrymose. "Be patient, my child," the maid whispered into the sobbing infant's ear, "Filomena will soon have a gift for you."

When the rag between her legs was saturated with the blood of the matriarchs of El Chocó, Filomena took it from her underwear and placed it in a pot with water. She let it boil until the cloth came clean and then strained some of the liquid into the baby's milk. But Ruthie rejected the brew, twisting her face away from the nipple of the bottle. It was Flora who ingested the liquor endowed with fortitude and longevity. She saw the half-full pot on the burner and, thinking it was beef consommé, drank three cups. Its power was readily apparent. The dark circles under Flora's eyes vanished and a pink flush spread across her cheeks.

Flora greeted Dave with a kiss when he came home for dinner. Her display of affection was unusual, but more peculiar was the brief quiet moment they experienced as their lips touched. They kissed again, this time their eyes focused on the baby in the bassinet. Ruthie's tiny fists beat the air but no sound emerged from her gaped mouth. Gaz-

ing into each other's eyes, they pressed their mouths together. The persistent crying submerged under their collective breath. Delectable silence filled their ears. For the
first time since Ruthie's birth, Flora and Dave could hear
themselves think. They allowed their lips to linger, enjoying the mundane thoughts that popped into their heads.
Flora planned the next day's meals and composed a shopping list. Dave calculated how much money would be
needed to open another store. That night they slept
soundly, lip to lip, able to hear the conversations within
their dreams previously muffled by the baby's incessant
weeping.

In the morning, the couple pondered their day over a
long good-bye kiss on the doorstep. Once they parted, it
occurred to Flora that Sol's lips might bear the same ef-
fect. Every day Flora doused his face with kisses. She'd
kissed Sol's chin, nose, eyes, but never his mouth. Flora
gazed at her son in the courtyard, bent over a boat made
from old newsprint. A boy was emerging from under the
baby fat. She snuck up behind him and placed her finger
inside the hollow of his now slender neck. When had that
plump roll of skin between his head and shoulders disappeared?

"Solly," Flora whispered in his ear. The boy turned to
face his mother. Flora cupped his head between her hand
and kissed his nose. Then, closing her eyes, she placed her
lips upon his. Inside, Ruthie continued to cry. Sol pulled
away and returned to his boat. Flora wiped the shame from
her mouth with the back of her hand.

After Ruthie did not respond to any of Filoména's con-
coctions, the maid decided it was time to consult the spirits. She had hesitated to call upon their expertise because
they were sometimes unreliable and apt to play tricks. But

Filomena saw the desperation in Ruthie's eyes and decided it was worth the risk.

At dawn, when Bolívariana's shuffling subsided and her shadow disappeared through the door in the patio, Filomena lifted the wailing baby from her crib and placed her beneath the altar. She lit the candles and whispered *"Espíritus, espíritus,"* into the smoke. Then, as the spirit that answered commanded her, Filomena warmed the rim of a jar over the ocher flame. She rolled Ruthie onto her stomach and pressed the mouth on the infant's back to create a seal between the skin and the glass. The jar filled with fumes. The baby's shrieks slowed to sobs and sputtered out. When the tears stopped flowing from her eyes Filomena pulled away the jar and replaced the lid. "There, *niña*. There. See. Filomena has fixed everything," she cooed.

The baby looked up at the maid defiantly. She squeezed her glassy eyes only to find her tear ducts drier than the desert. Ruthie opened her mouth to yell and only silence gushed forth. Her pale cheeks turned red with fury.

All day, Flora held the baby gingerly, afraid to jolt her out of her tranquil state. But Ruthie did not cry. Filomena had aspirated her tears and their sound.

"Be careful." Bolívariana stood in the doorway, watching Flora lift the baby from her crib.

"She's fine," Flora replied.

The old woman shook her head. She'd found the jar Filomena used the night before. When Bolívariana held the glass up to the light, she saw only tears. Filomena had pulled the glass away too soon, leaving sorrow and rage trapped under the baby's skin.

Ruthie grew up to be a woeful, nervous child who seldom laughed or smiled. She'd inherited the superstitions of another people, growing pale if a maid swept after dark and insisting on burning her nail clippings. It plagued her mother that Ruthie refused to have her picture taken. As a baby, she'd squirm and scowl at the photographer, unable to express that he was stealing her soul. Language strengthened Ruthie's determination. Despite her father's pleas and her mother's threats, she refused to sit for family portraits. Even when her father purchased a home movie camera, Ruthie refused to be captured on celluloid. While her brothers paraded back and forth in front of the camera and her mother feigned the coy shyness of Swanson and Colbert, Ruthie fled from the scene. The only time Flora managed to get Ruthie to pose was for passport pictures. In every one, she wore the same enraged countenance. Much to Ruthie's displeasure, her mother would have them enlarged and framed. They hung on the walls, a chronicle of her despair that multiplied year after year.

17

*T*he year after Ruthie was born, Harold turned orange. His alabaster skin exploded with color, at first a yellow so intense that it made people squint. Yellow clung to his gums and stained his teeth. It bled into his hands and fingers, turning the nail beds the color of sunflowers. Yellow even found its way into the whites of his eyes. At night, they glowed in the dark like a cat's.

Reesa shuddered while Fanny and Hava wrung their hands in despair. The Sisters could not help but remember the women who lived in the left wing of the clinic in Gomel where their father, Sol, a consumptive, had spent the last years of his life. Once, a door had been carelessly left open, and in the gray stone atrium where patients visited with their families, appeared two women dressed in canary yellow gowns. The Sisters had watched with amusement as the two waltzed across the floor. It wasn't until one began to climb up onto the sill that they realized their intent. Just as the nurse rushed in, one, in order to gain access to the window, pushed her companion into the glass. It shattered. The two women, their hands and faces studded with shards, were dragged from the room. They left behind a trail of blood and eerie laughter that lodged itself deep inside the Sisters' ears, making all laughter forever suspect.

And here was their brother, the color of insanity, refusing to eat meat, bloated and flatulent from the enormous number of vegetables and fruits he consumed in order to fill his stomach. Harold had also developed the nasty habit of spitting out anything that he didn't like. One morning, the Sisters were in the kitchen when they heard a dull thump against the wall. As Reesa stepped into the dining room to investigate, a soursop hit her between the eyes. Reesa slumped and struck her head against the sideboard. Hava and Fanny raced in just as Harold spit out a seed pod, sending it across the room.

"What has gotten into you?" Hava screamed at him as she revived Reesa with a cloth soaked in ammonia.

"Tasteless," Harold muttered. He picked up another soursop and tore into the green skin with the talon growing on his index finger. Despite his sisters' constant nagging, Harold refused to trim his nails, arguing that they came in handy for peeling oranges and breadfruits. He kept them razor sharp by filing them with the scrap of sandpaper stashed in his pocket.

The family, at Reesa's insistence, congregated at Dave and Flora's to discuss the situation. It had been easy to slip away, as Harold took his siesta on the verandah, dozing on a hammock he had bought at the market. Some nights he would slip from his bed and lay in the hammock, gazing up at the stars. In the morning the Sisters would find him outside, covered in sweet dew.

"He's insane," Reesa blurted out.

Benzi sat at one end of the table, with Mule on his right. Dave sat at the other end. Grecia, Zamie, and Leon sat between them while the Sisters paced around the table. Freida was not invited, and as Flora poured the coffee, she realized that had it not been her home, she, too, would have been excluded.

"Reesa." Benzi tried to mollify her. "It's just Harold. He's always been like this." Harold's naiveté and inability to perceive danger never came close to wounding him. He was like a cat, indestructible, landing on his feet every time, winning the wager, completely oblivious to the gamble or how close he had come to losing. He was blessed with a sort of luck that no one dared remark, fearing the mere mention would bring ultimate disaster.

"Not like this, Benzi. Not like this." Reesa pointed to the lump on her forehead.

"Is this not the same boy who invited the Russian Army home so he could say good-bye to his mother?" Benzi reminded his wife.

"Benzi!" Reesa cried. "He's the color of the sapotes he eats night and day." Indeed, Harold's skin had deepened to a luscious orange.

"Soon he'll be red like the government that is trying to put us out of business." Benzi laughed.

The government was also changing color. After forty years in power, the blue conservative party had been voted out and replaced by red liberals, who promised social and economic reform. The government, in order to promote industry, had curtailed the list of imported goods allowed into the country. It had become nearly impossible to get the religious statues, crystal, and kitchen gadgets that they sold. Empty shelves loomed throughout the store. Benzi knew it was only a matter of time before the cloth they imported to make the ponchos and women's shawls, their most popular items, would also be banned.

"He's fine, Reesa. Now, let us go back to work or we're all going to starve."

Benzi dropped Zamie and Grecia back at the store and drove to the barbershop. Somewhat fastidious about his appearance, Benzi liked a barber's shave every day. In the morning, he'd shave at home, but by noon, the bristles of his beard demanded attention. After he arrived in Medellín, Benzi spent a long time searching for the right barber, because as he put it, "You had to trust the man with a blade at your throat." He'd go to a barbershop, pull a billfold from his pant pocket, and place it on the counter before he sat down in the chair. Inside the bulging wallet were cut-out pieces of paper the size of peso bills. Benzi would chat with the barber in a friendly manner, get up, pull some coins from his pocket, pay for his shave, and then casually walk out. The wallet was never returned, not even if Benzi went back a few minutes later pretending to look for it. "A rotten lot, all of them," Benzi complained to his family.

"Not to mention the fact that you're spending a fortune on billfolds," Reesa admonished him.

By the time Benzi walked into don Ignacio's shop, he'd lost all hope. He'd been to almost every barber in the valley. "Ah, you're the foreigner who leaves wallets full of paper in barbershops," don Ignacio said to Benzi the moment he set the wallet on the counter. "I've been waiting for you to come into my shop."

"How did you know?" Benzi asked.

"We're a brotherhood." Don Ignacio smiled and began to lather Benzi's face.

"Then you're all thieves."

"And you, my friend? What would you do if a wallet full of money appeared at your feet?"

"Pick it up of course," Benzi replied. He enjoyed this kind of banter. It demonstrated intelligence, something Benzi respected more than honesty.

"Even if you saw the man who had dropped it?" Don Ignacio sharpened the razor against the leather strop.

"Only a fool is that careless with his money," Benzi said, laughing.

"Precisely." Don Ignacio pressed the blade into the base of Benzi's neck. He worked slowly and methodically, holding the blade firmly between his fingers as he eased it across Benzi's skin. After he was done, don Ignacio wiped the remaining soap off Benzi's face with a damp towel. Benzi got up and paid. The next morning when Benzi came into the shop, the fifteen wallets he'd set as bait were on the counter waiting for him.

"How did you know I'd be back?" Benzi asked.

"If a man closes his eyes while another holds a razor at his throat, he'll be back."

Throughout the years Benzi came to rely on don Ignacio. He went from barber to confidant. It was the closest relationship Benzi had with anyone. When Benzi traveled around the country peddling his wares, it was don Ignacio who recommended barbers for each town, as well as mapped out Benzi's trip so he'd never go a day without a shave. Only don Ignacio knew Benzi's schedule. If anyone in the family wanted to know where Benzi was or when he was coming back, they'd ask don Ignacio. At times, rather than leave Benzi at the mercy of an unfamiliar barber or worse—one who was renown for using a dull blade—don Ignacio pulled down the metal grate in front of his shop. Armed with a good blade, his strop, and his tiple, a twelve-string guitar, don Ignacio got into Benzi's Franklin and traveled the road with his client.

Don Ignacio's contacts extended beyond the world of barbers. When the president's barber suddenly died, don Ignacio was summoned to the capital. It was don Ignacio who temporarily kept the president's face smooth and his cuticles trimmed until the new official barber arrived from Europe. Don Ignacio groomed generals and politicians. Comfortable under his steady hand, secrets of government and war escaped their arched throats. His blade gently coaxed business ventures up onto the tongues of wealthy industrialists.

That afternoon, don Ignacio shared with Benzi a bit of information shaved out from under the nose of don Alvaro, the owner of the only textile mill in the city. A man in Laureles, a don Marco so and so, had two looms for sale. Old but never used. Left over from a business venture gone nowhere.

Unable to go himself, and Mule and Dave out on business, Benzi sent Harold.

Harold barely looked at the looms that sat in a shed off the main house. His attention was on the two mango trees perched on the hill above. He put down a deposit and went off to pick fruit. It wasn't until the men came back to pick up the looms that Dave noticed they were cemented into the ground. The original owner had poured concrete around the legs in order to safeguard them. Thieves notorious for pilfering entire herds of cattle, stripping homes down to the bare walls, and seducing young women about to take vows of chastity or betrothed to men they had never met, roamed the land.

The owner, don Marco, who had already gambled away Harold's deposit as well as the balance due, argued vehemently that sawing off the legs would not affect the performance of the machines. He refused to give them back the deposit. While Benzi, Mule, and Dave debated the issue, Harold went off to gather more mangos. Finally Benzi, noticing the patches of sweat on don Marco's shirt, came up with a solution. "How much for the shed?" he asked.

"Benzi, what are you doing?" Mule asked him in Yiddish.

"We're going to need a place to set them up. And it seems God and Harold have decided this is the place," Benzi answered him.

"But, Benzi," Dave reminded his brother-in-law, "You don't believe in God."

Benzi openly renounced the idea of a supreme being. "If there is a God, he is evil and merciless. If God were benevolent, he would not have taken my son, or forced me from my homeland."

"So then, do you renounce your religion as well?" Dave had asked him once.

"No. I can not renounce my blood. I will always be a Jew, Dovid."

Unable to decipher their words, don Marco watched the men. He knew about the Jews living in the part of town called La América. They owned a store downtown where the wealthy bought shoes made from leather. But he had never seen them until the day Harold came to inquire about the looms. Don Marco could tell by the accent that Harold was a foreigner, but it was his wife, doña Blanca, who pointed out Harold's slanted eyes and pointy nose. *"Judío,"* she stated after Harold left. "Watch out. They're shrewd business people."

"How do you know?" he asked.

"I've seen the wives at the market," doña Blanca replied.

"Don Marco, how much more for the shed?" Benzi asked again.

"Benzi, we can barely afford the machines," Mule argued.

Don Marco made a mental tally of his debts and tacked

on the price for the looms. "Two hundred pesos."

"Don Marco, we both know that shed is in need of repair." Benzi pointed to the thatch. "There are holes in the roof."

"I'll give you fifty pesos," Benzi said. He reached inside the breast pocket of his suit jacket and pulled out his wallet.

"No, Señor. Two hundred," don Marco insisted.

"Well that's too rich for our blood. So I guess we'll be needing our deposit back." Benzi held out his hand.

"One eighty." Don Marco looked down at the ground. The earth was black and moist, yet as long as he could remember it had lain fallow. "Worthless except to the tax collector," his father used to say.

Benzi pretended to misunderstand and pulled out eighty pesos from his wallet. He handed them to don Marco.

"No, one hundred and eighty," the man said, after waiting a moment for Benzi to give him the balance.

"Here's the twenty we owe for the looms."

Don Marco stared at the crisp twenty-peso bills in his hand. He could pay off a good portion of his debts. But Blanca would demand the money from the looms. So he tried one last time. "One fifty?"

Benzi reached out to take back the money, but instead don Marco extended his soft brown hand, and the two men shook on the deal.

rom the beginning, when it was nothing more than a small parcel of land with a dilapidated shed and two corroded looms, the men called it "the factory." It took months to get the looms running, for they had to be disassembled and reassembled several times before they worked properly, and even then, it was years before they stopped releasing their rust into the weave of the cloth. The first major decision, what to name the company, set a rocky precedent for future decisions to be made. Benzi insisted it should be called Tejidos Grossenberg, but Dave thought it too ethnic. Harold suggested Tejidos Paraíso, and Mule put forth Tejidos Medellín. "How about Telas Rusas," Grecia, always the patriot, scribbled on a piece of paper and passed it down to Benzi.

"Did you put any money into this purchase?" Benzi asked.

Grecia shook his head.

"Then stay out of it."

The battle escalated, pitting brothers against cousins, the Sisters against their husbands, especially Reesa, who thought it befitting to name the factory Tejidos Reesa, since she was, after all, the matriarch of the family. No one dared scoff at the idea except for Benzi. "That sounds like women's undergarments," he said, laughing.

Reesa's eyes turned to ice, and Benzi knew he'd lost an important ally.

One Sabbath dinner Flora grew tired of listening to them scream at one another. "If you're going to fight like this, you might as well call it Tejidos Leticia," she joked, referring to the town in the Amazon trapezoid for which Colombia had waged a war against Perú.

"Don't be ridiculous, Flora," Reesa sneered. "Name a company after a war zone?"

"Tejidos Leticia." Mule repeated the string of words several times, allowing it to sink into their angry ears.

"It's a cause Colombians felt very strongly about," Benzi recalled. "I'm in favor. Mule?"

"Yes. It's got a nice patriotic ring to it." Mule smiled at Flora. She blushed at his approval.

"Dave? Harold?"

"Yes," the brothers answered in unison.

"Tejidos Leticia it is." Benzi said. "Tejidos Leticia. It sounds great! Don't you think?"

"It's crazy, is what I think." Reesa folded her arms around her chest and stomped out of the room.

It was not the first time in recent weeks that she had accused her husband of being mad. When Benzi told Reesa about the purchase, she was furious. "You bought the entire shed? Are you insane? We don't have money to be buying property."

"It was the only way to get them," Benzi explained.

"Why do you need them at all? We do fine without looms."

"And what do you propose we sell? The shelves in the store are bare. Customs is tighter than my ass, pardon my French, wife. Not only do I have to feed you and Bluma, but your sisters and their good-for-nothing husbands and their children. Don't bother me with your foolish questions. I need to think." Eager to test the looms, Benzi had Zamie and Grecia comb the city for wool. Every lead turned up threadbare storehouses smelling of recent pillage and future emptiness. The only textile company in the city was quickly buying all the wool in the valley. Dave traveled to the capital and Mule searched the towns between Medellín and the city of Cali. Both returned empty-handed.

"If the good Lord wants you to be weavers"—the sarcasm rose in Reesa's voice—"he'll send you a flock of sheep."

Her ridicule slipped past Benzi's ears. His eyes had fallen on his wife's fingers, picking the lint from her cardigan. Benzi usually ignored her never idle hands, which smoothed the sheets and realigned blankets while she slept. Even when she ate, Reesa could not keep still, always getting up to refill someone's plate or to gather the empty dishes on the table. Now her hands were pointing to a solution. A few sweaters would provide enough wool to run a test on the looms. The Sisters and Flora were the only women in Medellín Benzi had ever seen wearing sweaters. Most wore mantillas of the same type of tightly knit cloth the factory was trying to produce. Benzi knew Reesa would never give him one of her sweaters, especially for something she was so dead set against. He would have to steal one.

Benzi waited until the next morning. After Reesa went downstairs to prepare breakfast he rifled through their armoire. He flipped through the hangers in the closet until he located her handwoven, gray cardigan. Aware of his wife's economy he didn't bother looking for more. All of Reesa's clothes could fit into one drawer. What she wore on Tuesday, was washed on Wednesday and worn again on Thursday. She stitched the runs in her stockings rather than throw them out.

Benzi shoved the sweater into his briefcase. After he finished dressing, Benzi knocked on Zamie's door and marched right in. "Get up, you oaf," Benzi hissed. "I need a sweater."

The bedsprings squealed as Zamie sat up. "What?"

Benzi opened the closet door and pulled Fanny's sweater off the hook.

"A sweater." Benzi hummed down the hallway toward Grecia and Hava's bedroom.

At the factory, Benzi proudly displayed his booty. Dave snipped the seams of Reesa's sweater and pulled on a loose thread. The wool snagged and fell apart. Another thread, another snag. By noon, the Sisters' sweaters lay shredded at their feet.

The men drove home in silence. Zamie rubbed his hands together to avoid stating the obvious. It would not be long before the Sisters missed their sweaters. They always wore them, even in December when the sun burned bright below the equator and heat, oblivious to man-made lines, spilled across the continent. Perpetually cold, the Sisters donned socks over their stockings to warm their icy feet, claiming that the Russian winters had forever frozen their blood.

As the car turned down Guayaquil, Benzi saw a flock of sheep at the end of the street. He stopped short. Zamie and Grecia collided into one another and Harold hit the windshield.

"Look!" Benzi pointed in front of him.

The Sisters were chasing the washwoman up the block. "Thief!" they brayed. "Thief!"

19

When Benzi awoke from the siesta, he saw a sheep in the corner of the bedroom, gnawing the spine of a book. He sat up, and it disappeared. As the men drove back to the factory, Benzi looked in the rearview mirror and spotted another sitting in the backseat of the car. He pulled over abruptly.

"What's the matter?" Mule asked his brother.

"Nothing. I thought I had to piss," Benzi muttered as he turned the vehicle back onto the road.

Don Marco was waiting for them by the entrance of the farm. He waved and then ran after the car as it snaked up the hill.

"Harold? You've been up in that damn mango tree again, haven't you?" Benzi asked.

"I only took one," Harold grumbled.

"Doña Blanca sells them at the market. At least pay her for them."

"I do! I pay double the price she gets at the market," Harold complained. "I say, 'Doña Blanca, think of all the trouble I save you. I pick the mangos myself and you don't have to lug them to the market.' But she still wants double. So I pay her double and then there's a worm in one. I figure she owes me a mango. So I took it. Ach!" Harold pulled out his handkerchief and dabbed his split lip. Every time he spoke, the wound opened up again.

"Don Benzi," don Marco panted through the window. His face was covered in the dust of the road. "Mi Señora asks that if you could please keep your sheep tied up to the tree." Benzi opened the door and stepped out of the car. "They ate her flowers and she's very upset."

"What sheep?" Mule asked.

"Those, *mi* Señor." Don Marco pointed to four sheep in the pasture next to the shed.

Benzi rubbed his eyes, but the sheep remained intact, busily chewing the grass in front of them.

"Benzi, where did you get them?" Zamie asked.

"I didn't," Benzi mumbled.

"Whose are they?" Harold asked.

"I don't know." Benzi stepped into the pasture, moving deliberately so as not to frighten them. He stooped down and gathered some clumps of watercress and began to call softly to the animals. They lifted their heads. Their eyes, unable to fix on him but on the space around him, saw only the tender grasses Benzi held at an angle from his body. One approached cautiously, and the others followed two steps behind. As they drew closer, Benzi bent down and examined their ears. "They're not tagged," Benzi called out as he walked back toward the car. "Don Marco? Do you know anyone who owns sheep around here?"

Don Marco paused to think. The city was encroaching, blanketing the valley in concrete and asphalt. His family had once owned all the neighboring property. But the land had shifted to new owners, who understood the value of land was not in cattle grazing or farming but in industry. They let it lay fallow, waiting for the seedling that would spring factories and houses. If one lay down its roots, then the rest would push up through the rich volcanic soil like weeds in an untended garden. "No, *mi* Señor," he replied.

Dave's Buick 8 sputtered up the dirt road. He pulled up alongside Benzi's car and got out, clutching one of Flora's sweaters.

"Dave!" Benzi patted his cousin's shoulder and pointed to the sheep. "It looks like we got our wool!"

Dave cupped his hand over his eyes and squinted toward the pasture. "Where did you get them?"

"God sent them. We need some rope," Benzi ordered.

"For someone who didn't believe in God, you've sure changed your tune."

"What do you want me to say?" Benzi grumbled. "My barber sent them? I don't know where the hell they came from. Just help me tie them up so we can shear them." Don Marco returned with some rope. Benzi took it and walked back into the pasture.

Dave ran after him. "But, Benzi! They don't belong to us."

"They do until someone says otherwise."

"Benzi, you've never sheared a sheep," Dave persisted.

"How hard can it be? Grecia! Zamie!" Benzi called out to his brothers-in-law. "Go into town and get the best pair of scissors you can find. No better yet. Go to don Ignacio's. Tell him to come with his best razor and scissors."

Twenty minutes later, Grecia and Zamie returned with don Ignacio. The barber trudged into the field toward his friend. "Don Benzi," he said tipping his hat.

"Don Ignacio! I have two new clients for you." Benzi slapped the barber on the shoulder.

"So I see." Don Ignacio circled the sheep, who eyed him momentarily and then went back to eating. "But may I ask? How do you propose we get them downtown and into the chair?"

Both men doubled over with laughter. Don Ignacio bent down in front of one of the sheep. He ran his fingers through the rough curls to determine the length of the fleece but could not locate the animal's flesh. "I'll need my scissors." He spoke quietly, afraid that the sheep might understand his intentions. But it remained calm, allowing him to rub its ears. Benzi nudged Grecia. He went off toward the car, muttering to himself. Grecia returned with the shears. The sheep stood motionless as don Ignacio stroked the broad bridge of its nose. Its front knees buckled, and it fell over into the grass.

Don Ignacio took the scissors from Grecia. He grabbed a clump of locks between his fingers and stretched it away from the belly of the sheep. He felt it yield. Don Ignacio got up and gently tugged at the wool he held in his hand. He handed the strand to Dave. "Walk slowly into the field," he whispered. As Dave stepped away from the sheep, it exhaled softly and surrendered the wool stored under its skin. "Is this long enough?" don Ignacio asked Benzi when Dave was five feet away. Benzi nodded his head, and don Ignacio snipped the strands. As Dave trudged back and forth, Zamie and Grecia stuffed the cut wool into some burlap sacks Mule borrowed from doña Blanca. After they finished, don Ignacio hypnotized the second sheep and robbed him too of his woolly robe.

"Take the wool to don Carlos," don Ignacio suggested. Don Carlos, another client of don Ignacio, was a local cutter Benzi had commissioned in the past to make the mantillas. "He might know how to wash the wool and spin it. Or at least he can send you to someone who does. I'd go with you but I've got to go to the military base and shave a lieutenant who's being made a colonel. They say this man will one day rule our country."

"Grecia. Take don Ignacio to the barracks," Benzi ordered. "Wait until he's done and then take him back to his shop. We'll go in Dave's car to don Carlos."

Zamie packed the wool into the trunk, and the four men drove downtown. They found don Carlos sitting outside his shop on Maracaibo, his hands folded across his lap. "*Buenos días,* don Carlos," Benzi called from the car. "Taking a little sun?"

"That's all I do these days," don Carlos grumbled. "No cloth being imported, no wool to make any, nothing needs to be cut. The Liberals and their economic development are going to put me out of business."

"We've got some wool," Benzi said, laughing.

"There isn't a strand to be had in the entire country. Even the mills are sitting around scratching their asses. Go play your jokes someplace else, don Benzi. I've got some sleep to catch up on before I die of poverty." Don Carlos tilted his chair against the wall of his shop and closed his eyes.

"We've got some."

"Where did you get it?" Don Carlos pretended to sleep.

"Where wool comes from. Sheep."

"There aren't any sheep in the valley. It's too hot."

"Well I have four at my factory," Benzi gloated.

"Yeah, and I've got a mountain of gold up my ass."

"Zamie, show don Carlos." Zamie got out of the car, walked to the back, and popped the trunk. The pungent scent of wet earth, grass, and manure filled the air, prying don Carlos's eyelids apart. The chair tilted forward and the front legs hit the ground. He stood up and scurried over to the trunk. Zamie opened one of the sacks and don Carlos dipped his hand inside. He rubbed the coarse wool between his fingers. "*Gracias, Madre mía,*" he whispered to the Blessed Virgin.

20

For centuries, the elite of the land secured their passage to heaven by bestowing a daughter to Christ for his collection of brides. To ensure her chastity, from the moment of her birth she had little contact with the opposite sex. Even fathers and brothers were kept at bay. The closest she came to men was at church, when she took communion or whispered her confession to the priest behind the screen. After the first blood trickled from her womb, the girl was taken to the nearest monastery and never seen again. Once inside, she was stripped of her clothes and hair and given a habit, several sizes too big. The girl was expected to fill the gown as she grew into her calling.

Benzi and Dave drove the wool up to the Sisters of El Carmel, a monastery located in the temperate mountains of Río Negro that sustained its small order by spinning wool. According to don Carlos, the nuns of El Carmel worked quickly and cheaply. "Las Carmelitas have nothing better to do at night," he said with a wink. "Once they set foot inside that door, they aren't allowed to see men again. Just leave the sacks outside with a note."

The men placed the wool at the entrance of the convent as don Carlos had instructed them. Resonant voices flowed from inside the monastery. Benzi, afraid that it might be stolen, rang the bell and then skirted behind the bushes to wait for someone to appear. A few minutes passed before they heard the bolt slip from its hinges. The door creaked open and a withered hand reached out and dragged the burlap bags inside.

The nuns prayed every waking moment. The stones of their fortress held the supplications of four centuries of women. As the wool came off their spinning wheels, their prayers became ensnared in the yarn as it twisted onto the spindles. They prayed for peace and harmony; they asked God to provide for the needy; and they begged him to forgive those who strayed or lost their way. But the shortage of wool throughout the land had brought idleness into the nuns' world. Their invocations became self-indulgent as their bins emptied. While one sister prayed that the cook might add more meat to the stew, another asked God to see that a certain sister bathed more frequently. And the day before Benzi and Dave dropped the wool in front of their door, a nun noticing the frayed hem and sleeves of her habit, had beseeched her Lord to provide some material for a new one.

After the wool was hauled inside, the convent flurried with activity. The nuns placed it in the shallow cement vats that lined the patio. Immersing the wool in water allowed any sediment trapped inside the fleece to sink. The nuns would pick through the clumps of grass and cicadas left at the bottom of the tubs. Sheep kept many secrets within their curls. The Carmelitas often found crucifixes, ceramic arrowheads, coffee beans, even emeralds. The Grossenbergs' wool emerged from the vats, leaving no trace of its past. The water remained pristine and the cement gleamed.

After the wool was washed, the Carmelitas spread it

across the courtyard. Squatting on the uneven cobble-stones, the nuns gently untangled the fibrous mass with their nimble fingers. Their black habits absorbed the intense mountain sun, preventing the fleece from scorching. Their hands transferred the delicate heat required to dry the wool and give it its sheen.

After morning prayers and a meager breakfast of dry corn cakes and black coffee, the nuns spent the day at their wheels, spinning to the rhythm of their prayers. When the bells for vespers chimed, the Sisters of El Carmel stood up and shook the rust from their legs. As they filed out of the room, one nun happened to notice that even though she had wound more than twenty spools, her basket remained full of wool. She chastised herself for her laziness and promised to work quicker. After a supper of watery soup, the nuns returned to the workshop to find all of their baskets brimming with wool. They looked at one another, simultaneously crossing themselves. "Ay Carmelitas," one nun whispered. "The Lord is in our presence. We must not be daunted by the task he requests." The nuns quickly took to their wooden stools and resumed their work. They spun throughout the night, sharing tales about other times God had found his way into their tiny convent. Once, when a mother superior died, the Christ in the chapel shed tears that bubbled the enamel on his face. People came from all across the land to see the crusted pool of salt at his feet. The Virgin once walked through their courtyard. "As she passed," the oldest Carmelita recounted, "the midday sky turned to night. When the sun returned, the sister who saw her was blind."

"I'd give my sight to see my dear Jesus," one nun sighed. The Carmelitas crossed themselves and nodded their heads in agreement.

At dawn, the wool in their baskets had yet to diminish. The Carmelitas began to wonder about the owners of the wool. Who were they? What did they look like? They decided to pack up the wool that was already spooled and to leave it outside the door with a note that the rest was forthcoming. Although they were forbidden to have contact with the opposite sex, they decided to look upon the men who had brought God into their convent.

Benzi and Dave returned the next day. They were elated when they saw the spools piled outside the door. Little did they know that a nun had been posted all morning to wait for them, and as she saw the car pull up to the convent, she had fetched her sisters from the workroom. They quickly gathered behind the door.

"More?" Benzi exclaimed in Yiddish after he read the attached note. "With this we can make fifty mantillas."

"How much do we owe them?" Dave asked as they packed the wool into the trunk and the backseat of the car.

"They speak a different language," a nun whispered to the others. Each took a turn looking out through a small crack in the wood.

"It doesn't say," Benzi replied. "I guess they'll bill us at the end." He slammed the trunk closed.

"It wasn't Latin," another Carmelita declared as Benzi started the engine.

"Perhaps French?" one suggested.

"It is the language of the devil." The Mother Superior stood behind them. The nuns froze under her icy glare. "Only the devil leads virtuous women to such temptations."

The nuns scurried back inside and resumed their work. They prayed loudly, so that if it was the devil's work that they did, he would be exorcised from inside their hearts and the walls of their convent. They would finish the job at hand, for they knew that setting the devil's work outside their door would only lead him to seep into the soul of the people. But the harder they prayed, the more wool brimmed from their baskets.

addy!" Sol cried when he saw the factory for the first time. "It's like the stick house in the three little pigs story Mommy tells me. One blow and—" Dave placed his hand over his son's mouth to stop him from uttering the end of the tale, which would lead Benzi to spend more money on securing the factory from the imaginary thieves that constantly plagued him.

Even though their legs were already cemented into the ground, Benzi, forever fearful of being robbed, fretted about the looms. He had Grecia and Zamie scour the city for the strongest bolts and installed three over the door. The small window on the rear wall also concerned him until he had it cemented over. But when Benzi locked the sheep in the shed overnight, Dave and Mule joined forces. Under duress, he conceded that the stench the animals imparted might not be good for business. Therefore, the sheep were left to graze in the pasture, tethered to a stake, so they would not wander off the property.

The sheep liked to eat the wild watercress growing on the knoll overlooking the shed. Perched above the factory, the animals circled the picket as they ate, changing direction when the wind shifted. One morning, as Dave drove up the road, he saw Benzi stomping around the field.

"What's the matter?" he asked Zamie and Grecia, who stood inside taking cover from Benzi's wrath.

"Dovid!" Benzi screamed down at him. "Someone stole my wool! My wool!" he cried, kicking up clumps of sod with the tip of his shoe.

Dave scaled the hill and walked over to the stake. The tethers lay limp in the dewy grass.

"Thieves!" Benzi continued to scream.

"They weren't ours, Benzi," Dave reminded him.

"Well they don't belong to whoever snatched them either," Benzi retorted.

"I don't think they were stolen. The ends look gnawed." Dave offered Benzi the frayed pieces of rope.

"Zamie! Grecia!" Benzi stormed across the pasture toward the shed. "Make yourselves useful for a change. Find my sheep! And don't come back until you do."

Zamie and Grecia searched for the sheep an entire week. They circled the valley, inquiring at all the farms along the perimeter of Medellín. Every place they asked, people scratched their heads and seemed truly perplexed by the question. "Sheep in the valley? No, Señores. It's too hot for sheep here."

They headed downtown, stopping in the neighborhoods along the way where cows, donkeys, and pigs roamed the streets unattended, nibbling flowers from window boxes. Yet, no one recalled seeing any sheep.

Zamie and Grecia even trekked up the Cerro de Nutibara, a wart smack in the center of the valley, thinking perhaps the sheep scaled up the foothill in search of cooler climes. From the top they could see the plaza in downtown Medellín. The market pulsed like a heart, contracting and expanding as people threaded in and out via the streets. The church bells rang in the evening hour and the beat slowed as the merchants packed up their stalls. When the plaza emptied, the two men returned home for the Sabbath.

At dinner Benzi continued to rant about the sheep. "I told you, Dovid, we should have kept them inside."

"The whole place smelled like a barn, Benzi. They were stinking up the cloth," Mule said, defending Dave.

From her corner of the table, Flora listened to the men bicker while they devoured the food on their plates. The Sisters stood by, eagerly dishing out second helpings.

"We lost our source of wool! We only got one batch to the Carmelitas. That's soon to run out. It's impossible to get any wool anywhere. We'll be out of business by next month thanks to both of you. Next time stick by your brother, Mule."

"May I please have some more meat, Aunt Reesa?" Sol asked.

"Of course, *mamashana*. You like your old aunt's cooking, don't you?" The boy nodded politely. "Flora, you're not eating," Reesa remarked.

Flora looked down at her plate. Potatoes, carrots, and meat sat neatly by one another, untouched.

"What's the matter? It's not tender? Don Mateo said it was very fresh. He saved it for just me, his favorite customer." Reesa dipped her fingers into the serving dish, pulled off a little bit of meat, and placed it in her mouth.

That morning while filling the Sisters' order, the butcher had asked Reesa when la señora Flora would be coming to the shop. "I bought her a treat at the slaughterhouse this morning."

"She's eating at our house tonight," Reesa answered. "I doubt she's coming today. Wrap it up and I'll give it to her this evening."

An hour later, Flora had strolled into the shop. "Señora Flora," don Mateo greeted her.

"*Buenos días*, don Mateo. I need some meat for lunch today."

"I just gave your sisters-in-law a package for you. They said you wouldn't be in."

"A package?"

"A surprise. Something almost impossible to get in the valley. Remember you asked me for lamb once? I got you a beautiful shank this morning. Señora Reesa has it for you. Let me know how you like it."

At lunch Flora had wanted to tell Dave what she discovered. But the children were in the dining room the entire time and she didn't want to upset Sol, who loved going into the field and feeding the sheep carrots. By the time she finished putting Ruthie and Sol down for their naps, Dave was already asleep. Flora left him a note on his nightstand: "Wake me before you go. I need to speak to you."

Dave ignored his wife's message, thinking it had to do with the Sabbath meal at Benzi's home. He knew how much Flora disliked going there week after week and didn't want to have another argument about "his" family.

There hadn't been time to speak before dinner. Dave arrived late and rushed them out the door. When Flora walked into the Sisters' house, the smell coming from the kitchen enraged her. Therefore, she kept silent and let them finish their supper.

new president assumed office, promising a more liberal Liberal protectionism and addressing the need for the import of machinery and materials to process the raw potential of the country. But the war percolating in Europe was spilling into the oceans, agitating the transports of his economic reform as well as Colombia's first lady, who impatiently awaited the arrival of two Louis Quatorze chairs for the presidential palace. Industry around the country sputtered and spit, depending on what the tide hauled into port. Yet amid the scarcity of supplies and parts, the factory managed a steady production of weaves thanks to the Sisters of El Carmel.

After the sheep disappeared, the order continued to provide wool leading the Grossenbergs to assume that the nunnery had a connection to a supplier. "Let's go up to Río Negro and see if the nuns have a little something for us this week," Benzi would say, unaware that the Carmelitas were still trying to rid their convent of the initial batch of wool.

Superstition kept the men from commenting on their good fortune. To ward off evil spirits, Benzi, Dave, and Mule masked their joy with nervous eye ticks, heavy sighs, and drawn faces. They constantly lamented that the looms, old and corroded, probably wouldn't last another month. They brought home swatches and sat for hours in the dining room, looking at the fabric with a linen tester, searching out every imperfection in the weave.

"Let me see," Reesa said one night. Benzi handed her the piece of cloth and the loupe.

"I don't need a magnifying glass," she said, rubbing the fabric between her thumb and index finger. "I can tell you right now that no one is going to buy this." She handed the material to Hava. Hava nodded her head in agreement and gave it to Fanny, who placed it against her cheek.

"Why?" Benzi asked.

"Because it feels like sandpaper," Reesa answered.

Mule, Dave, and Benzi sank their heads into their hands and uttered one long, plaintive sigh. Reesa was right. No one in their right mind would ever buy it.

The mantillas cut from the bristly cloth flew out of the downtown store and landed on the backs of women as far south as the capital. Orders poured in, causing the men more worry. "We'll never be able to fill them. Raw materials are scarce. And why don't the Carmelitas respond to our letters about payment?" they wondered. "Who knows how much we owe them and the supplier. The markup will probably be astronomical. It's a tight market. They'll cut us off if we can't afford to pay them," Benzi explained when Reesa asked for more household money.

"The only thing that is tight is your wallet," she retorted, enraged that Benzi tried to placate her with economic theory.

Benzi ran the family on a strict budget. Weekly allowances were distributed with meals and board deducted from the top. Even though Grecia and Zamie were charged extra for food because of their children, they weren't allocated more money. As far as Benzi was concerned, he supported Grecia's and Zamie's families, and they should be grateful that they got extra pocket money. Mule and Harold, bachelors, received an equal amount because they invested their own capital into the downtown store and later into the factory. Dave and Leon, who both ran separate households not by choice but at their wives' insistence, were given the same as everyone else and had to make do. But Reesa knew that only a portion of the board money went toward the rent of the house on Guayaquil. She was given the remainder with which to feed and manage the household. She'd discovered the food money in the till under Benzi's bed. "A safety net," Benzi claimed when questioned.

Reesa hurled the only insult that could penetrate her husband's thick skin. "Communist! You should have married Ganesa." Ganesa, the youngest Grossenberg sister, still remained in Russia. The family nicknamed her "the little Communist." Throughout the years the family had tried to convince Ganesa and Guita to join them. They sent care packages and coats with money sewn inside the linings. When Ganesa wrote that Guita had passed, the family assumed she would join them in Colombia. They sent more money, but Ganesa never wrote back. Over the years the Grossenbergs heard snippets about their sister from family and friends who made the journey from Russia to Medellín. They told tales of Ganesa living in a one-room apartment, surviving on black bread and tea, wearing coat upon coat to keep from freezing to death.

Many times Reesa accused Benzi of running the family like a Communist regime, and it never failed to incense him. He'd fly into such a rage that the family often wondered why she didn't hold her tongue. He never caved into her demand for more money, and often, she'd spend hours sweeping up broken glass. "I had the last word," she'd explain. Only after the founding of Israel and his reawakened interest in Zionism did Benzi come up with a reply. "More like a kibbutz, wife, a kibbutz."

23

*G*ender forbid the men to communicate with the Carmelitas directly. They wiggled and scratched but could not seem to ask one of the women in the family to help them. To need the help of a woman made their toes itch. And which wife? Flora or the Sisters? "A delicate situation," Benzi declared every time they pondered the problem. Freida wasn't even considered. Aside from the thought of Freida's satanic tongue inside the walls of a convent, Leon, the eldest brother, drew only their pity, not respect. They treated him like a frail child. Ill since his arrival, Leon worked only one or two days at the shop if his consumption or his wife weren't debilitating him.

The Sisters or Flora? The tips of their toes scaled. They hopped around the question unable to peel away their trepidation.

One afternoon, on the way back from an appointment downtown, Mule decided to pick Bluma up. Classes had just ended and the students at the Catholic girls school milled around the courtyard. Mule watched his niece chat with a few friends and then lost her in a throng of dark tresses among the uniformed girls. Bluma reemerged from behind a flock of nuns assigned to clear and lock up the yard. She spotted Mule standing by the gate and ran toward him.

"Uncle Mule." Bluma wrapped her arms around his waist and buried her face in his vest.

Mule bent down and kissed her forehead. "What are you doing this afternoon?"

"I'm going to Aunt Flora's to bake cookies."

"How about we swing by, pick up Flora and the children, and go for a drive?"

Flora was gathering the ingredients for her cookies when Mule and Bluma arrived. "I can't go anywhere looking like this." She laughed. "Besides the children are still asleep. They won't be up for a few hours."

"Leave them with the maid," Mule insisted. "We'll be back by dinner."

Flora wiped her hands on her apron. It was impossible to say no to Mule. "Okay." Flora winked at Bluma. "Give me a few minutes."

Flora stepped out of the house in her soft rose voile dress. Over her shoulders she wore a pleated cape made of the same sheer fabric. Mule opened the passenger door and she slid into the front seat.

"Where are we going?" Bluma leaned forward and rested her chin on the back of the seat.

"You're going to help me solve a little problem," Mule said as he put the car in gear. The black Dodge accelerated down the block and within minutes they were on the road to Río Negro.

The drive was delightful compared to the Sunday afternoon outings where the entire clan would cram into three cars and drive up into the hills to explore the many sixteenth-century towns built during the Spanish empire. Remarkably similar in layout, each town, no matter how small, orbited a plaza. Predictably, on one side of that square there'd be a church boasting a collection of crutches left behind by cured invalids, intricately carved woodwork, or a bloody Christ of distinction. But after the tedious journey along bumpy dirt roads, the family, numb from proximity, longed only to unwedge their hips and limbs. They fell from the cars, each hobbling their separate ways across the common.

"I think I should go in with her," Flora said after Mule explained his plan. He agreed and drove the car out of sight after dropping his cousin-in-law and niece on the steps of the convent.

Flora knocked. Footsteps echoed across the flagstone and halted. Peepholes concealed in the knots and cracks in the lower portion of the wooden door allowed the nuns to gaze upon the feet of callers and thereby gauge the sex of the visitor. Most who called on the Carmelitas arrived barefoot, making the task easy. The shape, hairiness, and arch seldom deceived. On occasion, espadrilles masked gender, requiring the visitor to present an ankle. The feet at present—saddle shoes and a pair of pumps—were unquestionably female. The bolt slipped through the hinges and the woman and girl stepped inside.

Flora and Bluma followed a nun down the cool corridor. She walked ahead of them, neck bent, her eyes concentrating on the stone tiles below her feet. Once they reached the courtyard, the nun pointed to a wooden bench and ordered Flora to sit. She took Bluma's hand and slipped around a dark corner.

Flora gazed at the sun beaming down in the courtyard. A small fountain gurgled in the center. She walked over and sat on the ledge surrounding it. Flora opened her purse and took out her mirror. She pat down her hair, mussy from the drive, and dabbed on some more lipstick.

Upstairs, a novice sweeping the balcony noticed a speck

of light dancing along the floor. As she tried to capture it with her broom, it scampered between the railing. She bent down to save it from falling into the courtyard and saw Flora face's lit by the sun. The novice swooned. The clank of the broom falling into the courtyard startled Flora. She looked up but blinded by the sun, could not see the body slumped on the balcony.

Flora got up and retrieved the broom from where it had fallen. She propped it on a pillar and went back into the shade of the corridor. What is taking Bluma so long? she wondered.

"*¡Hermanitas!*" a nun called from above. Three nuns whipped around the corner and flew up the stairs. Another two scurried behind them.

Flora was just about to step back out into the courtyard when a hand gripped her arm. "Let's go."

Flora turned and gasped. Bluma's hair had been lopped off by a mad barber. What remained stood on end. "What . . ."

Bluma steered her aunt toward the door. Flora's trembling fingers fumbled with the bolt. Together, they pulled the door open just enough for them to squeeze out. Bluma and Flora ran toward the car where Mule waited.

"What on earth?" Mule exclaimed when he saw his niece's hair.

"They thought Aunt Flora brought me to the convent to become a nun," Bluma gasped. "I kept trying to explain, but they wouldn't listen." Bluma ran her fingers through her hair. "My hair!" she wailed.

"Don't worry. We'll get don Ignacio to fix it." Mule started the engine. Bluma curled up in the backseat and cried herself to sleep.

"Flora?" Mule broke the silence. "Are you all right?"

Flora sighed. "I should have . . . What was I thinking?"

"No. This is my fault, Flora. I came up with the idea."

"You don't understand, Mule." Flora didn't care to explain. No matter whose idea it was, Reesa would blame Flora. Mule would be exonerated no matter how much blame he took.

"I'll drop you at home now. They won't even know you were there."

"But Bluma needs me."

"Don't worry about her. I'll take care of everything." Mule turned down Carrera Simón Bolívar. Dusk tinted the houses and trees in lavender light. Mule stopped the car in front of Flora's house. He placed his hand on hers. "I'm sorry I put you in this situation, Flora. I know they are hard on you. Don't worry. They'll never know. Bluma will stand by the story I tell her to."

Flora leaned over and kissed Mule on the cheek. She stepped out of the car and walked past the six eyes lurking behind the bushes.

Mule pried don Ignacio from his dinner to fix Bluma's hair. The barber slapped his thigh as he listened to Mule's tale. "Don't worry, my friend," don Ignacio chuckled, "I will fix everything."

"Not a word to Benzi," Mule pleaded.

"Your brother would enjoy this story, don Mule."

"But his wife," Mule reminded don Ignacio, "wouldn't."

"Don Benzi. I hear you're having a problem with the Carmelitas," don Ignacio said to his client a week later.

"What do you propose, don Ignacio?" Benzi lay back in the chair and the barber placed a hot towel on his face.

"This morning I shaved a priest on his way to see the Carmelitas. It seems one of the nuns had a vision. Anyway, I mentioned your dilemma and he remembered your cousin, don David and his wife. Apparently, they met on their way to Medellín." Don Ignacio removed the towel from Benzi's face. "He's willing to discuss the matter with them on your behalf."

"Bless you, don Ignacio." Benzi grinned at the barber via the mirror. "Bless you."

*F*or years the local parish of Alpujarras had been sending the Bogotá diocese letters regarding a little boy whose hand was inspired by God. The correspondence drew little interest until a cable arrived from Medellín's bishopric citing that a nun in a convent sixty miles away described an apparition identical to the one the boy drew. Father Belisario, recently appointed to study and verify divine manifestations, was sent to investigate. He arrived a week later in Medellín, exhausted from his journey up the Magdalena and train ride into the valley.

His first order of business was to visit Alpujarras. He examined the images now blackened by the smoke of candles left by supplicants throughout the years. Afterward, Father Belisario circled the square. An entire industry had sprung up from the patron saint they called Nuestra Señora de Alpujarras. Vendors peddled hand-painted prayer cards, ceramics, and woodcarvings of their lady, along with other religious curios. At one stand, he paused to look at a collection of porcelain Madonnas. Their uniform features, identical eyes and lips, size and dress, drew his interest. He picked one up.

"*Cinco* pesos, Padre," the vendor said.

"Where did you get this?" the priest asked. Father Belisario turned the statue over. On the base, written in red cursive, it read: MADE IN JAPAN.

"From the *judíos* downtown, *mi* Padre. They sell them to me for four pesos. Now because you are a religious man, I sell it to you also at four. You should take advantage, Padre. They told me last week that they won't be getting any more of my Madonnas or Christs." The vendor pointed to his selection of Jesuses. "Too hard to get now, they say. Where am I going to get my merchandise? No one wants the handmade stuff."

"I'll take a Madonna." The priest dipped his hand under his cassock and into his pocket to retrieve his wallet. The vendor wrapped the statuette in newsprint and Father Belisario walked over to the church where he was scheduled to meet the boy and his mother.

When her child stopped drawing Señora Flora, Lucha thought God had finally answered her prayers. But the religious fervor that Fernando's first paintings sparked refused to fade. People in Alpujarras continued to pay homage. And now the talking box called a radio was spreading a story about a nun in Río Negro rumored to have seen Alpujarras's lady walking through her convent. The news brought the devout from all over the valley. Some crawled across the city on their knees to show their respect. Others brought their sick to touch her face. Rich pious ladies also came, driven by their chauffeurs. The shiny cars idled in front of Fernando's paintings while the women inside pressed their faces on the glass and prayed. Sometimes they would have the chauffeur light candles for them and one even had her driver knock upon the door of a house and ask to buy the wall.

"I'd like to interview the boy alone, away from his mother," Father Belisario told the priest of Alpujarras.

"You won't get any answers that way," the priest answered.

"Why?" Father Belisario asked.

"He's mute," the priest replied.

Long ago, Lucha had silenced Fernando with her constant hushing. But as hard as she tried, Lucha could not stifle the images that continued to pour forth from her son's hand: obese politicians and magistrates, portly matrons with their overweight children, all enormous in body and diminutive in face. The previous day, Lucha discovered a portrait of a priest bursting from his cassock inside Fernando's notebook. Wrapped around the portly rendered fingers was a tiny rosary. Lucha had ripped it out, worried that one of the Jesuits at Fernando's school might see it.

Although Lucha and Fernando had met with the local clergy several times, it never failed to remind her that she had chosen God's wrath over that of her neighbors. The furor that her child and his subject sparked had turned an ordinary community into one of distinction. People depended on Nuestra Señora de Alpujarras not only spiritually but also economically.

Therefore, the information Father Belisario extracted from Lucha shed little light about Fernando and his inspiration. The child's father was dead and the woman had worked as a day maid until her legs were badly burned. Unable to stand for long periods of time, she now sold buttons made from tagua nuts at the market. Fernando was enrolled in the church's school, and his teachers characterized him as a sullen child, uninterested in his studies, always doodling in his notebook. As far as miracles, the portraits of the lady had ceased and everyone believed that he'd outgrown the ability to hear God or anyone for that matter.

Before he left for Río Negro, Father Belisario decided to visit Flora and Dave. Although only a few years had passed since their good-bye in Puerto Berreío, the priest had faded from Flora's memory, and he had to remind her where they had met before she asked him inside.

"And your husband?" Father Belisario inquired.

"He's in Bogotá, actually, buying some more looms," Flora answered. They spent some time chatting, Flora pretending to remember the river and the drought and the child almost mangled by the caiman. The priest held Sol and Ruthie on his knees. Ruthie played with his crucifix and at one point, drew it inside her mouth and sucked on it like a pacifier. He stayed through dinner and left, promising to return the next time he came to Medellín.

At the convent, Father Belisario listened to the Carmelita novice describe the vision she'd seen in the courtyard. It coincided with the one that Fernando had painted except for one detail. The image Fernando drew was a plump woman. The novice insisted that although the body was not slender, it was not fat. The fact that she didn't change her description after the priest queried her on this one difference convinced Father Belisario that the girl was not lying.

"Father, would you do us the honor of hearing confession while you are here?" the Mother Superior asked after he'd finished interviewing with the novice.

"Of course." For the next few hours, Father Belisario listened to nuns beg forgiveness from God for having glanced upon the men with the wool. By the time the priest emerged from the confessional, his ears tickled with their trespasses. Before he left, Father Belisario spoke to the Mother Superior on the Grossenbergs' behalf.

The priest stopped by the factory before returning to

Bogotá. Benzi greeted him and took him through the small production line. Father Belisario hoped Benzi might show him the source of the single bale of wool that continued to keep the nuns busy day and night. At the convent he'd held a clump of wool and watched it expand in his hand. "Who do you get your raw material from?" he asked casually, pretending to be interested in textile production.

"The Carmelitas," Benzi answered.

"No. I mean the raw wool," Father Belisario explained.

"The Carmelitas, Father. They supply us with all the product."

"But you brought them a bale of wool," the priest insisted.

"Only once," Benzi answered.

"Where did you get it from?"

"From four sheep that strayed onto the property."

"Where are they?"

"God giveth and God taketh. Especially in this land of thieves," Benzi answered. "So what do we owe the nuns?"

"They do not wish to take your money, don Benzi." A little coaxing convinced the nuns that the Grossenbergs were not devils, and that in this time of scarcity, they should look upon the wool as another act of God. Instead of letting their fingers and minds be idle, he'd given them a task to be completed.

"But we need them to continue working for us." Benzi grew concerned.

"And they shall. They do have one request. Some of the Carmelitas are planning a pilgrimage and they would like some cloth."

"Of course, Father. I'll have Zamie take some bolts up tomorrow."

◆

To avoid gazing upon men, the Carmelitas traveled the forty kilometers to Alpujarras by night. They set out after dark on foot, dressed in their old habits, marching single file down the road to Medellín. They walked all night, and when they felt the dawn mist rising from the earth, they took shelter inside the church of Santa Helena. Two days later they were in Medellín. They set out at dusk wearing the new cassocks they had stitched from the forty meters of cloth the Grossenbergs sent them. At the edge of Alpujarras, the Carmelitas lit their prayer candles. The first painting brought them to their knees. A soft rain began to fall and mingle with the tears they shed for the lady. Reciting the Lord's Prayer, the nuns wandered through the neighborhood the entire night. When dawn crept into the sky, the Carmelitas were unable to pry themselves from the images. The town awoke to find them standing deep in meditation, oblivious that their habits had shrunk up past their ankles, exposing their bare calves to the world.

25

*T*he Sisters' sharp eyes missed Bluma's shortened locks. The late afternoon stroll to check on Flora while Dave was out of town had upset their vision. The house was empty except for the old woman. Bolívariana, asleep most of the afternoon, didn't know where la Señora had gone. "The children?" the Sisters asked, nostrils flaring, trying to decipher the presence of the shiksa without having to inquire. Bolívariana shrugged her centenarian shoulders. While the old woman's bones squeaked back into their sockets, the Sisters sniffed for signs of dinner but inhaled only a cold stove. The notion of a house without a hint of supper drove them behind the hedge of the house next door to wait. An hour later, a car pulled up and Flora stepped out. The Sisters' eyes conveniently failed to recognize the make or the man inside. But the kiss and Flora slinking through the shadows, they saw clear as day. The image imprinted on their corneas played incessantly, allowing the Sisters to see nothing else but their sister-in-law's betrayal.

Determined to catch Flora, the three women abandoned their household chores to follow her. They threw breakfast on the table and hurried out the door on the pretext that they wanted to get to the market early. Instead, the Sisters lingered at the end of Flora's block, waiting for her to leave the house. All morning they trailed Flora through the market, hiding behind drays and baskets to avoid bumping into her. Every man Flora interacted with became suspect. Don Mateo, the butcher, smiled when he handed Flora her meat. Alvaro, at the dairy cart, gave her an extra dollop of cream. The man where she bought her potatoes put a few extra in her basket.

Suspicion drove the Sisters into doors, tripped them on stairs, and over cracks in the sidewalk. Their bodies were covered in scratches and bruises from trying to keep up with their sister-in-law. Finally, after days of crouching behind shrubbery and walls, their eyes spied a man entering Flora's home. Twilight interceded in their favor and concealed the Roman collar.

The Sisters flocked home. They stormed inside, waving their skinny arms in outrage. They panted and yelped and collapsed on the settee, begging for their smelling salts. When Mule returned from work, he found Bluma fanning the air around their colorless faces. At first they shook their heads, refusing to speak.

"What? What?" Mule urged. "A spider? A mouse?"

"No!" The Sisters wailed. "A mmmaan," they sputtered.

"A burglar?" Mule looked around the room to see if anything was missing.

"No. Flooorah." The Sisters paused to catch their breath. "And a mmman."

"What are you ladies saying?" The anger in Mule's voice made the Sisters pause. He was always soft-spoken and gentle.

"But Mule," they stammered.

"Be careful with your accusations. Flora is your sister."

"She's our brother's wife," Reesa corrected him.

"You are my brother's wife, Reesa. Therefore, are we not brother and sister?" Mule asked.

"But we are cousins, Mule. Related by blood," Reesa argued.

"No, Reesa. When you married Benzi, you became my sister as Flora became yours when she married Dave."

"Why do you defend her?" Reesa's eyes narrowed.

"I defend her as I would you," Mule answered curtly. "I am ashamed of you." He picked up his hat and left the room. He brushed past Benzi and Harold on the way out the door.

"Where are you going, Mule?" Benzi called after him.

"I'm going to Flora's for dinner," he said.

"Mule!" Reesa rushed outside and grabbed his arm. "Mule, dear. Let's not quarrel." She took his hand and led him back inside.

oña Blanca often compared her husband's luck to the Río Magdalena—dried up. "But like the boats," she bemoaned every time don Marco sold another acre of land in order to pay his debts, "the man still ventures, convinced he won't get stuck in the mud."

Doña Blanca witnessed the land that had been in don Marco's family for nearly two centuries slowly slip through his fingers into the open palms of the Grossenbergs. The section behind the shed was the first to go, and before the ink on the title dried, an identical shed sprung from the earth. Within a month the original building devoured her vegetable garden and buried the roots under its new poured-cement floor. She watched the inner walls of her former home collapse to make space for four wooden desks. One morning don Marco noticed his wife kneeling on the ground near the entrance of the property. "What's the matter?" he asked.

"You tell me." Doña Blanca pointed to some glass fragments poking out from the earth. Don Marco held his *carriel* close to his body. In the secret pocket of his purse was the deed to the last bit of land he owned. As he walked up toward the office, don Marco felt his wife's eyes poking a hole in his back. By sunset, a cinder block wall, studded with colorful shards of broken glass, girdled the property. A corrugated metal gate sprung up next to the adobe cottage that was now their home and don Marco exchanged his cotton poncho for a watchman's uniform and cap. Doña Blanca found herself standing in front of a cast iron soup pot in her former bedroom, now a cafeteria, ladling bowls of *sancocho* to the workers at lunchtime.

It was never the Grossenbergs' intention to own a plot of land the size of a city block. But the vitality of the wool infected the looms and each bolt of cloth. Every morning, wool brimmed from the storage shed that had been nearly empty the day before and a piece of fabric left overnight on the weaver had doubled in length. Nevertheless, Benzi kept the family's enthusiasm at bay by demanding economy. According to him, the factory verged on bankruptcy. Even when he lugged suitcases full of money to the bank, he'd complain to the teller that business was bleak.

Harold, however, was unable to conceal his euphoria. Since the day Benzi decided that the broad shady patch under the mango trees would be a good place to build a dye shed and purchased the land, Harold's thin lips had been fixed in a burlesquelike grin. His skin, now a burnished orange, glowed like a harvest moon, and his once dark brown locks had turned a brassy shade of red. He adamantly refused Benzi's suggestion or his sisters' pleas to go to don Ignacio's for a haircut, preferring to lop off sections that got into his eyes with a pair of shearing scissors. He'd also developed the nasty habit of humming. Day and night, he sang the Yiddish lullabies of his childhood, ignoring his sisters, who turned pale when he came to the table in the morning warbling a tune. "Ssht! Hatzkell. Ssht!" They pleaded with him and spit through their open fingers. But their admonitions about the bad luck in his future if he insisted on singing before breakfast fell on stone ears.

Harold hammered some wooden rungs onto the trunks and every morning, upon his arrival at the factory, he'd climb one of the trees and sit inside the leafy canopy eating sugar mangos. Invariably, Zamie would be sent to get him down. After Zamie climbed the hill, caught his breath, and wiped the sweat from his brow, he'd call up politely, "Hatzkell? Hatzkell?"

Sometimes, if he'd eaten his fill or had to go to the bathroom, Harold would come down. More often then not, Zamie came back to the office, his suit stained with mango juice, complaining that Harold hurled a pit at him. "Zamie, you think by now you'd know not to stand so close," Dave chided him.

"Dave, it doesn't matter where Zamie stands. Look at the size of him. He's impossible to miss," Benzi scoffed. "Get out of the tree, you monkey!" he screamed from the office door. "Or I'll chop it down."

The leaves of the tree rustled and soon a dusty leather heel appeared on the top rung, followed by a wrinkled trouser leg. Harold slipped down the wide trunk and stumbled down the knoll, wiping his hands on his pants. In the last few months he'd developed an awkward gait. He waddled around, favoring the outside arches of his feet. "Aim for Zamie's head next time, Hatzkell," Benzi whispered to Harold when he entered the office.

One morning, Harold noticed several mangos missing from the tree. Blame was immediately cast on doña Blanca. Harold rebuked himself with a song for providing such easy access to the fruit and ripped down the rungs. After all, the built-in ladder was only a luxury, a sign of ownership. Before the tree was theirs, the climb into the canopy came easily. It was best to keep those skills sharp. When Harold traveled on business, he often gathered his meals from the fruit-bearing trees along the road. He kept a rope ladder in the trunk of the car, but it was often more of a hassle to lasso it onto a branch than to just scale the tree. Besides, once a lassoed branch had given way, dropping him into a patch of prickly pear, and Hava had to pluck the thorns from his bottom.

The bandit struck hard the second time around, taking every blushed mango on both trees, leaving only the hard, green ones that gave Harold sour stomach. "The witch must have wings," he trilled. He decided to sleep in the field that night, stringing his hammock between the two trees. There was no convincing him otherwise. The men left him there, a sagging bulge, swinging back and forth under the mangos.

"Maybe one will fall on his head and knock some sense back into him," Reesa muttered when Benzi told her Harold's plan.

As the sky grew dark, Harold noticed that the broad green leaves in the trees were flecked with color. Magentas, oranges, and yellows glimmered over his head. "Hatzkell? Hatzkell?" Zamie's soft pleading made Harold sit up.

"What?" he called out.

"Hatzkell. Hatzkell."

"Where are you, Zamie?" Harold rolled out of the hammock.

"Zamie. Zamie. Hatzkell." The voice switched to Benzi's loud invective. "Get down or I'll chop it down. Down. Down. Monkey."

"Benzi!" Harold yelled. "This isn't funny."

"Funny. Funny." Followed by eerie, womanish laughter.

"Doña Blanca?"

"Witch must have wings." Now his own voice boomed down at him. Something warm hit his neck. Harold looked up and saw hundreds of parrots perched on the limbs of the trees. In their talons they clutched his precious mangos. Harold scampered up one of the trees and began to shoo the parrots off the boughs. They scattered, hopping onto branches beyond his reach. Harold climbed higher into the canopy and the parrots dispersed, taking with them the mangos that had softened and exploded with color that very afternoon. As Harold tried to grab one away, he felt a sharp crack under his foot. He fell through the tree, scratching his face and arms on the brittle young branches.

Harold awoke when a vulture pecked on his cheek. The sun peeked over the mountains. Harold looked up into the trees but could not see the parrots. The light of dawn had restored their protective green camouflage. He sat there, momentarily stunned, wondering what to do. "I'm going to get you!" Harold screamed, shaking his fist at the sky. The parrots buried their beaks deeper into their breast feathers and said nothing. "Acht!" he grumbled.

"Get who?" Zamie asked. He stood at the top of the knoll. His enormous frame blocked the emerging sun, casting a shadow over the trees. "What happened to your face?"

"Zamie? What are you doing here?" Harold asked. As he got up to untie his hammock, a flash of color caught his eye.

"Benzi sent me to check on you. Well actually, Reesa told Benzi to check on you and he told me—"

"Wait. Don't move!" Harold shrieked.

"What? What?" Zamie squirmed, brushing the shoulders and arms of his suit, afraid that there was something crawling on him. His gigantic body always seemed to attract all sorts of creatures. Once, an army of ants marched up the leg of his trousers. And then there was the spider that wove her web across his navel. But the worst was the cicada that flew into his ear, got stuck inside the canal, and buzzed incessantly until Hava yanked it out with a pair of tweezers.

"Sshh! Stand still." Harold searched the canopy. Under Zamie's shadow, flashes of red and blue burned through the leaves. "I see you!" Harold cried. "I see you!

"See what?" Zamie asked, trying to determine what Harold raved about.

"Look! Up there!" Harold pointed to the trees.

"What?" Zamie tilted his head up toward the sky.

"The parrots! Don't you see them?" Harold screamed.

Zamie stepped out of the sun to get a closer look and the colors vanished. He cupped his hand over his forehead and squinted. "I don't see anything."

"Acht! Come on." Harold gathered his hammock and walked to the car. "Drive me home."

◆

"Oh my God! What happened to you?" Reesa cried when she saw her brother storm in. "Zamie? What happened to him? Why is he all scratched up. Why is he limping?"

"He fell out of the tree." Zamie rolled his eyes and went to eat his breakfast. Reesa climbed the stairs after Harold, who headed in the direction of Hava and Grecia's room.

Harold burst into the empty room, opened the closet, and pulled out Grecia's hunting rifle.

"Put down that rifle!" Reesa screamed. "Benzi! Benzi! He's got a rifle. God help us. He's gone mad."

Harold brushed past her, ran down the stairs and out the door.

"Benzi! Benzi!" Reesa dashed into the dining room where the men were eating behind their newspapers. "Doesn't anybody in this house care that Harold's got a rifle?"

Benzi poked his head out from behind the paper. "Grecia? Is it loaded?"

Grecia nodded. "Follow him, Zamie, and make sure he doesn't hurt anyone." Benzi returned to his reading.

As Zamie wiped the crumbs from his face, a shot rattled the windows.

The family hurried outside. Bluma stood by the car, watching Harold hop up and down on one foot, holding the other in his hand. Blood dripped down the side of his arm. The rifle lay strewn on the grass.

"What happened?" Reesa shrieked.

"Uncle Harold tripped on a cobblestone and the gun went off," Bluma explained.

While Zamie fetched the doctor, Grecia and Mule carried Harold inside. Hava carefully removed his shoe and then cut away the sock. Everyone gasped in horror. His toenails were so long that they had curled and now dug into the flesh under his toes. "Why? Harold?" Reesa cried. "What possible need could you have for long toenails? To climb trees like the baboon you are intent on becoming?"

Harold said nothing. He scratched his scalp and pulled a piece of mango from his matted hair.

It wasn't until the doctor arrived and began to clean the wound that they realized Harold had blown off his left pinkie toe. The children were sent outside to search for it. "When you die, you must go back to the earth how you came in," Hava explained after they brought it back tucked in a napkin. They watched her seal it in a jar and then followed her outside to the garden, where she buried it next to the jar with the boys' and the mens' foreskins.

Harold's wound healed quickly. The gunshot sheared off the toe neatly and all that remained was a shiny bunionlike protrusion on the side of his foot. However, his other toes were so infected that the doctor assured the family that gangrene would claim them and possibly both his feet.

*F*lora stopped by to see Harold every day. She enjoyed sitting with her brother-in-law, as they often reminisced about their days in Paris. She always brought him a bag of tangerines or a bunch of the stunted bananas that he loved. One day Flora made the mistake of buying him a mango. His eyes had welled up as he bit into the top and pulled away the skin with his teeth. "Benzi is going to cut down my trees," he confided to Flora. Embarrassed by his tears, Flora stared at the jar placed under the foot of the bed, ready to collect any discarded digits.

"Whatever happened to your friend, the American with the blue eyes?" he asked during a visit.

"Dorothy?" Dave and Flora had run into Harold four days before Dorothy left Paris. During the few days that they had overlapped, Harold had never shown any particular interest in Dorothy. Therefore, his inquiry surprised Flora. "Actually, strange that you should ask. I received a letter from her just the other day. Can you believe it took over three months to get here?"

Mail delivery remained sporadic. Even though the postmen recently garnered bicycles, illiteracy demanded they stop at every door on their route. They sipped cups of espresso or a soda pop while residents sifted through the bag for their mail. Sometimes it took more than a day to cover a single street, as coffee or a cool drink provided an opportunity to chitchat with every pretty maid on the block. These flirtations were never discouraged by employers, unlike the ones between milkmen and housekeepers, which led milk to sour while the lovers stole away. On the contrary. A household considered itself fortunate if the postman fell in love with one of the servants. For a smitten postman made it a point to see his beloved at least once a day, if not twice, speeding up mail delivery.

Flora tried to recall what news Dorothy had written. "She's still living in Cincinnati, and I believe she said that she was working at a department store."

"Send her my regards when you write back."

That night, Flora felt a hand upon her cheek. She opened her eyes and saw her mother, Shana, sitting at the edge of the bed. "Mom?" Flora whispered.

Shana's caramel eyes gazed lovingly at her daughter. "I'm so sick, dear. So sick."

"What's the matter?" Flora sat up in bed.

Shana wiped away a strand of hair that had fallen over Flora's eye. "Remember when the baby died, Flora?" she asked.

"What baby, Mama?"

"I couldn't cry. People thought me strange. They said I didn't care. How can you not care for your own flesh and blood? Lotte was such a beautiful, sweet child. People always stopped to look at her. They always touched her and wanted to hold her. How was I to know?" Shana shook her head sadly. "Lotte got so hot. I made your father promise she'd get better. I made him swear she'd live. I was out of my mind. Her skin burned my fingers. My baby."

Shana fell silent. Flora reached for her mother's arm, but Shana shook her head again and vanished.

"Mother?" Flora sobbed.

Dave stirred. "What's wrong?" he asked.

Tears streamed down Flora's face. "She was here, Dave. She was telling me she was sick, that her baby was sick and died."

Dave held Flora's hand, trying to calm her. "It was just a dream. Just a bad dream."

"It just felt so real. Her hand stroking my face . . . I felt it, Dave. I guess I just miss my family." Flora sighed.

Dave yawned and fell back onto the bed. Flora lay beside him. Every time she was about to doze off, Flora would remember her mother's hollowed voice and be pulled away from sleep's grip. She finally gave up at two in the morning. Flora gathered a box of old letters and went into the kitchen. She poured through a stack, searching for phrases about her mother's health. But none of her brothers or sisters mentioned a word about Shana. Her father spoke of the grandchildren and how big everyone was getting. Flora compared the handwriting between letters her mother had written in prior years with the last one she received. Shana's beautiful cursive never faltered.

Flora returned the letters to the box. She chided herself for not having saved any of Dorothy's correspondence. Flora always scanned the letters, paying little attention to the details, and then threw them away. Now she longed for those crumpled pages that might have offered a clue about her mother.

Bolívariana shuffled into the room, dragging her rocker behind her. "A woman was looking for you," she said.

"When?" Flora asked.

"A few hours ago." Bolívariana sat down. The rocker creaked back and forth.

"This afternoon?" Flora inquired. It always took time and patience to gather information from Bolívariana.

"No. Around midnight," the old woman said.

"I didn't hear the bell. Who was it? Why didn't you wake us."

"She didn't ring the bell. She was in the courtyard. She was looking for you."

Flora's voice trembled. "What did she look like?"

"She looked like you, Señora. Like you, but old. I told her you were asleep in your room. Did she find you?"

A shiver raced through Flora's spine. "Yes," she whispered. Outside, an orange blaze burned on the horizon. Flora looked at her watch. Five A.M. The children would be up soon. She placed the kettle on the stove.

When Dave came into breakfast, Flora remained shaken. Her hand trembled violently as she set his tea down in front of him. The toast flew off its dish and onto his lap. Used to his wife's constantly trembling hands, sometimes exacerbated by fits of anger or frustration, Dave assumed he'd done something wrong, something to displease her. Sleep had wiped Flora's dream from his memory. Eventually, it will come out, Dave thought to himself, wiping the crumbs from his pants. Therefore, he said nothing, allowing Flora to keep Bolívariana's tidings to herself.

As hard as Flora tried not to believe the old woman's account, she could find no words to explain it. She tried to dismiss the image of her mother from her mind, but the memory of Shana's soft caress clung to Flora's cheek throughout the day.

The mailman seemed forlorn when he arrived at the Sisters' doorstep. He'd declined every beverage and treat along his route, covering the neighborhood with unusual speed. When he handed Reesa his bag, she noticed a tear in the inner corner of his eye. It slid down the side of his nose and dangled on his chin before dropping onto the stoop. As Reesa searched his pouch, she gathered the mail for her household as well as Dave's and Leon's. Benzi devised the idea to help expedite delivery after it had taken ten days for a letter Flora saw in the bag for Mule to reach them. After Reesa finished, the postman nodded goodbye and walked his bike to the next house. He rang the bell and sat down to wait for a cup of coffee the maid offered. Reesa watched the smile return to his face. She looked down at the stack of mail she held in her hand and felt the weight of bad news.

At lunch, Reesa handed Benzi a letter for Dave from Flora's father. "Her mother is dead," Reesa declared.

Benzi looked at the still sealed envelope. "How do you know?"

"Why else would her father write him?" Reesa was right. Flora's father never wrote to his son-in-law. After the couple announced they were moving to Colombia, Mr. Rosen had few words left for Dave.

"What's the matter?" Mule asked when he arrived and found Benzi and the Sisters talking.

"Flora's mother passed," Benzi answered.

"Oh no. She must be devastated. We should go over there right now."

"She doesn't know yet, Mule," Reesa said.

"Oh dear. How did you find out?"

Benzi handed Mule the unopened letter. His chest grew heavy and a lump welled up inside his throat. "Poor Flora," he sighed.

"What took her?" Benzi asked after he gave Dave the

letter. Zamie had pried Dave from his siesta and driven him back to the Sisters' house. They sat in the dining room, watching his eyes move across the one page letter.

"A cancer in the stomach," Dave said softly. He finished reading the letter, folded it up, and placed it back into the envelope

"When?"

"On the third."

"The third?" Benzi queried.

Dave pulled the letter out of the envelope and unfolded it. "Yes. The third of May."

"Dave, today is the fifth of May. It must have been the third of April."

Dave glanced down again at the letter. "No it says here May third. Look at the date on the top," he said, holding the letter under Benzi's nose. "May fourth."

"That must be a mistake. He probably wrote the wrong month," Benzi insisted.

"Look at the postmark," Mule suggested.

Dave flipped the envelope over. "It was stamped in Cincinnati yesterday," Dave mumbled. He put on his jacket. "Well whenever it was, I have to go and tell Flora."

"We'll have to prepare the house for shivah," Reesa said. "How many mirrors do you have, Dovid? They need to be covered. And you'll need a bench."

"But if she died last month, then it's too late to sit shivah," Benzi argued. He pulled the fruit bowl toward him, grabbed a tangerine, and began to peel it.

"Benzi, the letter says she died two days ago," Reesa retorted.

"The man was probably upset. He made a mistake on the date." Benzi popped a section into his mouth.

"Twice?" Reesa took the letter from Dave and waved it under her husband's nose.

"Then explain to me how it got here so fast in this land where everything takes forever," Benzi insisted. He spit a seed delicately into his hand.

"Bad news travels fast," Reesa replied.

"It doesn't matter," Mule interrupted. "We don't have a minyan." He was right. There were only six adult men and they needed ten. Conrado, Fanny and Zamie's eldest son, was just shy of thirteen.

"Dovid," Benzi said, eating another section. "She doesn't know yet. Let some time pass. Tell her in a couple of weeks. That way it will be too late to sit shivah. Anyway, no one wants to sit shivah. You'll be doing her a favor."

Dave rubbed his eyes. He got up and walked toward the door.

"Go home and pretend nothing is wrong," Benzi called after him. "Remember. It's for her own good."

Dave stuffed the letter in his breast pocket. He walked the ten-block distance between the two houses. He longed to spare Flora this grief. Being so far away and the mail so sporadic made it simple. When he approached the house, Dave noticed Ruthie standing with her nose pressed against the window. He tiptoed across the grass toward his daughter and placed his face against the glass, in line with hers. They stared into each other's eyes for a moment. Dave pulled away from her perpetually sad countenance. Once inside the house, he headed into the study. He took the letter from his pocket and jammed it through the crevice between the bookshelf and the wall. It fell behind the wood and disappeared.

$\mathcal{F}$ilomena sat in the kitchen with Sol and Ruthie perched on her ample thighs. A small suitcase stood by the wall. "I must go, Señora," she said to Flora. "I am needed at home."

"May I ask why? Is there something wrong?"

"Last night, I had a vision." Filomena bounced the children up and down on her knees. "The jungle of Quibdó was brighter than the sun and my people were dancing."

"You're leaving because of a dream?"

"It was a vision, Señora," Filomena politely corrected Flora. "I must go see what makes them dance." Filomena drew the children to her bosom. "Now, Señorito Sol, always take care of your mama. And Señorita Ruthie, try for Filo, not to be so outraged by the world."

"But Filomena, the children are very attached to you. We're very attached to you. Why don't you go and come back?" Flora pleaded.

"Señora, believe me. I asked the smoke from my candles the same question. I do not want to leave these children. But I am needed elsewhere."

After Filomena's departure, the newspaper reported a fire was raging in El Chocó. The intense heat was melting the gold in the mines. Liquid gold flowed through the jungle, plating all the vegetation and animals in its path. It coursed through the streets of Quibdó, turning them into golden rivers. A month later a package arrived. Inside were two gold-plated lovebirds. Filomena would send more objets d'art: a school of fish, a palm monkey, a lizard. Flora proudly displayed them in her breakfront. The artisan's ability for intricate detail and realism drew many compliments. Flora often took them out just to study them, unaware that beneath the coat of gold, hearts continued to beat.

Too busy tending house and trying to hire another maid, Flora failed to notice Ruthie's interest in the study. The child spent hours in the room, sitting on the floor, transfixed by the deceit lurking behind the books. "Eyeing the books, little one?" Flora asked her daughter one day, gathering her up off the floor. Ruthie struggled to break free from her mother's arms. "What is it that you like there?" Flora held the child up to the shelf. Ruthie ran her fingers along the spines and then kicked to be put down. Flora left Ruthie to feed her rage and went into the kitchen to make lunch.

Dave came home with a woman whom he introduced as their new maid. During a heated argument about common courtesy, just trying to help, I don't need your help, and how do you know this stranger won't steal the terracotta under our feet, the woman slipped out the door and ran down the street. Dave and Flora ate their meal in silence. Barred from the bedroom with a turn of the lock, Dave slipped a letter from Dorothy under the door and took his nap in the study.

Flora took the children to the park after the siesta. Sol marched back and forth, holding a small American flag that Flora had sewn out of old scraps of material. Ruthie sat by the edge of the fountain, dragging her palm across the water, watching her reflection ripple and bend.

"Ruthie," Flora called from the bench. "Take your fingers out of that filthy water." The child withdrew her hand obediently. Flora opened her purse and fished around for her handkerchief. "Come here. Let me wipe your hands." Ruthie declined with a shake of her head. Flora gave up and took out Dorothy's letter. The contents of her purse had battered the envelope, creasing the flimsy paper. Flora tore off the flap and began to read.

When Dave came home from work, the house was dark. He found Bolívariana asleep in her bedroom. Dave touched her arm. "Where are Flora and the children?" he asked.

"They went to the park," Bolívariana answered sleepily.

Dave knew something was wrong. Flora kept to her schedule. She always had dinner ready when he got home. Dave walked the block to the park. He saw Flora on the bench with the letter crumpled in her hand. Her head drooped like a newborn baby's. The children were by her side. Ruthie had fallen asleep in the crook of Flora's arm. Sol was picking at one of the loose stripes on his flag.

"Flori?" Dave placed his hand on her shoulder.

"My mother is dead," Flora mumbled.

"What?" Dave remembered Dorothy's letter. How could it have escaped him? Dorothy lived in Cincinnati, not far from Flora's family. Before they left for Colombia, Dorothy had stopped by to visit.

"My mother . . . Why didn't anyone write to me."

Dave helped her up. "Come. Let's go home, Flori. Come, children."

Dave lifted Ruthie and took Sol by the hand. Flora got up and walked ahead of him. Her first steps were tentative, and Dave feared she would collapse. But as they neared the house, her carriage gradually straightened and the muscles of her neck regained their strength.

Flora's recovery frightened Dave more than the fragility he'd witnessed in the park. She stifled sorrow and anger deep under the layers of her skin. He'd learned to look at his wife's hands to determine her mood. They refused to contain their rage or sadness, and therefore reminded him of a cat's tail, always betraying her calm demeanor. As Dave followed Flora inside the house, he watched her movements closely. She sat down at the kitchen table and with what seemed a steady hand wrote a short note on the tablet in front of her. After she was finished, she tore off the page and handed it to Dave. "Send this to my father via telegram."

Dave looked at the note. The handwriting was choppy, almost illegible.

"What is this? I can't read it, Flori."

"It says 'I'm sorry I can't come home now. I'm pregnant.'"

Dave stared at her. After Ruthie's difficult birth, the doctor had told them that Flora would never conceive again. "But I thought . . . "

"Well, obviously not."

"This is wonderful news." Dave embraced her.

"The telegram, Dave," Flora reminded him coolly.

"Yes. Of course. I'll be back soon. Solly!" he called. The boy came into the kitchen. "Come with Papa and Ruthie to the telegram office. We'll stop at the drugstore on the way home and get some candy." Sol took his father's hand and they walked toward the door. "Did Mommy tell you about the new baby?" Flora heard Dave ask the children on their way out. "Maybe we'll be lucky this time and you'll get a little brother."

lora's third pregnancy was uncomplicated and the labor uneventful. The baby wriggled out from between her legs, unwilling to wait for Zamie to return with the doctor. "Another textile engineer!" Dave laughed after Hava emerged from their bedroom and announced it was a boy. Mule sent a telegram to the mohel in Bogotá. Eight days later he arrived, and with a snip proclaimed him: Simcha, in memory of Flora's mother.

The Hebrew name, Simcha, was chosen because of the joy he brought his mother after being told that she would bear no more children. To his family, the boy was Semmie, short for Simon. Upon hearing the news, Bolívariana poked her head into the crib to determine if the infant was worthy of the appellation. "Simón," she said once and the baby, only hours old, stood at attention.

Semmie was no lackey. The apple of his mother's eye, the baby quickly moved up the ranks from little soldier to little general. At eight months he mastered command sentences and was awarded the title of "dictator." He refused to walk, demanding to be carried here and there. If denied, Semmie stomped and cursed until someone eventually picked him up.

At night, with a stern "go away," the golden-locked,

green-eyed child kept Dave from the couple's bed. His father tried to sneak back in the middle of the night, but Semmie always booted him out with a sharp kick. Semmie battled for his mother's undivided love, afraid that an intruder might one day lurk inside her belly. Eventually twin beds replaced the double mattress.

Banished from the bedroom until Semmie fell asleep, Dave listened to the news over the shortwave radio. He shook his head the entire broadcast, hoping disbelief might negate the events prickling his ears.

"It is no use, Señor, the world is rotting," Bolívariana said to him one night. He'd spread his map across the dinner table and was tracking the war with his pen. A tear fell on France. Dave wondered if it belonged to him or to the old woman, now so bent that she had to stretch her eyes to the top of their sockets to see above table level. Bolívariana shook her finger at Germany and walked away.

Dave couldn't help but agree. The world smelled of rot. Inside and out. No matter how many times he bathed or brushed his teeth, the rancid taste in his mouth and the scent that burned his nostrils refused to fade.

He carried the smell of the city's slums back from work every day. In the morning, the street urchins of Laureles waited for his car to turn onto the dirt road that led up to the factory. "Don David," they shouted. They ran alongside the vehicle, forcing him to slow down. Once he drove onto the property, Dave could see from his rearview mirror the children hanging on the corrugated metal door as don Marco pushed it closed.

Flora's nose picked up the scent, too. To her it seemed to be coming from inside her house. "It's not me," Bolívariana said when she noticed Flora sniffing around. "I smell aged. This is vile."

183

"Put on your shoes, Ana," Flora ordered her new maid. "It's time for a spring cleaning." Determined to wipe down every wall and corner, the two women began to drag all the furniture into the courtyard.

When Dave arrived at noon, Flora sat in the foyer, her suitcase by her side. The children sat beside her, dressed in their finest outfits. "I discovered what stinks." Dave took the yellowed envelope from Flora's trembling hand. She lifted Semmie from the bench and picked up her suitcase. Struggling to maintain her balance, Flora walked toward the door. "Come, children. Sol, please open the door for Mommy."

The boy slid reluctantly from the seat. He twisted the knob but had not the strength to pull it open. Flora put down the suitcase and helped him. "Let's go, Ruthie. Hold on to your brother's hand." Sol looked back at his father as Flora gently urged him outside.

"Flori." Dave touched her elbow.

"I cannot live with you. You are a liar." Flora pulled away. The look of disappointment to which Dave had grown accustomed had been replaced with icy rage.

"I've never lied to you," Dave defended himself. "I wanted to spare you."

"You lie by omission, Dave." Unable to look at her husband, Flora's eyes drifted and caught sight of Bolívariana slumped over the side of her rocker. Flora thrust Semmie into Dave's arms and ran to the old woman. "Dave!" Flora screamed from the courtyard.

Dave carried Bolívariana's limp body into her bedroom and went to fetch a doctor.

"What would you like me to do?" the doctor asked after he saw his intended patient.

"She's sick. She needs treatment," Flora cried.

"She's old, Señora, and there is no cure for age."

Flora tended to Bolívariana all night. From the mahogany bed came the crackle of bones as they crumbled to dust under her skin. Delirious, Bolívariana ranted about a single bullet that would pierce the heart of Colombia's people, until her own stopped beating in sympathy.

Preparations for the burial came to a halt after the mortician arrived to prepare the body. Flora found him in the courtyard among the furniture, searching for the corpse. "It's the room off the patio," she told him again.

"No, Señora. She's not there." Flora followed him into Bolívariana's room. The bed was indeed empty. "Are you sure she's dead?" the mortician asked after they searched the entire house.

While Dave combed the neighborhood, Ana and Flora moved all the furniture back into the house, hoping to discover the body under a table or a bed.

Confusion and exhaustion eased the sting of Dave's deception. Flora returned her suitcase to the closet and prepared the children for sleep. As she tucked Ruthie into bed, she noticed the child clutching a cloth doll the size of a pillow. Its features, beady black eyes and scraggly wool hair, were somewhat sinister. "Where did you get this?" Flora asked her daughter.

"Bolívariana's room," the child answered sleepily.

"Let Mommy wash it before you sleep with it." Flora tried to take the doll from Ruthie's arms, but the girl held on tight, refusing to surrender it. As they struggled for possession, the stitching gave. The doll burst at the seams. Batting spewed all over the room.

30

*D*orothy knocked on Flora's door six months later. Her wool crepe suit, glossy pumps, and tidy hair wound in a chignon so taut that it defied the morning's humidity gave the impression that she'd come from across the street rather than traveled over three thousand miles.

"This place is hotter than hell," she said, breezing past Flora, who stood frozen on the landing.

"What are you doing here?" Flora stammered. "How did you get here."

"Boat, boat, train, taxi." Dorothy laughed. "Oh, Flora, it's so good to see you. And you." Dorothy kissed Flora's once again pregnant belly.

"Ana!" Flora called. The maid scurried out from the kitchen. Flora shook her head at the sight of the woman's bare feet and said, "Help us lift this trunk."

"Señora, your friend is whiter than the Holy Ghost," Ana whispered to Flora as the three women dragged the footlocker into the house.

It was true. Although Dorothy had been aboard a ship from New York to Colombia and then on the steamer down the Río Magdalena, her skin remained the color of milk. The ship's captain remarked that the sun dared not ravage such an exquisite face, yet he could not resist kissing those perfect cheeks. After the ship docked in Puerto Colombia, he personally escorted Dorothy to Barranquilla. The captain begged her to marry him, but Dorothy declared that she was promised to another. As he watched her set sail down the Río Magdalena in the boat of another captain, his tears cascaded into the river.

"Now I understand why you seldom wrote," said Dorothy, after Flora introduced her to the three children. "You've been quite busy."

Flora looked down, still a bit shocked by her bulging stomach. "We had a fight," she stammered.

"Aah. Must have been a doozy," Dorothy teased. "Looks like you made up."

"Ana, bring us some juice," Flora called out to the maid. She led Dorothy into the living room. Dorothy kicked off her shoes and threw herself on the sofa. "Why are you here?" Flora asked again.

"I've come to marry Harold." Dorothy pulled a packet of cigarettes from her purse. "Where is he?"

"Marry Harold?" Flora burst out laughing. "He never said anything about you two getting married."

Dorothy tapped a cigarette against the table, placed it in her mouth, and struck a match. Her blue eyes flickered mischievously. She took a deep drag before she continued speaking. "All the details haven't been worked out yet." Smoke billowed from Dorothy's mouth.

"Have you two been corresponding?" Flora asked.

"Not exactly."

"So when did this romance start?"

"Your last letter." Dorothy opened her purse again.

"My last letter?" Flora tried to remember when she had written to Dorothy.

"Here it is." Dorothy handed Flora the letter.

Flora opened the envelope. It was the note she'd sent Dorothy, thanking her for the condolence letter. "I don't understand," Flora said.

"Harold sent me regards." Dorothy leaned over and pointed to the bottom of the letter, where to fill the empty space on the page, Flora had added Harold's regards.

"Are you joking?" Flora stood up. "You came all this way because Harold sent his regards? What in the world made you think that was a proposal?" Ana entered, carrying a tray with two glasses of blackberry juice. "Ana, *los zapatos,*" Flora reminded the maid as she left the room.

"Obviously he's interested in me or else he wouldn't send them." Dorothy took a sip of her juice. "After all, Harold is a man of few words."

"Well I'm sure this will make him speechless," Flora quipped. "Dorothy, you've gotten more marriage proposals than anyone I know. Why on earth would you want to marry Harold?"

"Why not? It's time for me to marry and I have chosen Harold."

"But life is very hard here, Dorothy," Flora explained. "You'll be so far away from your family and friends. If you married someone in the States, your life would be simpler."

"Oh, Flora!" Dorothy laughed. "I don't want life to be simple. I want it to be an adventure! Just getting here was the most exciting thing I've ever done."

"Adventure?" Flora was incredulous. "Having to boil your water every day so that the amoebas don't devour your intestines is not an adventure, Dorothy. They have electricity but the maids are afraid to answer the phone or turn on the light. I have to plead with Ana so she'll wear shoes. They are like children. You have to supervise everything they do. I can't leave written instructions or ask them to follow a recipe. They don't know how to read or write." Flora took a swig of juice and immediately spit it back into the glass.

"I think it has salt in it," Dorothy said quietly.

Both women burst out laughing.

◆

Harold and Dorothy traveled to Bogotá to be married at the new synagogue downtown. The rabbi, a recent arrival to the mountain city, fell asleep as the bride circled the groom seven times. The paid witness, a stranger Harold hired off the street, nudged the rabbi awake. He began again. In the middle of the service, the rabbi's memory faltered. His blessings got mixed up and he ended the service with a prayer to be recited at a Jewish divorce. No one in the room spoke enough Hebrew to catch his error. Dorothy and Harold left the synagogue unmarried and divorced under Judaic law. The civil ceremony required by Colombian law for people not married by the church could not undo the rabbi's mistake. His prayer split them apart, sending the couple on separate paths that would rarely intersect.

Back at the hotel, Harold realized that he'd lost his passport. Dorothy, not willing to forgo her honeymoon, kissed him good-bye and sailed for Cuba, where she danced the nights away with a gentleman by the name of Batista.

"Who goes on their honeymoon without their husband?" the Sisters cried when Harold returned alone. No one expected Dorothy to come back. But she did, four months later. A single kiss and Harold moved into the small home Dorothy rented down the street from Flora and Dave.

Harold's indifference toward his wife's outlandish behavior ceased to concern the Sisters when they realized their brother had grown oblivious to the world and its rules of convention. Harold often failed to come home, preferring to sleep where slumber came to him. Arrested and jailed overnight for not having proper identification (he never bothered to replace the lost passport), Harold emerged nonchalant, as if he'd spent the night in a hotel. Engrossed in a book about organic farming and unable to check it out because he lacked identification, Harold slept in the reading room of the public library until he finished the book.

A week after his son was born, Dave and Mule dragged Harold to visit his wife and baby. "At times," Benzi recalled, "we wondered if Harold even knew Dorothy was with child." Harold couldn't understand the fuss. "What's his name?" he asked Dorothy.

"Norman," she replied.

Harold looked at the infant but remained unimpressed. "I'll see you," he said and disappeared again.

Dorothy took all of Harold's antics and strange behavior in stride. One morning she heard him speaking Yiddish to the maid. "If I talk very slow," Harold explained to his wife when she asked him what in God's name he was doing, "they understand."

Fastidious about the fruit he consumed, Harold preferred to pick it out himself. Therefore he insisted on going food shopping with Dorothy. While he haggled with the vendors in the plaza, Dorothy bought staples and meat. One morning, after they finished shopping, Harold backed their car into a military vehicle. Before Dorothy could stop him, he got out and began to direct a tirade of insults at the driver and his passenger, a General Rojas Piñilla.

"Harold!" Dorothy screamed. "Get back inside before you get us both shot." She dragged him away and pushed him into the car. "You back into a general's car and then you start yelling at him? My God! Now sit there while I go and apologize."

Dorothy got out of the car, straightened her skirt, and walked over to the general's car. The chauffeur opened the door for her and she stepped inside. Half an hour later she got out, promising to send the general one of the factory's new products: a blanket.

Her gift prompted the general to place an order for a thousand blankets for the new military barracks in the western plains of Los Llanos. The blankets never made it to their destination. Horsebacked insurgents, dressed in chaps like cowboys, intercepted the military vehicle on the road to Villavicencio. They drove the truck south, giving away blankets to men willing to join their cause or to peasants who provided food or shelter from the encroaching army. The blankets' coarseness worked to the guerrillas advantage. Those who used them awoke with a prickle of discontent and realized their dissatisfaction with their living conditions, government, and country. Women who slept with these men became infected with their lovers' discontent. Boys and their fathers joined the insurgents. The countryside erupted in violence. The army ordered more blankets for the troops sent to quash the rebels. Some made it to the military camps and others got diverted by the guerrillas who quickly learned how to identify the trucks carrying blankets of insurrection. Colombia was in chaos, close to another civil war, but thanks to Harold, the factory was making a fortune.

31

When Harold and Dorothy moved to 17 Carrera Giradot, they set off a chain reaction. Dave and Flora bought number 20 in the middle of the same street. And Benzi, to shorten the gap created by their departure, bought the house with the turret, number 12, that stood at the top of the block. Leon's illness prevented him from driving, thereby forcing him and Freida to stay put in their home only two blocks away from the shop.

Carrera Giradot was lined with jasmine. The ocher flowers opened at sunset and infused the block with their fragile fragrance. But their wondrous perfume could not diffuse Flora's irritation arising from living under the constant eye of the Sisters. From the turret, they could see all the gardens and patios of the houses on the block. Flora kept her curtains drawn day and night until she realized their eyes could see through the imported damask.

"You shouldn't let Ruthie play with that filthy rag doll, Flora. You shouldn't let that mangy dog inside the house, Flora. It's got fleas. Tell the shiksa she needs to shine the tile in the dining room, Flora. It's very dull."

Once she let the light seep back into her home, Flora also noticed the dust accumulating on the new furniture. Dave woke up one night to find his wife dusting the headboard of his twin bed. "What's the matter, Flori?" he asked.

"This house is too big for Ana to clean by herself," she answered. "During the day I have my hands full with the children and the cooking."

The next night, the smell of silver polish invaded his sleep. He switched on the light. Flora sat in her bed surrounded by silverware. Dave was about to ask his wife what she was doing when he realized that her eyes were closed. In the morning Dave suggested Flora hire another maid to help with the housework.

"I don't need two maids," Flora responded, unconscious that she rose from her bed every night to clean.

"The house is filthy." Dave set the bait, knowing that it was the only way to get Flora to agree. "Either you hire another maid, or I'll find one for you."

Marina came highly recommended by the neighbor's housekeeper. "A hard worker, Señora. An excellent cook," the girl told Flora.

Flora agreed to meet Marina and hired her on the spot. She moved in the next day and that night dazzled the family with her beef stew.

One evening Flora entered the kitchen holding a thin rectangular box and a small silver dish. "Marina?"

"¿Sí, Señora?" Marina stood at the sink washing the dinner dishes.

"Is the coffee ready?" Flora asked.

"Sí, Señora." Marina pointed to the tray on the counter that held a coffeepot surrounded by eight cups and saucers.

Flora ran a jagged fingernail down the center of the box to perforate the cellophane wrap. The maid stretched her thick neck to see the contents of the box. Inside, sitting in crisp white paper liners, were little brown squares, circles, and rectangles. Some were smooth, some had swirls embedded in their tiny shapes and some sported pale brown curls across their tops. Flora carefully pulled each one out, and arranged them on the dish.

"Marina?" Flora picked up the dish.

"¿Señora?"

"Please bring in the coffee. Oh, and please don't throw this box out." Flora pointed with her elbow to the empty box on the counter.

"*Sí*, Señora." Marina turned off the faucet, dried her hands quickly, and picked up the tray with the coffee. She followed Flora out into the living room.

Dorothy sat on the sofa surrounded by the four American businessmen who had come to Colombia to sell the Grossenbergs some looms. Harold sat across the room, slouched on the wing chair. His wild blue eyes circled in their sockets. When Marina entered the parlor they stopped, focusing on the thin silver crucifix around her neck. Marina set the tray down on the coffee table. She poured a cup of coffee, placed it on the saucer, and handed it to Flora.

"Would you care for some coffee, Mr. Edwards?" Flora held the cup to his ear, but he didn't respond.

"Mr. Schneider?" Flora repositioned the cup in front of Mr. Schneider, who sat to Dorothy's right. The china cup rattled against its saucer. Mr. Schneider looked up. "Would you care for some coffee?" Flora asked, pushing the cup in front of his long thin nose.

"Excuse me, gentlemen." Dorothy stood up. The four men followed her with their eyes as she walked out of the living room.

"Coffee?" Flora asked again.

"A remarkable woman," Mr. Schneider said, taking the cup out of Flora's hand.

"Chocolate?" Flora offered him the tray. Marina watched Mr. Schneider's delicate manicured hands select a smooth rectangular chocolate. He bit into it. A thread of the soft white center clung to the right corner of his lip. A chalky tongue darted out of his mouth and licked it away.

After she finished serving the coffee, Marina returned to the kitchen. While washing the dishes she fantasized about the insides of the little coffee-colored shapes. Were all the little pockets filled with the same creamy white substance? Did it taste like cream? The white box on the counter caught her eye. She turned off the faucet, leaned over the counter, and reached for the box. She opened it, and the smell of chocolate that had permeated the thin cardboard flowed out. Marina had her nose pressed against the inside of the box when Ana entered the kitchen.

"From America," Ana said. "Señor Mule brings them for la Señora when he goes to the States. Or don David brings them back from his trips to Barranquilla where you can get lots of American food. Señora Flora has boxes and boxes, upstairs in the closet. I saw them one day while I was waiting for her to give me some cans of vegetables for dinner."

"Have you ever tasted them?" Marina asked.

"Yes. *La niña* Ruthie saves me the ones she doesn't like."

After the guests left, Ana straightened the living room. She stacked the cups on a tray in sets of two and then made a pile of saucers. The white candy liners scattered on the coffee table were gathered, pressed into one another to form a miniature paper tower. Ana gathered the cloth napkins into her large apron pocket. As she picked up a stray cup left on the table next to the wing chair, Ana noticed a crumpled napkin shoved between the cushion and the seat. She reached for it and felt something inside the cloth. Inspection revealed a half-eaten chocolate, its firm green jelly center exposed. Ana smiled, dropped the morsel into the top candy liner and carried the tray into the kitchen.

"Look what I found," Ana called out to Marina as she pushed through the swinging door.

Marina stared at the chocolate. "Should we give it to Señora Flora?" she asked. "She came in and put all the left-over ones back into the box."

"Someone already took a bite out of it. It's trash." Ana's cold serpent eyes fixed on Marina. "Do you want to split it?" She reached for a knife sitting on the drain board and divided the tidbit into two equal portions. Ana popped one half into her mouth. She held out the other to Marina. "Don't you want it?"

Marina stared at the offering sandwiched between two leathery fingertips. There were two slight ridges where the chocolate had been bitten.

"Go on, take it." Ana dropped the plum into the maid's hand.

Marina put the treat in her mouth and rolled it around with her tongue, carefully sucking away the thin layer of chocolate from the gelatinous center. She spit out the brilliant emerald square into her palm. "I'm saving the rest," she said, delicately placing her prize into a candy liner.

A week later, Flora gave Marina a bag of red-striped peppermints to place in a candy dish. Nineteen of the mints met their destination. One managed to find its way into Marina's brassiere, where it lay nestled through teatime. When she pulled it out, the stripes had bled into each other. That evening, as Marina was clearing the din-ner dishes, she spied the bowl sitting on the sideboard. She reached in, spreading her fingers wide to gather as many as possible. Nothing short of a handful would do. She was stopped by the clicking of heels against the marble floor. They grew louder, quickly approaching the dining room. Marina hastily pulled her hand away. In the process, a peppermint shot into the air and landed in the crevice between the wall and the sideboard. It hung there precariously, but before Marina had a chance to remove it, Flora entered the room. Marina quickly resumed clearing the table, reciting a silent prayer of forgiveness to her Lord. Her lips moved as she stacked the dishes on the tray.

"Marina, dinner was very good tonight." Flora approached the sideboard and picked up the crystal dish. "Oh! How did this get here?" Flora asked. She reached behind the sideboard, retrieved the candy, and dropped it into the bowl. Flora was halfway out the door when she paused.

Marina held her breath.

"I guess I mean to say that I'm very pleased with you," Flora said with a smile.

"Thank you, Señora." Marina exhaled a sigh of relief and then made a promise to the Virgin del Carmen never to steal again.

Marina was putting away some tablecloths in the linen closet when Flora beckoned her upstairs. Marina followed her into the master bedroom.

As Ana had said, behind the closet doors were several stacks of the long white rectangular boxes. Cans lined the shelf three deep. Their bright labels had illustrations of yellow corn kernels, tiny green peas, and purple beets. Flora reached up and grabbed two cans with forest green labels.

"For dessert." She handed Marina the cans. "Put two in a cup for each person. I think two cans should be enough."

Marina carried the cans down to the kitchen, staring

hard at the picture: two egg yolks butting up against each other. Who would want to eat egg yolks for dessert? What did those fancy letters across the bottom mean? While the family ate dinner, Marina opened the cans. Five giant yolks bobbed up and down in a thick translucent liquid. As she lifted one out with a slotted spoon, the slime that surrounded the yellow mass slipped back into the can, leaving the orb wet and shiny. Marina touched it, poking her finger around the slippery exterior. It felt firm, not delicate like an egg yolk. She flipped it over, palpating the frayed center. Her finger instantly gravitated toward her mouth. A drop of sweet syrup fanned out across her tongue. The ringing of the crystal bell signaled the family was ready for dessert. Marina grabbed a tray and hurried into the dining room. She quickly cleared the plates and returned to the kitchen. Using a fork, she speared the peaches and placed them in the dessert bowls. Marina then drained both cans of their liquor, sucking it down eagerly, oblivious to the jagged metal edge cutting into the corner of her lip.

"Where's the syrup?" Semmie cried out as Marina placed a bowl in front of him.

Bernie, the baby, began to wail.

Marina cringed. She felt something sticky on her lip. Her tongue darted out and quickly licked it away.

Flora looked down and noticed her two peaches looking rather dry in their bowl. "Oh, Marina, we like to drink the syrup from the can. Could you get it?"

"Señora, I'm sorry. I threw it away," was Marina's instant reply. "I didn't know you ate that part." Semmie glared at her. The tight curls surrounding his face trembled slightly.

"Oh well, you'll know for next time." Flora jabbed a peach with her fork. Juice squirted from her lips and dribbled down her chin as she bit into the peach. Marina reached across the table to retrieve an empty vegetable bowl. A drop of red fell on the remaining sauce. She was wondering where it came from when another one landed on the tablecloth. Marina looked up. The entire family was staring at her.

"Marina!" Flora got up and pushed a napkin at her.

"¿Señora?" Once again, there was something warm and sticky on her chin. She wiped it and her hand came away smeared with blood. Marina quickly accepted the napkin from Flora. As she held it to her face, they all rushed around her. Marina kept insisting that it was more bloody than serious. "It must have been a bent tine on the fork with which I ate my dinner, Señora." The next day Flora bought a new set of silverware for the help.

Marina satisfied her daily sugar cravings with impromptu midafternoon jaunts into the living room. All subsequent behavior hedged solely on the status of the blue crystal candy dish on the coffee table. If full, Marina would help herself to three or four pieces. If not, she'd take only one and then proceed to the other rooms of the house. The den usually had a stash of caramels inside the right drawer of Dave's mahogany desk. Offering to help Ana dust provided easy, unquestioned access. Marina also volunteered for chores that involved being upstairs, like taking up the laundry. On the bookshelf upstairs sat a jar filled with brightly colored sour balls.

Parties, teas, and dinner guests provided splendid opportunities for collecting scads of sweets. After the guests left, Marina gathered handfuls of candy from the crystal dishes in the living room. La Señora, good hostess that she was, never questioned how much her company had eaten.

The closet, with its cache, became Marina's obsession.

Every time she dropped off the laundry in the master bed-room, Marina tested the door to see if, on the off chance, la Señora had left it open. But Flora never failed to secure the closet, and the key ring, attached to her body like a magnet, never left her side.

The kitchen turned into a laboratory. Marina tested sleeping potions on Cupcake, the dog. After a while, the poodle became wary of eating anything Marina offered him because of the ache it produced in his French belly. Suspicious, Cupcake sniffed and usually turned up his nose. But the bowl of milk sweetened with honey he lapped up eagerly.

"Flora. That dog of yours is dead." Reesa's voice cack-led over the phone.

"What?" Flora looked out into the yard. Cupcake lay on his side. "He's sleeping."

"He hasn't moved since yesterday. I tell you, he's dead."

Flora put the receiver down. She stepped out into the patio. "Cupcake," Flora called out. "Cupcake!" The dog didn't budge.

"There's a band of thieves roaming the neighborhood," Benzi informed the family when they gathered for the Sabbath. "They throw pieces of meat laced with poison to ward off watchdogs. I've been thinking of putting a roof over our garden. You know, one of those metal corrugated roofs like the one in the factory."

"Benzi, you don't have a dog," Flora pointed out.

"I know. But this way no one can get in through the yard."

"No one can get into your garden, Benzi," Dorothy in-terrupted. "Not with all the broken glass and barbed wire you've run along the wall. The place looks like a prison."

A mothball was Marina's demise. She was hanging a

dress in Ruthie's closet and noticed the open tin. She picked up a glistening white lump and placed it in her mouth. Ruthie entered the room and saw the maid's chubby face contorting.

"Marina? What's wrong?"

"Nothing." Marina brushed past the girl into the hall-way. She raced down the steps spitting the ball into her palm. Sputtering crystal particles, she made her way into the kitchen, where Flora was baking a cake. Marina burst through the swinging door and flew to the sink.

"Marina? What's the matter?" Flora rushed over to her.

Marina flushed her mouth several times, trying to get rid of the bitter-tasting naphthalene that coated her palate and was making her woozy. "The candy. The candy!" Marina wailed, still clutching the mothball in her hand.

"What's that smell?"

"Candy from the tin in *la niña's* closet." Marina threw up into the sink. "I'm sorry, doña Flora," she gasped. "I'll never do it again."

Flora was willing to overlook that one indiscretion. She guided Marina into the maids' room and helped her into bed. Flora opened the closet to fetch her a nightgown. The box of Wittamer chocolates Mule had brought her from his last trip to Europe, the Whitman's Sampler Dave bought for the children from his trip to New York, and a box of after-dinner mints stood in a ziggurat on the shelf. Flora pulled one out. Inside were rows of caramels, gum-drops, peppermint candies, sour balls, and chocolate kisses neatly tucked into slightly crumpled candy liners.

$\mathcal{F}$lora and Ana stood behind the garden gate, watching Marina trudge down Carrera Giradot clutching the small suitcase that contained the candy she had accumulated during her two-year employment with the Grossenbergs. "What a pity," Flora muttered, tapping the toe of her shoe three times against the cement walkway. "What a shame. She wasn't a bad cook."

Ana nodded, pursed her lips, and folded her arms across her chest in a gesture of solidarity.

Marina stopped at the corner and glanced back at the two women. She sighed heavily, recalling her own mother's prediction that her sweet tooth would only bring her disgrace. God looked unkindly on those who were easily tempted. And for that reason he had placed Marina in a house teeming with sour ball candies, chocolate kisses, and chewy caramels. Marina slipped around the corner too absorbed in her fate and a prayer to Saint Joseph to notice the young girl that brushed past her arm.

The girl, propelled by the slight sway of her underdeveloped hips, moved slowly up the incline of the street. Every couple of feet she'd pause, tilt her head up toward the pink sky, and inhale deeply. When she reached Ana and

Flora, the girl stopped, flared her small nostrils, and asked, "What's that smell?"

Both Flora and Ana scrunched their noses and took in the aroma. "The jasmine." Ana pointed to the tree, outside the gate.

The girl closed her eyes and inhaled again. Color slowly flowed into her pale face. She walked over to the tree, wrapped her long arms around the trunk, and pressed her lips against the bark. She giggled softly to herself, turned to Flora and asked, "Señora, do you need help in the house?"

Flora and Ana stared at the girl. "No. I don't need anyone. Thank you. Probably from the insane asylum," Flora whispered to Ana. They retreated into the house to watch the girl from the living room window as she do-si-doed with the tree, swinging from arm to arm, gathering momentum until she finally fell exhausted onto the grass.

Flora rapped her knuckles on the window pane, to get the girl's attention. "Go away!" she ordered. "Go!" Flora shooed her away with her hand. "Get!" The girl stood there for a moment watching Flora's eyebrows furrow. She got up off the grass and walked a few feet up the street, out of Flora's line of sight.

The next morning, the Sisters' keen eyes honed in on a foot dangling from the jasmine tree in front of 20 Giradot. "Flora. There's someone trying to break into your house," Reesa hissed over the phone. Before Flora put down the receiver, the Sisters were outside her gate. They tiptoed under the tree and spied the girl sleeping on a branch, her head resting against the trunk. The girl awoke to Reesa's strong grip around her ankle. She jerked back, trying to shake free, but then Fanny's rough, calloused hand seized her thigh and Hava reached out and grabbed her other leg. With a silent count of three, the three women yanked the girl from the tree. She landed with an "Ay!" on the grass in front of them.

The Sisters surrounded her, their beady eyes scanning her small frame. The girl's matted hair was sprinkled with jasmine petals. "What were you doing up there?" Reesa demanded.

"Sleeping." The girl rubbed her hip.

"Who sleeps in a tree? What are you, a monkey or something? You were trying to get in through that bedroom window, weren't you?" Reesa pointed to the window that was several feet from the nearest tree branch.

"No, Señora."

"Someone better get Flora. Let her know," Reesa said. With that, Fanny separated herself and walked up the path to the house. Hava bent down to examine the girl.

Flora emerged before Fanny knocked on the door and flew down the steps. "I told her to go away yesterday. She was hanging around here acting crazy. Is she hurt, Hava?"

"No bones broken. Can you get up?" Hava addressed the girl.

"I think so." The girl stood up.

"Flora, I think we should call the police," Reesa said. "She's probably working with some gang of street urchins trying to get into houses. She's small enough to climb through a window."

"No, Señora. I wasn't going to steal anything. I was just resting in the tree. I had nowhere to sleep."

"A likely story," Fanny interjected for Reesa's approval.

"Flora, go call the police. Have her arrested," Reesa repeated.

"Have who arrested?" The women turned out of their

circle to face Mule, who had sneaked up behind them. They all quickly patted down their hair and tried to smooth away the dowdiness of their housedresses. Reesa took Mule's hand.

"Mule! Good morning," she croaked. "I'm so glad you're here. You can help us. We saw this girl in the tree. We think she was trying to sneak into Dave's house. By the way, did the shiksa serve you the latkes I made for you?"

Mule smiled. "Yes, thank you, Reesa. They were delicious. But what's this about the girl?"

"I'm going to call the police," Flora said assertively. "She was hanging around the house yesterday, acting strange."

"What's your name?" Mule addressed the girl.

"Luz. Luz Alba Rodríguez," the girl stated proudly.

"Luz Alba. Dawn Light. What a beautiful name," Mule declared. "Now, Luz Alba Rodríguez, were you trying to break into this house?"

"No, Señor. I was just sleeping up in the tree."

"Why?"

"Because I have no place else to go."

"A likely story!" Hava cried. "Mule, don't you think we should call the police?"

"No." Mule took Luz's hand and helped her up. "Are you hurt?"

"No. Just my rear end is sore."

Mule chuckled. The four women reciprocated with tight-lipped smiles, somewhat embarrassed by the girl's reference to her anatomy.

He opened his double-breasted jacket, removed his wallet from the inside pocket, and pulled out a wad of crisp bills. Mule flicked through them, finally selecting a five-peso note. "Here." He handed it to Luz Alba.

"*Gracias,* Señor." Luz took the money, touching Mule's smooth hand in the exchange.

"Luz Alba, come back to the house and we'll give you some food," Hava said emphatically.

Reesa glared at Hava, wishing she had thought of it first. "Yes, Luz Alba. Come back to the house. I have a daughter your age. I might have some clothes for you."

"Ladies, you have a good heart." Mule patted Reesa's arm.

"Luz, I need a girl for the kitchen," Flora piped in. "Do you know how to cook?" The Sisters glared at Flora.

"*Sí,* Señora," Luz Alba replied, crossing her long fingers behind her back.

"Good. Then you can start today if you like."

"But first she has to come to our house to have something to eat," Reesa scowled. Flora had outdone them.

"She can eat here, since she is going to be working here," Flora replied.

"What about the clothes, Flora? She needs to come and get the clothes." Reesa took Luz Alba by the elbow.

"Just bring them over later, Reesa." Flora ushered Luz Alba Rodríguez through the gate. "Mule, do you want some coffee?" Flora called back to him.

"No, thank you, Flora." Mule turned to the Sisters. "Ladies, I'll see you at lunch." He kissed them each on the cheek and then walked back up the hill, toward his car.

◆

Luz Alba Rodríguez could not cook. She could sing and dance along to the music from the small transistor radio in the kitchen. She knew every character in every radio soap opera and could summarize the plot of each one. She kept current on all the gossip on the block. The most recent tidbit to come her way was that the milkman was in love with the girl who worked in number 18 Giradot. Unfortunately for him, that maid was in love with don Mateo, the butcher where doña Flora purchased all her meat.

Luz loved the butcher shop. On Tuesdays, she would sit in the backseat of Flora's Ford and head downtown to help with the marketing. Flora's last stop was always the butcher shop. As don Mateo filled Flora's order, Luz would lean her bare legs against the cool glass counter and stare out at the crowded street. Her presence always distracted the butcher and often made him bang his head on the refrigerated case when he pulled out a cut of beef.

"She's burning everything. All the pots are ruined," Flora complained to Dave after every meal.

"Switch her. Let Ana cook and Luz can do the cleaning," Dave answered.

"Ana can't cook either. Besides, Ana's the best cleaner I've ever had. She never leaves any dust. Luz has to go before we starve."

It was not the first time Flora had asked Dave to fire Luz Alba. He'd been ordered to dismiss her in the past but always came away without having accomplished the task. In the few weeks Luz had worked for the family, she'd blossomed. Her hair, at first stringy and oily, was now thick and shiny. From underneath her gritty skin had emerged a flesh smoother than satin. But it was the small black mole on the right side of her chin that prevented Dave from bringing up the subject that brought him into the kitchen.

The same mole was discussed ad nauseam by his three sons. "Do you think there are more?" Bernie, the ten-year-old, had asked his older brothers.

Sol had tried to find out. One day, he discovered the maid dancing in the kitchen with her broom.

"Teach me how to dance, Luz," Sol pleaded.

"Well, I'm just learning myself. How can I teach someone?" she asked.

"Please?"

"Okay." Luz stepped toward him, placing his plump hands on her waist. Her hips began to sway to the mambo music playing on the radio. "No, *niño*," she said, laughing, the mole dancing up and down on her chin as she pushed Sol's eager hands away from her newly developed breasts. Sol stared at her bosom, which seemed to be tugging at the buttons of her uniform while Luz readjusted his hands on her waist. "Don't be fresh," she said after his hands wandered back in the same direction a few moments later. He was exploring the curve of her waist, inching his fingers down Luz's hips, when the sound of his mother's voice cut through the house.

"The roast! The roast! Luz!" Smoke billowed from the oven.

"Did you do it this time?" Flora asked Dave one afternoon as he sneaked around the bedroom. Instead of starting his siesta right after lunch, Dave had taken to lingering about the house, pretending to search for some important piece of paper. He'd wait for Flora to give Luz Alba and Ana instuctions about their chores and then follow her up the stairs, admiring the width of her hips. The friction between Flora's satin underwear and the cotton of her dress created a soft rustle as she climbed each step. When she reached the top, Dave scrambled up behind her.

"No," Dave answered. He propped the pillows on his bed and lay back. As his wife prepared for her nap, Dave pulled a little yellow book from the breast pocket of his jacket and began to leaf through it. Even though Flora had asked him the title several times, all she could remember was that it started with a "K" and sounded Chinese or something. The previous night, she'd asked if she might read it when he was done. Dave had smiled and placed it under his pillow.

"Oh, Dave! What now?" Flora undid her apron and laid it over the chair.

"Flora, she has nowhere to go. We can't just put her out." Dave crossed over to Flora's bed and sat down next to her. She felt his hand on her neck as she took off her shoes.

"That's what you said last time. We're not responsible for them."

Dave slowly unzipped the back of Flora's housedress, slipping his hands in between the cloth and her warm body.

◆

Flora sat in the kitchen, dunking a burnt cookie into a cup of rancid coffee. She was at her wit's end. She had a cook who couldn't boil water without ruining it and a husband who was requesting highly imaginative sexual positions in the middle of the afternoon. Luz stumbled into the kitchen, readjusting her uniform over her newly curvaceous hips. Her eyes were swollen, the thick lashes surrounding them slightly parted.

"Doña Flora, can I get you anything?" she asked.

"That uniform is too small. What size is it?"

"I don't know," Luz answered.

"Let me check, so I can get you a larger size this afternoon when I go out shopping." Flora walked over to the girl, lifted the collar of the uniform away from Luz's musky skin, and peered inside.

"Luz! You're not wearing any underwear!" Flora exclaimed.

"No, Señora," she answered shyly. Her breath smelled

like jasmine.

"Why not?"

"I only have one pair and I wear it on Sundays to church."

Twenty minutes later, Flora sat in the driver's seat of the Ford, mumbling something about the peasants, God, and forsaken countries. Luz sat in the back, squirming in her damp underwear, which Flora had forced her to pull off the clothesline. She rolled down the window, and stuck her face out the window. The hot breeze whipped her face as they drove downtown. Flora pulled up in front of a shop. The mannequins in the window were dressed in night-gowns. Luz followed Flora inside. Flora spoke in soft tones to the saleswoman, who kept nodding her head at Luz.

"Venga." The woman called Luz over. Luz walked toward the woman, who held a yellow tape measure in her hand. She measured Luz's chest and hips. Then she cinched the cord around Luz's stomach. The saleswoman stopped and looked up at Flora with concern. Her eyes moved back to Luz, who stood with her arms held high above her head staring at the window, mesmerized by the man-nequins.

lora."

"Yes, Reesa?"

"Your undergarments are flying away. Tell the shiksa she needs to pin them." From the turret, the Sisters watched a bra float over Flora's garden wall. It fluttered in the wind until the bougainvillea snagged it with its spiny leaves. A minute later, the Sisters saw Flora dash out of her house to retrieve it.

The last five days the Sisters had eaten lunch alone, bickering among themselves about who could skin a potato with the least waste, or whose brisket was juicier. "Do you think the men will eat lunch there today?" Hava dared to ask.

"They eat there every day, Hava," Reesa grumbled.

"Not Zamie," Fanny said proudly. "My Zamie comes home for lunch."

"Your Zamie eats at Flora's before he comes home, Fanny," Reesa informed her sister.

"He does?" Fanny's face dropped.

"Yes, he does," Hava confirmed.

"Then why does he come home to eat again?" Fanny wondered out loud.

"Because he's a *chazer*," Reesa snarled. " Or haven't you

noticed that he weighs close to three hundred pounds?"

"Don't call my Zamie a pig," Fanny said, defending her husband.

"Why do you think they're eating there?" Hava pondered.

"I'm not sure. But I intend to find out," Reesa answered.

It wasn't that they missed the company of their husbands. On the contrary, the Sisters had been enjoying the men's absence. It was Mule's recent defection to Flora's table that had left its sting. The men had taken their dull conversation to Flora's house and left the Sisters with Mule's adventures in the Far East. He complimented every dish and flushed their cheeks when he noticed the color of their housedresses. They fought to receive the bouquet of flowers he sometimes brought to decorate the table. Each Sister was secretly convinced the flowers were for her, especially Hava, who had once, when they were children, promised herself to Mule.

"I'm the reason Mule never married," Hava liked to boast.

"You're the reason many men never marry," Benzi would reply.

Everyone knew Mule's true love was Ganesa. The family took care not to mention Ganesa in Mule's presence, for his big brown eyes would fill with tears and he would admonish himself for not having stayed with her to fight the cause in which she so believed. The Sisters would cry that Mule was a saint and Ganesa had always been a foolish girl, full of pride and not worthy of his tears.

Last Monday, Mule never arrived. The Sisters had sat at the table waiting for him, eyeing one another nervously. When Zamie arrived, Fanny quickly served him and then sat down again to her empty plate. Zamie drank his soup under their intent gaze. They watched him chew, the grease of the meat and potatoes shining his lips until Reesa could stand it no longer and spoke.

"Zamie. Should we wait for Mule or is he tied up at the factory?"

"He went to Flora's for lunch," Zamie answered through a mouthful of potato.

The Sisters' hearts sank simultaneously, deep into their soft bellies. Hava and Fanny looked to Reesa, who drummed her long bony fingers on the table. Reesa studied Zamie as he finished his main course and ate his dessert. Feeling uncomfortable under the weight of her stare, Zamie ate quicker than usual and ended his meal with a resounding burp that stirred the women out of their catatonic state.

When Mule returned that night, they regarded him with cool indifference. Throughout dinner the Sisters made comments about Flora and how her cooking must have improved, since everyone preferred to lunch there. They secretly vowed to make a trip up the block to expose their sister-in-law's culinary secrets.

Flora was just as perplexed. The men flocked to her house at lunchtime, yet Luz's cooking had not improved. In fact, it seemed to be getting worse. Every day, the dining room table was so crowded that Flora was considering breaking lunch into two seatings.

Leon had been the first to arrive after he and Freida had another one of their spats. The fight was no different from the fight they had once a day, about Leon letting his younger brothers take advantage of him. Depending on Freida's mood, the accusations came with a varying degree of nastiness. That morning her tongue had been razor-sharp. Therefore, Leon decided it was best to avoid home and eat lunch with Dave and Flora. Leon, always sickly pale from the consumption that would ultimately kill him, had sat at the table, pondering what the thick brown juice in the glass in front of him might be. He watched Flora put the glass tentatively to her mouth and take a minuscule sip. Her large lips instantly puckered. She reached for the small crystal bell in front of her and shook it furiously. An instant later, Luz Alba appeared from behind the swinging door.

"Luz, what kind of juice is this?" Flora asked.

"*Banano*, Señora."

"Banana?"

"*Sí*, Señora," Luz answered.

"Luz, which bananas did you use to make it?"

"Those big green ones in the basket in the kitchen."

"Take this away and bring the next course," Flora snapped.

Leon's yellow eyes fixed on Luz's hips as she retrieved the glasses and walked back into the kitchen.

"She can't even make a simple juice. The girl doesn't know the difference between a banana and a plantain," Flora complained to Dave.

Luz reemerged from the kitchen carrying bowls of soup. As she placed a bowl in front of Leon, he suddenly felt aroused. His penis, inactive from years of verbal abuse, steadily swelled with each spoonful of the slightly bitter soup. When Luz returned to clear the table, Leon's eyes rolled into the back of his head and his body lurched forward.

"Oh my God!" Flora screamed. "He's having a seizure."

Dave and Flora rushed to his side. Leon's eyes slowly opened. He felt a sticky ooze drip down the right leg of his pants.

"Leon! Are you all right?" Dave asked.

"Just fine. Absolutely fine," Leon kept repeating during the rest of the meal.

Leon returned the next day with Grecia, who was now also working at the shop. Harold, after overhearing Leon telling Grecia about the juicy morsel at Flora's lunch table, popped in a few days later. Benzi, concerned that Grecia, Leon, Harold, and Dave might be plotting to cut him out of the business, joined them. He invited Zamie along in an effort to gain his loyalty in the event of a power struggle. But Benzi's fears dissipated as soon as he set eyes on Luz. The instant Flora picked up the crystal bell all eyes fell on the kitchen door in anticipation of Luz's face behind the round glass window.

The day Flora decided to fire Luz Alba herself, Mule arrived at the house for lunch.

"Flora, I hope this isn't an inconvenience," Mule said, handing her a small cylindrical package wrapped in white tissue paper.

"No, Mule. Of course not. You are always welcome." Flora lead him by the hand into the dining room where Grecia and Leon were fighting over a seat. "Come sit next to me," Flora motioned.

Flora sat down and untied the satin ribbon holding the package together. It fell apart revealing three embroidered handkerchiefs. "Thank you, Mule. They're beautiful," Flora said, taking one out and holding it up. "Grecia, you sat there yesterday. Let Leon sit there today." Flora's stern voice ended the argument. Leon and Grecia took their designated seats.

When the men finally arranged themselves elbow to elbow around the dining room table, Flora rang the bell. Luz Alba entered carrying a soup tureen. She leaned between Mule and Grecia and set it on the table.

"Is this Luz Alba?" Mule looked up at the girl whom he hadn't seen since the day Flora had hired her.

"*Sí,* Señor Mule. *¿Cómo está?*" Luz Alba greeted him.

"My, my . . . Well isn't she just doing fabulous, Flora?" Mule patted the beaming girl's soft hand. Flora forced a smile. "Just fabulous," Mule repeated as Luz Alba went back into the kitchen. "Flora, how very good of you to take her in. What a wonderful woman this is," Mule announced to the table. "Dave, you are a lucky man." And with those words, Mule reversed Luz Alba's impending dismissal as all the men at the table nodded their heads in agreement, silently acknowledging that Dave was indeed a lucky man. Lucky to be living with such a wonderful creature as Luz Alba.

34

*T*he morning the Sisters descended upon Flora, they swooped into the kitchen, lifted the lids off of pots on the stove, dipped their fingers into bowls in the refrigerator, and opened every cupboard. "Flora," they croaked in unison when she entered the kitchen. They pecked Flora's pale cheek with their dry lips.

"Reesa, Hava, Fanny," Flora coolly greeted her sisters-in-law, retrieving a bowl of day-old hollandaise from Fanny's hand and returning it to the icebox. She took out a brick of butter. "To what do I owe this surprise? Luz Alba!" Flora called out for the maid.

"We were just off to the market and wondered if you needed anything," Reesa said.

"¿Señora?" Luz Alba entered the kitchen.

"No thank you, Reesa. Luz, I'm going to make a cake for dinner tonight. Please get the flour, sugar, baking powder, and four eggs from the pantry."

"*Sí,* Señora."

"Is that a new shiksa you have?" Reesa asked as the girl retreated into the pantry.

"No, it's Luz Alba," Flora answered curtly.

"Who?" Reesa asked.

"That mangy girl from the tree?" Hava was astonished.

217

"Yes, Hava."

"So, she's the secret you've been keeping." Reesa's eyes twitched. "She must be some little cook, Flora."

At that moment, Flora discovered the perfect way out. She could get rid of Luz without losing face with Mule. "She's a quick learner, Reesa. I teach her once and then she does it by herself. She made a wonderful casserole last night. Now don't you try and go steal her out from under me. Excuse me for a moment. I have to go upstairs and get some vanilla extract from the closet." Flora made her staged exit.

Reesa approached Luz after she returned with the ingredients from the pantry. "Luz Alba." The girl backed away from the older woman, who smelled of onions. "Do you remember me?"

"*Sí*, Señora." Luz walked over to the kitchen counter and took four eggs from the basket.

"Do you like working here?" Reesa asked.

"Oh *sí*, Señora! I love it here." Luz gazed lovingly out the kitchen window, admiring the jasmine in the front garden.

"Do they treat you well here?" Hava asked.

"*Sí*, Señora. El Señor David is very kind."

"How much do they pay you?" Reesa asked.

"Fifteen pesos a week," Luz answered proudly. She placed the eggs in a bowl.

"Fifteen pesos? Would you like to make sixteen pesos?" Reesa suggested.

"Sixteen pesos? Where?"

"Working for us," Reesa answered eagerly.

Flora, who had been listening behind the door, reentered the kitchen. "Here we are," she said, retrieving the bottle of extract from her pocket.

"Think about it and let me know," Reesa hissed into Luz's ear.

"*Sí*, Señora." Luz walked the bowl of eggs over to the table where Flora was measuring out ingredients.

"Luz? Let me show you a quick way to separate eggs." Flora took an egg and handed it to Luz Alba. "Crack gently against the side of the bowl and then open it up carefully." She led the maid through the motion, tapping the egg against the rim of the bowl. "Gently," she reiterated. The shell gave way, slightly exposing the casing. "Okay, now open it." Luz pulled apart the brown shell. "All right, now before it all drops out, let me have it." Flora retrieved the egg and was about to shift its contents between the two shell halves. "Well! Would you look at that!" Luz Alba's eyes grew wide. "A double yolk." The girl swooned and collapsed.

"Luz!" The Sisters rushed over to the girl, who lay unconscious on the floor. Her face was the color of ash. "Get some ammonia," Hava said. "That will bring her around."

"Ana!" Flora yelled. "Ana!"

Ana walked into the kitchen holding a dustpan. "Señora?"

"We need some ammonia! Luz just fainted."

Ana scurried to the broom closet and returned with the bottle of ammonia. She handed it to Hava. While Hava waved it under Luz's nose, Ana noticed the egg with the double yolk that had run out into the bowl.

"Twins," Ana mumbled.

"What?" Flora looked up at Ana.

"A double yolk means twins," Ana said. "My cousin Carmen cracked open an egg with two yolks and two months later, she had a pair of twin boys joined at the hip. At least these yolks aren't touching." Ana lifted the bowl to show the women. The small orange yolks sat at opposite ends. "Carmen's were connected."

"That's just an old wives' tale," Flora said.

"In the country, pregnant women never crack open eggs," Ana kept on. "They always have someone do it for them, just to avoid problems."

"Ana, that's ridiculous! It was just a coincidence that your cousin had Siamese twins," Flora exclaimed.

"Well what about my mother's friend, Hortensia? When she was carrying her first child, she opened an egg that had no yolk. Only white. Her baby was born without a heart."

"That's impossible. How could a baby not have a heart?" Reesa asked.

"My mother, may the Lord protect her in heaven, saw it with her own two eyes, Señora Reesa," Ana said. "She told me that the baby came out dead and in its chest there was only a hole. A big empty hole." Ana crossed herself for emphasis.

"Tanya ate a rotten egg when she was pregnant and she got a rotten son," Fanny reminded her sisters. The three women nodded their heads simultaneously.

"Who is Tanya?" Flora asked.

"Tanya was our father's mother's sister," Reesa answered. "She had sixteen children. Poo poo poo." Reesa spat into the air.

"Tanya had a son named Isaac," Fanny continued. "He was rotten to the core."

"He was a thief," Hava interjected. "He stole our father's mule and sold it to the butcher as horse meat."

"Well what does it matter?" Flora cried, exasperated by their superstitiousness. "No one here is pregnant. This conversation is pointless. Hava, let me try." Flora took the bottle from Hava's hand. She bent down and held it steady under Luz's nose.

35

*T*he first to arrive was don Mateo, the butcher. He stood in the doorway, his hairy arms extending almost a foot past the sleeves of his borrowed suit. He carried a delicate bouquet composed of balsam, pigweed, and a stem of a quereme, a rare plant used by fortune-tellers and witches to concoct love potions. Tucked under his armpit was a parcel wrapped in brown paper and tied with butcher string. Ana led him into the kitchen, where Flora sat drinking a cup of tea.

"Doña Flora, *¿cómo está?*"

It took Flora a moment to recognize him, as she had never seen the butcher out of his white, blood-spattered jacket and pants.

"Señor Mateo? What are you doing here?" Flora asked.

"Señora, I come on a personal matter." The butcher lowered his voice to a whisper. "The child is mine. I am a responsible man. I will take care of Luz." He offered Flora the package. "Please accept this gift as a form of apology for any trouble that I have caused."

"That is very decent of you, Señor Mateo," Flora answered, ignoring his outstretched hand. "Have you told Blanca?"

"Who?"

"Blanca. Your wife," Flora reminded him.

The butcher's eyes remained flat. The first time Luz came into the shop, she took with her his every thought. Her image cluttered his head. Every carcass was her body. The suckling pigs he carried from the freezer bore her tender face. Even his wife, trimming meat behind the counter, became Luz, and the screech of her knife across the sharpening stone turned into a ballad.

"It doesn't matter," Luz Alba said after don Mateo left, taking his tenderloin with him. "He is not the father." Flora and the girl stood on the stoop watching him walk down Carrera Giradot. Luz pulled the quereme out from the bouquet and twirled it between her delicate fingers.

"Then why did he say he was?"

The girl shrugged her shoulders.

The question bouncing around inside Flora's head fell out of her mouth. "Do you know who the father is?"

"Oh *sí*, Señora."

"Who?" Flora braced herself. Once the doctor confirmed Luz's pregnancy, uneasy eyes lurked everywhere.

Luz pointed with the stem of quereme toward the jasmine.

"Are you trying to protect someone?" Flora demanded.

"I tell you, Señora, and you don't believe me . . ." Luz's eyes filled tears.

"A tree didn't do this to you." Flora pointed to Luz's distended belly.

The gardener, don Germán, knocked on the door an hour later. Even though he had scrubbed his hands until they were raw, he still had soil embedded under his yellow nails.

"Señora Flora." Don Germán tipped his hat. "Señora, I

must see Luz on an urgent matter." His eyes never left the ground.

Flora led him to the patio, where Luz sat resting her swollen legs. He left through the garage door a few minutes later.

"He's not the father either? " Flora asked.

"No, Señora." A blade of grass hung from between her pouty lips.

Flora belched silently. Acid filled her mouth. "Are you sure?"

"Yes," the girl replied.

"Why can't you just marry one of them? It would be so much easier for you," Flora pleaded with the girl after the milkman left with tears streaming down his cheeks.

"But I don't love any of them, Señora," Luz wailed.

"Love? Love?" Flora muttered. "Do you love the father of this child?"

"With all my heart," Luz Alba answered. The conviction in the girl's voice brought tears to Flora's eyes.

"Flora? What are you giving away?" Reesa called to inquire one morning.

"What are you talking about?" Flora asked her sister-in-law.

"There's a line of men standing outside your door."

Flora peered out the window. Twenty men, some in ponchos, some in suits, stood waiting to see Luz. One clutched a chicken, another had a pig on a leash. But it was the short, curly-haired one with a book strap that sent Flora flying down the stairs and out into the street.

"Bernie?" The boy looked up into his mother's petrified eyes. "What are you doing out here?" Flora asked him.

Bernie shuffled his feet. "I had to go to the bathroom.

When I tried to go in, I was told to go to the end of the line."

Flora took Bernie's hand and escorted him back inside. His words did not bring her relief. The dark hair sprouting around his knuckles and the creaks in his voice made him a suspect.

During dinner, Flora observed her sons. When had Sol grown into the man that sat at the table? His lean body reminded Flora of her brother, Joe, but his face belonged to Dave's side of the family. His brown eyes darted nervously in their sockets, unable to make contact. Semmie fidgeted in his seat, shedding his baby fat before Flora's eyes. By the time dinner was over, the girlish curls surrounding his face had tightened and coarsened.

Flora spent a sleepless night. Suspicion tossed her body back and forth on the mattress until daybreak. "What did they say?" Flora asked Dave after she sent him to query their three sons.

"They all confessed," Dave replied. "But I think we can rule Bernie out."

"Why?" Flora asked.

"He said something about rubbing her belly button." Dave laughed.

"What was he doing rubbing her belly button?" Flora wrung her hands, unable to see the humor when the other two might very well be speaking from experience. "Should we ask Luz?"

"Let's not put ideas into her head," Dave answered. "We'll know soon enough."

Although Flora knew Dave was right, his words didn't sit well. They bubbled inside Flora's stomach, making her queasy. Her appetite waned. Perpetually exhausted, she'd collapse on the sofa and sleep all afternoon.

"Flori? What's the matter?" Dave asked when he noticed her sitting in the corner, staring out at nothing.

"It's the change of life." After menopause, Shana's face sported a beard and mustache. The prospect of the same coarse facial hair that defied tweezers filled Flora with melancholy. Tears slid down her cheeks and dropped onto her lap. Dave stared at the puddle in the sag of her apron. Uncomfortable with woman issues, he left the room without saying a word.

For weeks, Flora moped about the house. While Luz's body swelled with life, hers was shutting down. She tried to fill the void with sweets plucked from the closet. She baked cookies and cakes. Clothes that once hung loosely on her frame soon stretched at the seams.

One morning, Flora felt a sharp jab in her side. The pain was followed by a vaguely familiar fluttering sensation in her stomach. Flora put down her darning and raced to the bathroom. She pulled up her dress and stared at her stomach protruding over the elastic of her underwear. She felt the flutter again and the skin on her abdomen rippled. When it stopped, there was a lump sticking out from under her ribcage. Flora traced the shape with her hand. "Oh my Lord," she whispered.

"Oh my Lord," Dave repeated that night when his wife placed his hand on her stomach and he felt the tiny foot jutting out from Flora's side.

"Oh my Lord!" the Sisters cried after the couple announced that Flora was pregnant.

The house that always felt spacious with its ample bedrooms and living spaces shrunk at the prospect of another child within its walls.

"Pack your bags, Flora," Dave's voice crackled over the phone line. "Remember that French Revival house we saw on Carrera Benalcazar? I bought it."

"You bought a house without me?" Flora screamed.

225

"It's beautiful, Flori. You're going to love it. It's got ten bedrooms."

"I don't care if it has three swimming pools. You don't buy a house without asking your wife's opinion. Return it." Flora hung up on him.

"Did you return the house?" Flora inquired when Dave knocked on the bedroom door and asked to be let in.

"Flora, you can't return a house." Dave laughed. "Come out and we'll go see it now."

"I'll come out when you return the house," Flora answered. "Until then, don't bother me."

Infuriated by her stubbornness, Dave decided to wage his own war. He paraded rental agents back and forth in front of the bedroom door and announced that the house would be vacant within a month. He wheezed and coughed and complained loudly about the film of dust settling over the entire house. Even Reesa's voice ordering Ana to take down the curtains and wash them didn't lure Flora out.

After a week, a defeated Dave hired a contractor. Plans for a new bedroom on the second floor were drawn. Workmen hauled wooden support beams up the stairs and dragged furniture out into the corridor. The sound of a sledgehammer breaking through wall sent Flora bolting from the bedroom. "Are you insane?" she shrieked. Flora considered returning to the sanctuary of her bedroom, but the unsightly mess was more than she could bear. On her way to get some sheets to cover the furniture, she saw the blueprint coiled up in the corner.

"Why on earth would an infant need a balcony, Dave?" she demanded to know a few minutes later.

"The branches of the tree, Señora," a construction worker answered, pointing to the jasmine. "It makes room for the tree."

"It's an invitation to disaster," Flora said. "Cut down the tree."

"But Señora, the tree provides the house with some shade from the sun," the architect interjected.

"Cut down the tree and extend the room. And put a window on the other side, too." Flora crossed her arms over her chest.

"Señor David. The room will be an inferno," the architect argued.

"Do what she wants," Dave answered.

◆

The next morning, don Germán and another gardener climbed into the canopy of the jasmine and began to trim the tree, snapping the brittle young branches with their machetes. Luz sat on the stoop watching the intermittent shower of flowers that fell from above. Every few minutes, she'd ease herself off the step and gather the felled twigs from the lawn. "Look," she called up to don Germán. Luz Alba held a branch up to the sky. Jasmine rained down on her face. "They're blooming." At noon, Luz went inside to help Amparo, the new cook, serve lunch. After the family finished eating, Luz and Ana cleared the table and set it again. "Go tell don Germán and don Jairo that lunch is ready," Ana told Luz. "I'll go upstairs and get the construction men."

"Don Germán," Luz called from the front door. "*Almuerzo.*" The gardeners continued working. The sound of hammers and saws coming from the second floor drowned out her voice. Luz walked downstairs and under the tree. "Don Germán!" she shouted into the canopy, startling the gardener. Don Germán's foot slipped and he grabbed the trunk of the jasmine to save himself. His machete dropped through the branches and landed on Luz Alba's head, killing her instantly.

Unable to trace any of Luz's family, Dave had the young woman buried in the cemetery adjacent to the site destined to be the new airport. No one knew the date of her birth, so the small headstone read solely "Luz Alba Rodríguez." One day, a groundskeeper noticed a sapling growing over the grave. He tried to pull it out, but the tree clung to the soil. After he fetched a shovel and began to dig up the earth around the grave, the caretaker discovered an extensive web of roots below. He continued to dig until his shovel hit wood. He cleared the dirt over the casket and found that the tree was sprouting from the center of the pine coffin. Not willing to disturb the dead more than he already had, he refilled the grave and moved the stone marker in front of the tree.

Flora went into labor the day Jorge Eliécer Gaitán, the populist presidential candidate, was shot. Rioters took to the streets of Bogotá and burned down the plaza. Their rage sparked fires across the country. Flora, determined to deliver at the recently opened hospital on Junín and not at their new home on Carrera Benalcazar, insisted that Dave drive her there. "I want to have this baby the civilized way. I'm tired of having to use my own sheets and I don't want doctors trampling mud on my new carpet," she screamed at Dave after he pointed out that it might be dangerous.

After a potato flew into the windshield, cracking it, Flora conceded. "Okay. You're right. Let's go home."

But it proved impossible to turn around. They were stuck. Worried that Flora might deliver in the car, Dave decided they should get out and walk. Unable to open the driver's side door because of the crowd, he tried the other doors to no avail. The couple was sealed inside until a woman, standing by the passenger window, cried out, "*¡Nuestra Señora de Alpujarras!*" She pointed to Flora. The people around the car fell to their knees, allowing Dave to push open the door. Flora stepped out. "*Nuestra Señora de Alpujarras,*" they chanted. The crowd parted, allowing Flora and Dave to move past them. Terrified that their chanting might turn hostile, Flora and Dave broke into a run. Two blocks later, they were in front of the store. Dave pounded on the metal grate until Leon, who had been holed inside for hours, let them in. A few minutes later, Flora gave birth to a baby girl on top of a bed of prickly blankets.

*T*he new baby, named Gracie after her paternal grandmother, Guita, absorbed time. Before the family had a chance to adjust to her presence, Sol had been accepted to the Philadelphia Textile Institute and moved to the States. As Bernie read from the Torah in celebration of his bar mitzvah, a Star of David flowered on the cupola of the abandoned church in downtown Medellín. Despite Benzi's ardent disapproval, Dave and Flora allowed Ruthie to enroll in a girls' college outside Philadelphia. "Why waste money on educating a girl," Benzi protested. "I can find her a husband in Bogotá, Dovid. Lots of Jewish men in Bogotá. Look how well my Bluma married. I never have to worry about her again."

Don Abraham, Bluma's father-in-law, owned a large hardware store in Bogotá. Over the years, Benzi purchased many locks and bolts from the shop in La Candelaria and therefore knew the family well. At Benzi's suggestion, Bluma's dowry was used to open an annex in Medellín. His plan insured an income for his daughter, a job for his son-in-law, and his padlocks at cost.

"But you hate your son-in-law," Dave reminded him. Benzi rarely spoke to Isaac, and when he did it was to scold him.

"I hate him because he is my son-in-law. If he weren't, I'm sure we'd be the best of friends," Benzi had laughed.

After Ruthie's departure, years slipped between Dave and Flora's fingers, evading them until Sol's wedding, where time alighted upon Flora. Its weight made her gasp. As Gracie walked down the aisle tossing flower petals from a wicker basket, Flora concentrated on the Band-Aid pasted across her daughter's small knee to keep from fainting.

The cantor's nasal voice set Flora's mind adrift. Twenty-four years. She'd not been home in twenty-four years. And now she stood in Philadelphia, crowded under a chupah with the bride's parents and four grandparents. Flora squeezed Dave's arm so hard he winced.

"Sol should have married your daughter," she whispered to Mrs. Lerner, the maid of honor's mother, when she came through the receiving line. At the reception, Flora found herself repeating the same words to friends of the bride's parents who mentioned their daughters. She even suggested it to the bathroom attendant who showed Flora a picture of her daughter pasted inside the door of the supply cabinet.

Flora thought Bobbie and Sol an awkward couple. A ballet dancer, Bobbie's carriage was tall and confident, while Sol stumbled about to please her. The previous summer, at Flora's request, both had traveled to Medellín. "I want her to know what's she getting into," Flora told Sol. "I want her to know what her life will be like here."

"I can't understand a word they're saying," Flora heard Bobbie complain a few days after her arrival. Flora was passing by the study and the anguish in their voices drew her ear to the wall.

"You'll learn Spanish. We'll enroll you in a class after we get back from our honeymoon," Sol sobbed.

Bobbie clutched the emerald pendant Mule had given her as an engagement present. The two-carat, square-cut diamond ring Dave had purchased for Sol to give to his bride shimmered on her finger.

"It's not worth it," Flora wanted to cry out. Her son's weeping stopped her.

After the wedding, Dave returned to Colombia with Bernie and Gracie. Flora stayed behind to get Semmie set up at the textile college. Then she traveled to Cincinnati and visited with her family. A month later, Flora landed at La Playa airport in Medellín.

Gracie and Bernie waited outside while Dave slipped the guard five pesos and himself inside. He saw Flora standing by the baggage truck. He hired a porter and walked out onto the tarmac toward her. "Flori." Dave kissed her on the cheek.

"I've got a lot of luggage. Hire another porter," Flora ordered. She pointed out her suitcases to the baggage handler. He climbed up onto the truck and began tossing them down to the other porter Dave brought over to assist them. The men arranged the fifteen bags onto two hand trucks and pushed them over to customs. The inspector, who had been pacing the length of his table, looking officially bored, perked up when he saw Dave approaching with Flora. He extended his mulatto hand to Dave's.

"Don David. ¿Cómo está? Doña Flora. Did you have a nice trip?"

He waved the porters through without bothering to open a single suitcase. "So good to see you, don David. So very good to see you. Bienvenida, doña Flora," the inspector said, pushing the bills Dave handed him deep into his pocket. He smiled as the formation slowly filed out the door and headed toward Dave's shiny black Ford.

Once at home, Gracie followed her mother into the bedroom. While Flora unpacked, she sat on the bed, peeling off curly bits of loose leather from the sides of Flora's old battered suitcase and rolling them between her fingers. Clothes, towels and sheets, appliances (a toaster, an iron, and a new transistor radio) emerged from inside the shiny new suitcases. After each one was emptied, Gracie dragged it into the hallway closet. "Gracie, stop destroying my suitcase." Flora took the bag from the floor and placed it on the bed. Her hand trembled as she inserted the key into the lock and released the catch. The top popped open. Boxes of chocolate, bags of licorice, and hard candies spilled out onto the bed. Cans of fruits and vegetables lined the inner walls of the suitcase. Bundles of clothing unfurled, revealing the jars of grape jelly and maraschino cherries hidden in their centers. Gracie inspected each item before surrendering it back to Flora for storage in the closet. She pressed her chubby finger into a caramel, trying to imagine its taste.

"Stop poking the caramels," her mother scolded and took the candy out of Gracie's hand. Flora looked at it for a moment and then gave it back to her daughter. "You might as well eat it, since no one else is going to want it all smushed like that." She continued to line the canned goods along the closet shelf.

Once everything was put away, Flora shut the closet doors and pulled out the large brass key ring from her housecoat pocket. The keys jangled as she searched for the one with the dab of red nail enamel. She inserted the key into the lock, turning it several times. Flora placed the empty suitcase alongside the others in the hallway closet.

"I want peaches for my birthday dessert," Gracie said as she followed her mother into the kitchen.

"We'll see," was Flora's response, heavy with implication that Gracie should be on her best behavior. Being the youngest, the child had full control over her father. Her every desire became reality. If Gracie wanted to eat only ice cream for dinner, it was fine with Dave. No doll was too expensive or any gift too lavish. Flora, on the other hand, kept a tight reign on the five-year-old. If Gracie wouldn't eat her dinner, it showed up on her breakfast plate. She ignored Gracie's tantrums in the supermarket, steering her cart down the aisle away from the screaming child.

The night of Flora's return, Gracie fell asleep in the living room. Dave carried her upstairs and tucked her into bed. Later, as Flora combed her hair at the dressing table, there came a sharp pound at their bedroom door. She opened the door and Gracie barged in, visibly upset that the door had been closed.

"Gracie? What's the matter?" Flora asked.

"You put me to sleep in the wrong bed, mama." Gracie climbed into Flora's bed and pulled the covers over her.

Flora glanced at Dave, who sat in his bed reading. "You haven't been letting her sleep here?"

Dave said nothing.

"Dave!" The pitch of Flora's voice shook his silence.

"But Flora," Dave defended himself, "we all slept together in the hotel room in Philadelphia. She was scared when we got back and I didn't have the heart to make her sleep alone in her room."

"Come on, Gracie." Flora lifted the covers off her daughter. Gracie yawned and rolled over.

"Gracie, I know you're not asleep."

"Why don't we let her stay tonight, Flora?" Dave suggested. "Then tomorrow we'll make sure she stays in her room."

Exhausted from three days of traveling and too tired to argue, Flora climbed into bed with her daughter.

The next night Gracie refused to sleep in her room. Each time they tucked her in, she climbed back out and shuffled into their bedroom. When Flora locked the door, Gracie threw herself down on the floor and screamed so loud that the lizards scaling the walls of the neighborhood lost their grip and splattered on the ground. Worried that someone might call the police, Dave opened the door and let Gracie in.

"You may sleep in this room, but not in my bed," Flora said to her daughter as she tried to climb into bed.

Gracie shrugged her shoulders and cut across the room to Dave's bed.

"Don't you dare, Dave," Flora warned her husband. "If we make it comfortable, she'll never leave. Gracie. Take a pillow and some blankets and make a bed for yourself on the rug."

Dave spread out a sheet for Gracie on the rug, got her a pillow, and placed a blanket over her. He bent down to kiss her goodnight and whispered something in her ear. When Flora awoke the next morning, Gracie was fast asleep in her father's bed. Dave snored loudly beside her.

At breakfast, Flora sat at the table with her arms coiled over her chest. Feeling the burn of his wife's basilisk glare, Dave ate his toast behind his newspaper. Late for school, Bernie stood at the table, shoving large amounts of egg into his mouth and washing them down with gulps of juice. He kissed his mother and sister good-bye and sped off to catch the bus.

Gracie nibbled her eggs, quietly observing her parents. She knew better than to break the silence between them. It was just a matter of time before her mother unleashed her anger.

Gracie was accustomed to Flora's dramatic exits. It was not uncommon for her mother to storm upstairs and lock herself in the bedroom for days at a time. Armed with a can opener and a fork stashed inside an old purse, Flora survived on food from the closet and tap water from the bathroom sink. Boredom tended to deplete her stamina. Therefore she kept several long books (*War and Peace*, *The Iliad*, and *The Odyssey*) inside her night table. The outbursts were so frequent that Dave kept an extra supply of toiletries and a week's worth of clothes in the guest bedroom.

Much to Gracie's surprise, Flora didn't say a word. She just sat there until her father finished his breakfast. Dave excused himself and went to brush his teeth. He returned a few minutes later and kissed Gracie on the head. "Bye, baby. Bye, Flora," he added on his way out.

"Finish your breakfast, Gracie." Flora's voice contained a certain eerie calmness that Gracie had never experienced before. She ate her eggs and then asked to be excused.

A few hours later, Gracie spotted her mother sitting on the bench in the foyer. She'd shed her housedress for a skirt and jacket and held her purse on lap. The old suitcase stood by Flora's feet.

"What are you doing, Mommy?" Gracie sat down next to her mother.

"I'm leaving," Flora answered.

"Leaving?" Gracie's face grew frightened. "Why?"

"I can't take it anymore. Don't worry. Your father will take good care of you." Flora stood up and picked up her suitcase.

"But . . ." Gracie's eyes filled with tears. "No, Mommy," she begged. "Please don't go." Gracie clasped her arms around Flora's legs.

"No. I have to go. You and your father don't mind me.

Why should I stay? I'm not needed here." A car outside blared its horn. "There's my taxi. Good-bye, sweetheart." Flora kissed the weeping child on the cheek and opened the door.

"No!" Gracie shrieked. "Mommy! I promise I'll be good. I promise. I'll sleep in my room."

Flora turned around. The child was sobbing uncontrollably. She stepped outside and waved the car away. "Maybe I'll stay through lunch. That way I can say good-bye to your father and brother. But then, I'm going." Flora closed the door. She put down her purse and went into the kitchen to help Amparo prepare lunch.

Dave returned home to find a teary Gracie sitting on the bench clutching her mother's purse. "Mommy's leaving after lunch," she sputtered.

Dave gathered Gracie in his arms. He understood the child's fear. Flora's silences still made him squirm. "Come, let's eat."

After lunch, Gracie took her nap on the bench in the foyer, just in case her mother decided to slip out during the siesta. She kept guard the rest of the day, until it was time to go to bed. Then she obediently went into her room and tried to go to sleep. But the dread that her mother would leave in the middle of the night kept her awake. Every hour or so, she'd slip out into the foyer to make sure the suitcase was still there. In the morning, Gracie appeared at breakfast with dark circles under her swollen eyes. After she finished her entire breakfast, Gracie quickly resumed her post by the door.

Gracie kept vigilant guard over the foyer for over a week. In the morning, she'd bring her dolls and coloring supplies downstairs and set up camp. Only at meals did Gracie abandon her watch. She sat at the table, watching her mother's every move. If Flora stepped away from the table, the color drained from the child's face until her mother returned. She ate her food without being coaxed, hoping to ease Flora's anger. But the suitcase remained by the door and Ana had taken to dusting it along with the other furniture in the room.

One afternoon, as Gracie was rocking her doll to sleep, her elbow accidentally hit the suitcase and knocked it over. She returned the bag to its upright position, and its lightness drew her curiosity. She pressed her finger on the latch. It snapped open. Gracie looked around. She could hear her mother talking to the maids in the kitchen. She carefully triggered the other latch. The two sides parted and Gracie peeked inside.

Flora's suitcase was empty.